Cupcake

Cupcake

COOKIE O'GORMAN
AUTHOR OF *ADORKABLE*

Entangled Publishing, LLC
10940 S Parker Road
Suite 327
Parker, CO 80134
rights@entangledpublishing.com

Entangled Teen is an imprint of Entangled Publishing, LLC.

Visit our website at www.entangledpublishing.com.

Edited by Stacy Abrams
Cover design and illustration by Elizabeth Turner Stokes
Title lettering: Elena_Si/Shutterstock
Cupcake: nastasyaalt/pixabay
Interior design by Toni Kerr

ISBN 978-1-64937-032-7
Ebook ISBN 978-1-64937-045-7

Manufactured in the United States of America

First Edition November 2021

10 9 8 7 6 5 4 3 2 1

an imprint of Entangled Publishing LLC

To all the plus-size, chubby, curvy,
voluptuous, "big" girls of the world.
You are beautiful.
You are worthy.
You deserve love, kindness, and every good
thing life has to offer.
At any size.

At Entangled, we want our readers to be well-informed. If you would like to know if this book contains any elements that might be of concern for you, please check the back of the book for details.

Chapter 1

"If you could date an Avenger, who would it be?"

Okay, my best friend and I talked about everything under the sun, so that was a completely legitimate question. I thought about it a second.

"I'm not sure," I said. "My instinct says Captain America because he's kind, confident, loyal, and just yum. But it's hard because Thor is gorgeous, too, and he could probably pick me up if I ever fell down a hill in the rain."

Toni snorted as she braided my hair.

"That was random," she said.

"Not really. I watched *Sense and Sensibility* last night."

I heard her sigh. "Again, Ariel? You know they make new movies every year, right? You don't always have to watch the same things over and over."

"Yeah"—I rolled my eyes—"but I know what I like. And romances nowadays just aren't what they used to be."

I couldn't see her, but I knew Toni was smiling.

She loved to tease me about my obsession with romance movies, but we both knew she'd discovered plenty of her favorites because of me.

"Who would you pick?" I asked. "From the Avengers?"

"Black Widow," she said. "No question. She kicks butt, and I'd love to ask her where she gets her cat suits and that red hair dye."

"Ooh, good choice."

"Thanks."

"Hey," I said, touching a strand of my dark brown locks, "speaking of hair. I was thinking of adding some highlights. Do you think you could—"

She *tsked*, then gave a sharp tug, making me gasp.

"Ouch! What the heck?" My eyes shot to the front of the classroom, but there was no need to worry. Our substitute teacher was currently nose-deep in his crossword.

Toni and I were seniors. This was Health, our final class of the day, and he'd given us the last ten minutes to talk. It was all good.

Well, except for my hair-pulling bestie.

"What was that for?" I asked.

"You ruin a mane like this with cosmetic enhancement and I'll never forgive you," Toni warned, running her fingers through my hair. She always made me look like I'd just visited a professional stylist—the girl could've charged for her amazing skills. "Don't even think about it. Your natural mahogany already has hints of auburn in it anyway."

I frowned. "But you color your hair. You change it up nearly every month," I pointed out.

"I'm an artist," she said, as if that explained everything.

"Hey, I'm creative, too."

Toni laughed. "Yeah, but that's just with tasty treats."

She finished by pinning the Swiss braids over the top of my head, then had me turn around to pull out a few tendrils.

I lifted a brow. "I didn't see you complaining when you were eating that jasmine vanilla cupcake I brought you earlier."

Toni's eyes closed as she groaned. "Oh, girl, that was sooo good! And pretty, too."

"Thanks," I said. "Keep the flattery coming, and I might just forgive you for that crack about my art. Making food that looks beautiful *and* tastes good takes skill, you know."

"Oh please, I didn't mean it like that," Toni said. "My love affair with your food is my longest relationship to date."

I laughed.

"Seriously A, you've been doing it since you were what? Six?"

"Five," I corrected. "Grandma D always stressed how important it was that the food not only tasted good, but looked pretty, too. We eat with our eyes first—that's what she always said."

My grandma Duncan had started me out early. We baked cupcakes every Sunday, and she'd let me choose the decorations and guide my hand as we frosted them together. My mind traveled back to those days of baking in my grandma's kitchen, and I couldn't help but smile. They were some of the best times of my life.

"Deep." Toni gave a nod. "And true for more than just food."

"Yeah, she was the best. I miss her."

"Well, at least her baking lives on through you," my best friend said. "I can't even cook spaghetti, let alone make those little yummy flowers made from that stuff…what is it called again? Farquaad?"

"Nope, Lord Farquaad would be the short guy from *Shrek*." I grinned. "The flowers are fondant. I've been working on them the past few days. Helps me keep in practice for the baking competition next month."

"Well, they're beautiful." Toni twisted one last piece of my hair around her finger, released the curl, then nodded and pinched my cheeks. "And so are you! Seriously, give me that hair, and I could rule the world."

"Toni, you play too much. Your hair is awesome! That magenta really suits you."

"You think so?"

"Yes," I said, "total rock star art goddess."

"You're right." She nodded, fluffing her ever-changing bob, then looked down at herself. "Hair wouldn't be a problem, but for true world domination, I would definitely need your amazing rack."

I nearly swallowed my tongue. "Toni!"

"What? You have great boobs."

"My breasts thank you for the compliment," I murmured as heat rose to my cheeks. "But seriously, you're gorgeous, and you know it."

"I guess my girls are perky, if a little small," she said.

I shook my head. "Stop that! You're my best friend, and your boobs rock. Just accept it."

Toni suddenly grabbed my hand and placed it against the center of her chest.

"What are you doing?" I asked.

"Just giving our little eavesdropper over there something to smile about," she whispered and tilted her head to the side. Sure enough, out of the corner of my eye, I caught sight of Ben Shultz watching us with avid attention. He was pretending not to look, but his gaze kept coming back to my best friend and me. The small smile on his face was filled with awe.

"How long has he been watching us?" I asked.

Toni shrugged. "No idea. But I think he's enjoying all the boob talk."

"I think you're right." I leaned forward and kissed her cheek, chuckling when I heard what sounded like a notebook hit the floor. Leaning back, I snuck a glance just in time to see Ben retrieve his binder and then look at Toni. "Bet he's happy about that, too."

"Yeah," she said. "Ben's a sweetheart…if a bit of a perv."

I scoffed with a smile. "Says the girl who was checking out my 'rack.'"

Toni's gaze narrowed. "Did you just air-quote me?"

"Sure did," I said. "You are quite quotable."

Toni thought about that a second, then grinned. "I am, aren't I?"

The intercom system beeped, and the end-of-school-day announcements began a second later.

"Hello, students of Honeycomb High! This is Principal Maxine. I have some exciting news for you today."

"Is it just me," Toni whispered, "or does Principal Max sound extra happy?"

I shrugged. "Her voice is always upbeat."

"It's about Homecoming Court," the principal went on, and I could feel the whole room shift to listen. "As you know, ballots went out at the beginning of the week, and now the results are in. There will be princesses and princes representing every grade, so please pay attention."

"Hey, how did you do on that test in Bio?" I asked, but Toni waved me off.

"Eh, not bad. Let's listen."

"Why?" I laughed. "I thought we didn't care about Homecoming. Every year the popular people get voted in and fawned over, and we usually stay home, binge-watch rom-coms, and eat ice cream."

"Yeah, but who knows? There could be some surprises this year."

"I still—"

The girl a couple seats in front of Toni turned around to give us a glare.

"Will you two please be quiet?" Lana said. "Some of us care about our school traditions."

"Sorry," I said and meant it. "I didn't think we were being loud."

Lana rolled her eyes. "Whatever, Cupcake, just keep it down. Some of us actually have a chance at getting our name announced."

Okay, so most of the school called me "Cupcake" in a sweet way, an endearment of sorts (though there was little warmth in Lana's voice), thanks to my love of baking. And I wasn't really offended by the Homecoming comment either— it was the truth. Girls like me were never chosen, and I was totally cool with that. I didn't even want to be a princess.

But my bestie seemed to take Lana's words personally, as she narrowed her eyes. "You sound real sure of yourself there, Leavengood. You rig the ballot box or something?"

"As if I'd need to," Lana said, dropping her voice to a whisper. "Unlike you two, I have goals and a reputation."

With that, she dismissed us with a flip of her hair and turned back around.

"Yeah," Toni mumbled, "a reputation as a snotty brat."

If Lana heard the insult, she didn't show it. Principal Max was still talking, announcing the sophomore and junior nominees. Lana was listening hard; she even seemed to be taking notes. A little overboard if you ask me, but hey, I guess some people took this Homecoming stuff seriously.

To be honest, Lana *was* a bit of a snot, but it wasn't totally her fault—the whole senior class fed into her obsession with herself. And yeah, mean girls weren't supposed to exist. In this day and age, girls were supposed to be lifting one another up instead of tearing one another down—but I guess Lana had never gotten the memo.

She had two faces: the one she showed to the people she thought could help her get ahead, and the one she showed when those people weren't looking. Obviously, Toni and I were beneath her notice, so we saw glimpses of her dark side. But to everyone else? Lana was an angel. She'd been elected to Court every year we'd been at Honeycomb High, so there was next to no chance she'd be left out this time.

"And now, we have our senior nominees! Oh, this is so exciting," Principal Max gushed. "Four princesses and four princes will represent Honeycomb High this year."

I leaned over to tug on Toni's shirt.

"Why do you think they need so many?" I whispered. "Is it like the *Hunger Games*? Will only one survive?"

"They nominate two girls and guys from every class," she said as if it was common knowledge. "Except seniors, who get more because it's our last year and all."

I guess that made sense.

"And our first senior nominee is…" The principal paused. "Can I have a drumroll, please?"

To my surprise, an honest to goodness drumroll played through the speakers.

"Must've gotten someone from the band," Toni murmured. "Nice touch."

Principal Maxine spoke again after a loud cymbal crash. "Lana Leavengood! Congratulations, Princess Lana, and welcome to the Honeycomb High Court!"

Lana's friends hugged her and tittered as she pretended to wipe away a tear.

"I can't believe it," she said insincerely. "Thank you guys *so* much! I couldn't have done it without you."

Of course Lana would be the first girl announced, I thought. Of course.

No one else probably noticed the haughty glance she threw Toni, but I did. My best friend answered her with a scowl.

"Did you want to come over after school?" I said, trying to cheer up my BFF. "We could watch *Crazy, Stupid, Love* again."

Toni gave me a look. "Ariel. You know I never get tired of seeing Ryan Gosling without a shirt."

"And our second nominee is—" The drumroll came

again as the principal's voice rose, followed by the cymbal. "Bryleigh Davis! Congrats, Bryleigh!"

"But I'll only come," Toni went on, "if you promise to make more of those awesome red velvet cupcakes."

I gave her a smile. "You got it."

Toni looked up to hear the third nominee announced— it was Tessandra Mendoza. At that, my bestie let out a sigh. She seemed so invested in this. I wasn't sure why, but I was growing concerned.

"Something wrong?" I asked.

"Huh?" she said, then shook her head. "Oh no, it's nothing. I was just hoping someone we could actually root for would be nominated this year."

"Like who?"

"I don't know." Toni shrugged and gestured in Lana's direction. It looked like she was still giving her acceptance/ thank-you speech. "Someone more genuine and less...well, fake."

I lifted my shoulder in return. "So would I. But you know how these things go, Toni. It's all shallow fluff anyway."

"I guess you're right." Toni smiled. "So, for the movie, should I bring the chips and salsa?"

I was just about to say *heck yeah* when Principal Maxine's voice came over the speaker again.

"Only one more princess to go," she said, her voice echoing out to the entire school. "Who will the lucky girl be? I'll tell you in a moment!"

"You were right," I said on a laugh. "She is *really* into this."

"I know," Toni said, "it's like she's puking up rainbows

with every new name or something."

The visual of Principal Max spewing rainbows everywhere soon had me giggling. But that would disappear in the next second.

"Our final princess is…Ariel Duncan!"

An earthquake right here in Georgia would've been less of a shock.

Chapter 2

"Way to go, Ariel, and welcome to Court!" Principal Max continued as if the school hadn't been hit by a tornado like in the freaking *Wizard of Oz*, taking us to a completely new land. I wouldn't have been surprised if little orange men with green hair and overalls jumped out and started doing a jig. "Those are our four princesses, and one of them will be your queen! Congratulations again to all the nominees! Now, on to our princes—"

My ears cut out at that moment.

It was like I was in a wind tunnel or something. No sound broke through except the whoosh of my own breathing. My head felt a bit light, like I might pass out from lack of oxygen.

Toni was in front of me, saying something as she grinned from ear to ear. But for a few seconds, I couldn't make out a thing.

What had Principal Max said?

Had she really called my name?

Was this some kind of cruel prank?

Unable to help it, I looked up—but nope. There was no bucket of pig's blood waiting to drop on my head. I guess me not being *Carrie*'d was one mark in the positive column. But seriously, what the heck?

Toni gripped both sides of my head, forcing my eyes to meet hers.

"*Ariel,*" she said, shouted really, her voice finally breaking through. "Did you hear that? You made freaking Homecoming Court!"

"I thought I might've been hallucinating," I said, still shocked.

"Well, you weren't."

"Good grief," I muttered as the reality sank in. "How did this happen? There must be a mistake. I don't even remember my name being on the ballot."

"It was," Toni said matter-of-factly. "Right between Wendy Dulluth and Jessica Eakes. There were, like, forty names listed, just for the senior girls, and yours was one of them. You should really pay more attention, A."

I shook my head, trying to make sense of it all. "But that means someone had to nominate me."

Toni nodded. "It means more than that. People actually voted for you, my friend!"

"But no one even knows me."

"Of course they do or they wouldn't have voted," she said. "You're a member of the debate team—"

"Which I suck at," I put in.

"—which you do suck at," Toni agreed, "but only

because you're so nice. You're also in art and helped with the school's theater production last year."

I lifted my hands. "So did you. I helped a little, but you were basically in charge of that. I just touched up the scenery and made the celebratory cake at the end of the year."

Toni grinned. "Must've been some cake."

"Come on, Toni. Be serious."

"I am," she said, then examined her nails. "And you know, there was that time you were on TV."

"But I was, like, nine years old!"

It was my one brush with fame. I'd submitted to be a part of this kids baking challenge and earned a spot with my cute pigtails and Easy-Bake Oven. I went home after round two, but it was a good experience. Then in middle school, I'd started a baking vlog which now had a decent following. It paired two of my favorite things: desserts (cakes, cookies, cupcakes etc.) with my favorite movies. But that was just for fun.

"People love a hometown star," Toni added. "I'm just saying."

"Wow," I breathed.

"Yeah, wow and yay and all the other words used to convey happiness!" Toni laughed at the look on my face. "Why aren't you more excited about this? Ariel, this is incredible!"

"This is going to be a disaster," I mumbled.

Lana stepped up to my desk, and I realized people had already started leaving the room. The bell must've rung while I was in a Homecoming-induced stupor. Gah.

"Well," Lana said, eyeing me up and down, "congratulations on making Court."

I blinked. "Thanks, Lana. You too."

"I don't know how you did it," she went on. "But this should at least be entertaining. I'll see you after school, Cupcake."

We both watched her go, Toni with a satisfied grin and me with a frown.

"That sounded ominous," I said. "What do you think she meant by that?"

Toni shook her head. "You really were in la-la land for a second, weren't you?"

I shrugged.

"Everyone who was nominated is supposed to meet in the cafeteria after school," she said.

"Why?"

"To hear all about Court, what's expected of you, the works."

I smiled. "Well, that shouldn't be hard. Homecoming Court is just walking out on a football field at halftime and accepting some flowers, right?"

Toni chuckled while shaking her head at me.

"Riiight," she said in this drawn-out way that made me think it was so much more. But how could it be? I'd never been to Homecoming, wasn't interested in football, and I preferred to keep my dancing skills confined to my bedroom.

But it was just one night. There wasn't much to it.

"You better go, A. Wouldn't want to be late."

As I walked to the door in a daze, the principal's words

kept replaying in my mind.

Me? A princess?

I bit back a laugh. Yeah, right.

If I was, I must've been Sleeping Beauty, because I was obviously still dreaming.

Chapter 3

*I*f it was a dream, it was definitely one of those alternate reality ones where you can't wake up. People kept stopping me in the halls to congratulate me. Me! I couldn't believe it.

"Hey, congrats on the nom," Kendra Claire said. She'd been the lead in last year's theater production of *Hairspray* and was sensational. We'd bonded after I brought everyone in the cast and crew rose-shaped macarons on opening night.

Kendra had said she'd been doing the theater thing for years, and that was the first time anyone brought her flowers. I'd responded that with amazing talent like hers, it definitely wouldn't be the last. "It'll be nice to see a real girl on the Homecoming stage for once."

"Thanks, Kendra," I said, not really knowing what she meant.

I kept walking but was once again sidetracked by Teddy "The Tank" Kowalski.

"Yo, Cupcake!" he said, stopping me a few feet from my locker and holding his fist out. "Heard you're a princess. That's cool."

I rolled my eyes but tapped his fist with my palm. "Well, not really."

He lifted his chin. "They going to give you one of those girly crowns to wear?"

"A tiara?" I asked. "I hadn't really thought about it."

"If they do, you know it's legit," he said and gave my shoulder a pat. "Congrats."

I blinked. "Thanks, Teddy. Say hi to your little sister for me, okay?" He nodded, then walked off.

We'd had classes together since elementary school but never really spoke before last year. Teddy had come to me out of the blue, saying it was an emergency situation. His sister's tenth birthday was coming up, and he was supposed to have ordered something special (a cake, cookies, doughnuts etc.) to celebrate. His parents had given him the money weeks in advance to ensure they'd get an awesome surprise for their baby girl. Guess who'd promptly forgotten the cake, found the cash in his bag days later, couldn't remember what the money was for, and spent it on a new pair of Nikes?

Yeah, that would be Teddy.

The birthday party had been the next day. He'd looked so pitiful, begging for my help, and I couldn't find it in me to say no. I'd whipped him up a two-tier minion-themed cake with one layer of chocolate and one of vanilla. I'd even used yellow dye to make twelve little marshmallow minions, one for each of the party attendees as well as the birthday girl.

Teddy and I had been friendly ever since.

Mrs. Reeves nodded as I passed her biology classroom and stopped at my locker. We got along great—okay, I was on good terms with pretty much all of my teachers, but Mrs. Reeves and I shared a common love of movies and sweets.

"I heard the news," she said, beaming. "Way to go, Ariel. I know you'll do Honeycomb proud."

"Really?" I joked. "I wish I felt that certain."

"What do you mean?"

I shrugged. "Pretty sure I'm not the typical princess, Mrs. Reeves."

Translation: I'm confident and love myself just the way I am. But society might not see me that way. My look didn't exactly scream "princess."

Mrs. Reeves didn't seem to get my meaning.

She pushed her glasses up her nose. "Oh? Is there some criteria for high school royalty I don't know about? I thought it was just based on who got the most votes."

"You're right. It is," I said. "I just don't understand why anyone would vote for me."

"Again," Mrs. Reeves said, probing me with her shrewd gaze, "why wouldn't they?"

I didn't have an answer for that but decided to try.

"Well, I'm awkward and quiet."

"I'd call you friendly and sweet," she put in.

I nodded my thanks. "It's just… I'm like a turtle. I love my shell, and I'm very content in the shadows. I've never really wanted to be in the spotlight, you know?"

"I do know. But even turtles have to venture out once in a while. Sometimes life chooses your destiny for you."

Mrs. Reeves smiled a second later. "That was in my fortune cookie last night. Thought it would be appropriate here."

"I guess so," I said.

"Good luck, Ariel. And don't worry. I'm sure you'll knock 'em dead."

I didn't want to kill anyone, I thought, just to get through this debacle unscathed.

Several more people stopped to offer their congrats, and a few even said they'd voted for me. It hit me then for the first time: maybe I wasn't as under the radar as I'd thought. Other students noticed me...and they seemed genuinely happy for my success.

It was actually kind of awesome.

Because of all the pit stops along the way, by the time I left my locker, it was nearly twenty minutes after the final bell. The halls were less crowded, most of the students eager to be home or to start their after-school activities. The emptiness was good, since I needed to book it to the cafeteria. I walked as fast as I could. The only thing I hated more than the spotlight was walking in late—which automatically ensured attention I didn't want.

I'd just looked down at my phone to check the time... when I ran straight into a brick wall.

Or that was what it felt like.

I rebounded hard, falling to the floor and landing on my butt.

Thank goodness I had some extra cushioning back there, I thought. Otherwise, the cold tile (which had to be layered over concrete) would've hurt like a mother. My bag, books, and phone had gone down as well, creating a little circle of chaos around me. Cringing, I surveyed the scene — until my eyes latched on to what had caused me to fall in the first place.

My eyes traveled up over thighs encased in black workout pants, a muscular chest covered by a long-sleeved HHS T-shirt, strong shoulders, square jaw…and stopped on stormy blue eyes.

Gah, I thought. This was so cliché.

What am I, the heroine in a rom-com?

The guy I'd run into was frowning at me.

Rumor had it Rhys Castle rarely smiled, so I tried not to take it personally.

He'd certainly never smiled at me.

"Nice one, Cupcake," he said. "You okay?"

I blinked. My brain must've been addled because all I could think in that moment was, *Wow, even Rhys knows my nickname*, and on the heels of that thought, *I've never seen such a pretty wall*.

Seriously, Rhys could've given Captain America a run for his money.

I watched in a daze as Rhys collected my things off the floor, then looked at me again.

"Need help getting up?"

I snapped out of it at that. Ugh, if Honeycomb's golden boy quarterback had to help me, it would only add insult to injury. Trying to calm my blush, I struggled to my feet.

"No, but thanks," I said as he handed over my stuff. "Sorry, I didn't see you, thought I'd walked into a wall or something — which is pretty out-there, since obviously you're very much human."

"You walk into walls often?" he said, and I couldn't tell if he was joking.

I smiled anyway. "It's been known to happen once or twice."

My attempt at humor was a fail. He didn't crack; his lips remained stuck in a firm line.

"Are you okay?" I asked. Maybe I'd hit him harder than I thought, and that was what put him in a bad mood. "I hope I didn't hurt you."

"Oh, I'm good," he said. "Girls throw themselves at me all the time. Just not quite so literally."

"I didn't—"

"Maybe you should go out for the football team." That made the words I'd been about to say die on my tongue.

"Why would I do that?" I asked slowly.

"Just saying, that was a decent hit." I might've been imagining it, but I could've sworn I saw his lips twitch. "With a little practice, you could probably take me down."

I shook my head in disbelief. "Do I look like a football player to you?"

Rhys gave me a once-over, and for some reason when his eyes met mine again, I could feel my cheeks blushing.

"Watch where you're going next time," was all he said, and then he sauntered past me down the hall.

"Pretty *and* rude," I said under my breath. "Should've seen that one coming."

Chapter 4

*S*haking my head, I continued my walk to the cafeteria, which was thankfully in the opposite direction of Mr. Personality. Out of all the guys in school, I just had to run headfirst into Rhys. The guy gave new meaning to the word swoon, but wow, did his surly attitude suck.

Try out for football? Blah.

I couldn't believe I'd fallen under his spell for even a second.

Luckily, no other obstacles (human or otherwise) impeded my progress, and I got to the cafeteria right on time.

A petite blond woman, wearing a green and white sweater dress, met me as I walked through the door. She had an easy smile. Her teeth were blindingly white, and she wore a sparkly pin in the shape of a crown on her left breast.

"You must be Ariel!" she said brightly and handed me a packet of papers. "I'm Juliana Weaver, Honeycomb's

Homecoming director. I'm so glad you're here! We're still waiting for one more, but we were just about to get started."

"Thank you," I said softly. "Are there assigned seats or...?"

"Oh no, honey." She laughed. "Just pull up a chair! Feel free to sit wherever you'd like!" This woman's entire demeanor was like one big exclamation point.

Trying not to worry about all the eyes on me, I made my way to the back and sat down. My gaze searched the faces dotting the cafeteria, and it was like a who's who of Honeycomb High. Lana was there, of course, and she narrowed her eyes as I passed her. She was seated at a table that included Bryleigh Davis, Tessandra Mendoza, and three guys I knew to be some of the most popular in our grade: Daniel Pascale, Jon Wu, and Zander Albritton.

Daniel was our student body president, a total hottie, and one of the smartest people in the school. Jon, drum major of the Honeycomb High marching band, was also a member of several clubs (including debate, which he rocked by the way). He waved as I looked at him, and I waved in return. Zander was a member of the wrestling team who knew basically everyone; he also played defensive lineman for our football team and was nearly as big as Tank. With his Hawaiian heritage and easy smile, Zander kind of reminded me of a young Jason Momoa.

I made a mental note.

So these were the princes.

All of them were popular and good-looking.

Actually...glancing around, I noticed that was a common theme. Bryleigh, HHS head varsity cheerleader, had always looked like she stepped straight out of a magazine. Her hair was the color of ebony, falling in long waves down her back, her skin black and beautiful. Her makeup was light and nearly as perfect as Lana's. Tessandra should've looked out of place sitting next to them, but she didn't. Even if she was a so-called "nerd"—we'd all known Tess would be valedictorian of our graduating class even when we were in middle school—her tomboyish clothes couldn't hide either her flawless olive skin or her smarts. She fit with the others for a simple reason: Tessandra was extraordinary. So was everyone else sitting at what I belatedly realized was the unofficial senior table.

I was betting the freshman, sophomore, and junior nominees each had something special about them as well. They all looked completely at ease in this crowd.

Ugh, I felt like such a poser.

I so did not belong in this room with these people.

Maybe I could sneak out the back before anyone noticed. I was just about to make my escape when two things happened at once.

"Well, I guess we should get started!" Ms. Weaver said, pulling us all to attention. "Though we seem to be short one prince."

And the door to the cafeteria suddenly opened and in walked the quarterback, looking just as good and unhurried as he had out in the hall.

"Rhys Castle, I presume?" Ms. Weaver said, smile extra bright. "How nice of you to join us! I'm glad you could fit us into your busy schedule."

"No problem," he said, gesturing back to the door. "I was going to skip, but Coach told me I had to come."

The wattage in Ms. Weaver's smile dimmed.

"Oh?" she said. "Well, I'm glad Coach Feinnes persuaded you. Homecoming is a big deal here at Honeycomb High!"

"If you say so," he said.

"I do! This should be something very special for you! Please take a seat."

Rhys nodded, then sat right in the front at an empty table.

Okay, so it wasn't me—he was just a cold fish. I guess that should've made me feel better.

"It's my pleasure to welcome you all to this year's Homecoming Court! As I said, my name is Juliana Weaver, Homecoming director, queen for the class of '88." No surprise there, I thought, mentally cataloging her nonstop bubbly persona and general friendliness. "I'll be helping you all through this wonderful time in preparation for the big day!"

I gave a mental scoff. Only in the small southern town of Honeycomb, Georgia, would this be considered *big*. They loved their traditions here almost as much as they loved football. Keyword: almost.

"There are only three weeks until Homecoming, and that time will be packed full of fun. If you'll open your packet to page one, you'll notice a court calendar and itinerary of events." She held up a finger. "These will include, but are not limited to, the following: the annual Homecoming parade, bonding exercises, formal dance lessons, pep rally, and Homecoming football game culminating in the announcement of king and queen, as well as the big dance!"

My eyes widened as they moved down the page. This

was definitely more than I'd bargained for. Ms. Weaver confirmed as much with her next words.

"For the next month, everyone in this room is Honeycomb royalty." She beamed at each of us in turn. "You are all now princesses and princes, voted in by your peers to represent Honeycomb in this time-honored tradition. Oh, it's just so exciting! Does anyone have any questions?"

Tessandra raised her hand. "Will this affect our school-work in any way?"

Ms. Weaver shook her head. "Most Homecoming activities will be held outside of school hours, and those that aren't have been agreed upon by the faculty and staff. So you won't be penalized for leaving class early or anything like that."

One of the junior boys raised his hand next. "What about sports? Will this interfere with practice?"

"The coaches are all aware and fully supportive of our Homecoming traditions."

My eyes went to Rhys as he grunted. Looked like he didn't approve.

Lana was called on next, and she actually stood.

"I don't have a question," she said, "but I just wanted to say thank you so much, Ms. Weaver. I'm so proud of myself for being a Honeycomb High princess for the fourth year in a row. It is such an honor."

Juliana Weaver nodded. "It is, Lana. Thank you. Does anyone else—"

"Actually, I wasn't done," Lana said, cutting her off. "I also wanted to add that keeping in shape and making sure to look my best has always been a top priority, and I cannot wait for the chance to be Honeycomb's Homecoming queen. Some people were born for things like this, and I'm so glad to be in good company." Her eyes sliced in my direction, then quickly away. "But there can only be one queen. And we all know who that should be."

With that, she sat, looking very pleased with herself. I found myself biting back a smile. Lana was just so over-the-top.

Rhys spoke next. "What if we're supposed to play in the Homecoming game?"

"Good question," Zander said. "What happens then, Ms. Weaver?"

"Or if we're cheering," Bryleigh put in.

"Or leading the band," Jon added.

Juliana Weaver had been staring at Lana with what looked like disbelief, but the questions shook her out of it.

"There shouldn't be a problem," she said. "At halftime, you'll simply abandon your posts and assume your royal capes, so to speak."

"Do we get capes?" Zander said as his smile widened.

"Not literally," Ms. Weaver said slowly, but seeing the disappointment on Zander's face, she quickly added, "but the girls do get tiaras and sashes, and the boys each get a scepter."

"Dang," he said, nudging Jon with his elbow. "A scepter is like a sword, right? I'm going to rock that so hard."

The two high-fived as Lana rolled her eyes and held up her hand once more.

Ms. Weaver looked wary as she called on her.

"When will we find out who our princes are?" she asked.

My ears perked at this. What did she mean by that? All the princes were already here, I thought.

"I was just about to get to that," Ms. Weaver said as she leaned down, picked up and placed something covered by a green silk sheet onto the table. "Every princess has her prince, and the opposite is also true. That's actually our first order of business! I can tell some of you are confused, but don't worry. All will be made clear in a moment."

With a flourish, she withdrew the sheet to uncover...two large, antique-looking cups.

They seemed to be made of bronze with hints of pearl and a few emeralds shining through. Honestly? My mind immediately jumped to Harry Potter. That happened a lot. I'd already done several desserts dedicated to the Hogwarts crew.

"This matching set was gifted to us by one of the founding members of the school. They are called the Honeycomb chalices. Each year, we put the nominees' names into the cups and draw to see who will be paired with whom. The chalice never lies."

Okay, it was official. There were literally two goblets of fire sitting before me. Harry, Ron, and Hermione would probably walk in at any moment. Where was Toni so we could geek out over this together?

One of the sophomore girls timidly raised her hand.

"Yes?" Ms. Weaver said.

"Do we *have* to be paired up?"

"Most of the activities do require a pair—such as the bonding exercises and dance lessons. Oh, those are just wonderful!"

Considering the fact that I'd always been too chicken to dance in public, I wasn't so sure about that one.

The other sophomore girl raised her hand.

"Are the pairings always girl-boy? Or can we be a little more inclusive and have a girl with another girl?"

Ms. Weaver blinked twice. "Well, I'm sure we could… if that's what you wanted. There's nothing that says it has to be divided by gender. Though, for the underclassmen and juniors, that would mean your pairs are already chosen, since there are just two girls and two boys. Is that what you'd like to do?"

This led to some conversing, and in the end, it was decided that the sophomores would be paired girl-girl and boy-boy. Everyone was cool with that decision, including Ms. Weaver. She drew names for the freshman and junior representatives. Then came the seniors' turn. The first two pairings ended up like this:

Tessandra and Jon.

Bryleigh and Daniel.

Lana's name was drawn next, and from the way she kept throwing glances at Rhys, I knew she was hoping to be paired with him. Secretly, I hoped that, too. He was beautiful, there was no doubt about that. But Rhys wasn't my type, and I wasn't his—case in point, he used to date Lana back in the day—so I wasn't eager to spend more time with him.

Unfortunately, my prayers went unanswered.

"And Lana's prince will be…Zander!" Ms. Weaver smiled as she put the two names on the table together, and then placed her hands in the glasses one last time. "So that means our final pairing will be Princess Ariel"—she read my name from the paper in her hand and then switched to read the other—"and Prince Rhys. What delightful pairings!"

Were they really? I wondered. Rhys had looked my way when she read my name, but I couldn't tell what he was thinking. Probably something like: *Great, it's her. The girl who walks into walls.* Ugh.

Of course, Lana had something to say about the results.

"Can we draw again, Ms. Weaver?" she asked, then lowered her voice, though we could all still hear her. "I think the chalices may have made a mistake. I should be with Rhys, and Cupcake should have Zander. Those pairings make more sense. Plus, they would just look better, don't you think?"

I couldn't deny that I saw what she meant.

Though wow, what a brat for saying it out loud.

She and Rhys were cut from the same cloth. I wasn't ugly, but Lana was gorgeous. Although Zander had a cute face, Rhys was debonair in a way he'd never accomplish, something that obviously called to Lana. And yes, either of them would probably look better on her arm than on mine. But geez.

"I'd be okay with that," I said, just so no one thought I was holding Rhys against his will. As if. No matter what he thought, I wasn't one of the girls who would fall at his feet. Well, I mean I *had*. But I wouldn't do it again. Not on purpose. Also, it was really crappy of Lana to throw Zander under the bus like that. "I'm cool with switching partners if everyone else is."

"Awesome," Lana said, then looked to her right. "Zander,

are you good?"

He shrugged. "Sure."

"Well, I'm not," Rhys said, surprising all of us.

"What was that?" Lana said in her sweetest voice. "Did you say something?"

"Yeah. I don't want to switch. I want to stay with Cupcake."

Lana's face fell. "But—"

"That's enough," Ms. Weaver said and held up a hand to stop any further protests. "The chalices are never wrong, Miss Leavengood. The homecoming pairings have been chosen, and they are final."

Lana's mouth snapped shut but then opened once more. "Oh well, that's fine. I was just thinking about the optics, that's all."

I rolled my eyes at that, then caught sight of Rhys watching me, and looked away.

Why did he want to stay with me anyway? The only other time we'd talked, I'd run smack into his chest and ended up making a fool of myself. Not to mention he'd been a colossal jerk. Let's be honest: I was pretty sure Lana was right, and they'd fit together better than we ever could.

"Everyone be sure to review your packets," Ms. Weaver said, still smiling. "I'll meet you all here tomorrow at the same time to discuss our first Homecoming activity. Being on Court is a once-in-a-lifetime opportunity! I hope you enjoy every second!"

As I was about to leave, Ms. Weaver came over and placed a hand on my arm.

"I hope you weren't offended by what Lana said." She spoke quietly so only I could hear. "I want to believe she didn't mean anything by it, I do. But I've known that girl for the past three years and her mother far longer. They aren't the…nicest people."

I smiled at her concern. "I wasn't. It's all good, Ms. Weaver. Honestly, I think she was more upset that she didn't get her preferred prince. Zander's an okay guy, though. I wouldn't have minded the change."

"Ah, ah, ah," she said, "the chalices know what they're doing, my dear. You just have to trust the process!"

"Okay," I said.

"You know, Ariel was always my favorite princess," she said with a wink.

"You and my mom have that in common." I sighed. "See you later."

I walked away in a bit of a daze.

Princesses, princes, and chalices. It felt like I'd suddenly been thrust into a fantasy novel. And Ms. Weaver was sweet, but…

Goodness gracious, a whole month of homecoming activities?

Ugh, I knew I should've bolted when I had the chance.

Chapter 5

*M*om's car was in the driveway when I got home. I wasn't eager to tell her about my homecoming news, so I opened and closed the door as quietly as I could. Luck seemed to be on my side—the hinges didn't make a peep. As I tiptoed toward my room, stealth was my middle name, my steps so silent I could've been a ninja extra in a movie.

Unfortunately, my mother had hypersensitive hearing— or a sixth sense that told her when I was trying to hide something.

I was only a few feet away from my room when Mom walked out of the kitchen in yoga pants and a black tank top with Elsa, snowflakes, and the words Keep Calm & Let it Go on the front.

"Oh yay, you're here," she said, smiling at me. "Weren't you going to say hi?"

"Thought you might be busy," I said, and it wasn't even a lie. I *had* hoped she'd be doing something to keep her from questioning me. "It's been a long day, Mom. I was just going to take a nap."

"Well, don't hurry off. Come sit and chat for a bit. I feel like we never see each other anymore."

I gave her a look. "Mom. Come on. We spent like four hours this weekend watching Disney movies."

"I thought you enjoyed that."

"I did," I said. "Maleficent is now my new BFF, and you know I salivated over Belle getting to be around all those books. But you can't say we don't hang out when we do. Our mother-daughter relationship is on point."

"Still." She walked to the couch, took a seat, and patted the cushion next to her. With a sigh, I sat. "See? Was that so hard?"

I shrugged. "No, but seriously, there's nothing to talk about. I had a test today. I think I did a good job."

"You are one smart cookie," she said. "Anything else?"

I couldn't meet her eyes. "That's pretty much it."

If you don't count me being Honeycomb royalty.

But I couldn't say that to Mom. She'd blow it waaay out of proportion.

"So nothing interesting happened?" Mom pressed. "You're home a little later than usual."

"Oh yeah, I had to stay after," I said quickly.

"For what?"

Hmm, how to answer that…

"There's this thing," I began, then didn't know how to finish.

Mom nodded after a moment, gesturing for me to keep going.

"Well, it's nothing really. Just…there was this thing."

"You said that already, Ariel," she reminded me gently.

Gah. Why was this so dang hard?

I should just tell Mom the truth and get it over with. I opened my mouth, but at the same time my phone rang, saving me from having to explain.

"It's Toni," I said with relief. "I should take this."

"Of course." Mom's face was serene. "I'll wait."

"You don't have to—"

"I'll wait," she repeated and reached across to pat my hand.

After I hit the accept button, Toni's voice came streaming out before I could say a word.

"*Rhys Castle!* Oh my gosh, you've gotta be kidding me!"

I winced. "Hi, Toni."

"Yeah, yeah, hi to you, too. But seriously…Rhys freaking Castle!" she said again—shouted really. There was no way Mom wasn't getting an earful. "You get paired with a guy that fine, and you don't even tell your best friend? How does that work, A?"

Turning away, I lowered my voice. "I was going to but didn't get the chance yet. The omecoming-hay eeting-may ran long."

"Are you speaking pig Latin?"

"Es-yay, why?"

"Ugh, you are so weird."

"But you love me and all my quirks," I said.

"Yeah well… *Anyway*, you have to be home by now, so what kept you?" she said. "It better be something good."

"My mom wanted to 'talk' when I got home." I dropped

my voice even more. "She's been acting kind of strange, actually."

"Ah, okay." Toni was silent a beat then, "But it's Rhys! Ugh, he is so…gah!"

"I know," I mumbled. "Listen, can I call you later? I promise we'll discuss all this then."

"No problem. But next time something this big happens, A? I better receive a text, smoke signal, a good old-fashioned skywritten message. Okay?"

I couldn't help but smile at that. "You got it, Toni. I'll have a carrier pigeon on standby. Talk later."

"Sure, sure," she said, and I heard her mumble Rhys's name and the words "can't believe it, so hot" just before she hung up.

When I turned back to Mom, her look was expectant.

"Sorry about that." I laughed, putting my phone on the table. "You know how Toni can be."

"She sounded excited about something," Mom remarked.

I shrugged, silently hoping she hadn't heard the entire conversation—or one name in particular.

"So who's Rhys Castle?"

Ugh, why me?

"Ariel," Mom said when I didn't respond immediately. She waited until I looked at her and then said it again. "The guy Toni couldn't seem to stop talking about—Rhys. Who is he?"

Just play it cool, I thought. She's only asking because my bestie was overly enthusiastic, not because she knows anything.

"He's a boy from school," I said, but it was clear Mom

wanted more. "Rhys is the quarterback of the Honeycomb High football team. Word on the street is he's very good, already has college scouts looking at him."

"Ah, I knew I'd heard that name before."

Unlike me, Mom actually liked sports. Lord knew why.

"But why did Toni call you about him?" Mom asked.

"We kind of got paired up for this thing," I hedged.

Mom tilted her head. "The same 'thing' you had to stay after school for?"

"Yeah," I said, then abruptly stood from the couch. "But it's no big deal. Like I said, Mom, my day was boring as usual. I have a lot of homework. See you later."

"Okay, sweetie," she said then added, "but you know, it's the strangest thing."

Her tone made me freeze in my tracks. Looking at her, I saw a sparkle in her eyes that hadn't been there a second ago.

"I got an interesting text about ten minutes before you walked in."

I couldn't help it. I took the bait, hook, line, and sinker.

"Oh yeah, from who?" I asked.

"A woman I've never met," she said while lifting a brow. "Like I said, it was so unexpected. Her name is Juliana, and she said that you were selected to be a princess for Homecoming Court today."

I gulped as Mom's hands went to her hips.

"She also said something about being excited to work with you this month—which implies it is, in fact, a big deal."

My mouth opened, but no words came out. It was okay, though. Mom wasn't done talking.

"What I don't understand is why you, my wonderful daughter, didn't tell me about this yourself."

So busted.

"Mom, I—"

She held up a hand. "Just tell me one thing. Is it true?"

I nodded, wincing as her smile bloomed.

"Ariel!" she squealed then grabbed me up in a hug. "This is so exciting! I can't even… Why wouldn't you tell me? It's like a dream come true!"

"Ugh, not really," I said, and Mom took in my face.

"Why aren't you more excited about this?"

Hmm, let's see. *1) Homecoming is an antiquated idea. 2) I love my body, but I'll never fit the mold of what society thinks a princess should be. 3) I never want to be the center of attention, avoid it pretty much like the plague. 4) I've been paired with Rhys Castle, and I'm 99.9 percent sure he's a jerk. 5) If people are going to judge me based on some unattainable ideal of perfection…uh thanks, but no thanks. I'd rather stay home.*

Instead of saying any of that, I shrugged.

"Ariel, what's wrong?" she asked. "This is going to be so fun! Juliana was telling me about all the cool things coming up. And ooh! I can't wait to let all the girls at work know."

"Mom, don't go overboard," I said. "It's just Homecoming."

She sniffed. "Must you steal my joy? You are a princess whether you like it or not."

I laughed at her mulish expression. "It's not like I'm marrying into the royal family."

"This is the next best thing," she declared. "And it's

going to be amazing! Just you wait."

"Yeah. Amazingly awkward," I muttered.

"Oh pish, you're going to love it." Mom grabbed my hands and met my eyes. "You are the sweetest, loveliest, most wonderful girl, and I love you."

I blushed. "Love you, too, Mom."

"I know you do," she said. "Now, is there anything else I need to know?"

Her eyes were penetrating, but the cat was out of the bag. So I figured why not tell her everything?

"Rhys Castle, the guy we were talking about," I said.

Mom nodded. "The one who according to Toni is 'gah, so hot'?"

"That's the one," I said. "We were divided into pairs at the meeting, and he's my prince."

"I see. And is he gorgeous?"

"Unfortunately, yes," I said.

"Got it. So, you're a reluctant princess with an unfortunately hot prince. Is that everything?"

I thought it over. "Yeah, that's the gist."

Mom's smile was slow. "So, do I have to bow to you now? Since you're royalty and all?"

I rolled my eyes. "Mom."

"Yes, your highness?"

"Ugh! I'm going to my room now."

Mom laughed and actually did curtsy as I walked past her, and I bit back a smile.

"You know, this is all your fault," I said.

"Me?" she asked.

"Yes." I held out a hand and gestured to her. "Jeez, you

even named me after a princess. You hoped something like this would happen. Don't even try to deny it."

"Maybe I did. Or maybe I just watched *The Little Mermaid* one too many times."

Mom suddenly got this faraway look in her eye.

"My baby girl is a princess. Ooh, I can't wait to tell everyone!"

And I knew she would the minute my door closed, but there was no help for it. As I was about to enter my room, I switched course, heading straight for the kitchen. Lifting my apron off the hook and over my head, I started pulling down ingredients.

It had been one heck of a day. The kitchen was my happy place, and it was time for some major baking therapy.

If I happened to eat a cookie along the way, so be it.

Goodness gracious, I thought as I stirred the dry ingredients together, unable to clear my mind. The homecoming packet we'd received was mocking me from where I'd placed it on top of my bag across the room. I could already hear Mom in the living room, telling her friends the news.

Cookie dough, I decided.

This definitely called for a spoonful or two of the good stuff.

Chapter 6

un fact: I read a study once that said 40 percent of people eat more and/or skip meals in response to stress. I used to do that sometimes.

But typically, I took the road less traveled.

Instead of stress eating, I liked to stress *bake*.

Measuring and mixing ingredients together, following instructions, focusing my full attention on a recipe really put me at ease. The act of creating something out of nothing was so satisfying.

And okay, yes, I'd snag a little taste here and there.

But hey, I had to test the results! It was a rule. No one could eat anything I made until I tried it myself first. This was for their sake as well as mine. I wanted my food to provide comfort, joy, and add a little sweetness to someone's day. If I forgot an ingredient by accident, I didn't want to make anyone sick (which hadn't happened yet, thank goodness). Plus, I cared enough about my baking skills to always strive for the best.

It could take a few tries to get there, to completely de-stress.

That was why I ended up taking two large containers of cookies to school the next day.

"These are so good," Toni said as she chewed. "There is literally a party going on in my mouth."

"Am I invited?" I said.

"That depends. Can I get a second cookie?"

I didn't even bother to answer, just handed her one.

"Okay, I guess you can come." Toni winked.

"Hey, Cupcake," Jon Wu called out as he came even with my locker. "What have you got today?"

"Chocolate chip cookies," I said back.

"Can I get one?"

"Sure." I tossed him a cookie. "Hope you like it."

"You rock," he said, giving me a nod as he took a bite and kept walking.

"Seriously," Toni said, "look at all of them loving your food." She nodded to the students up and down the halls with cookies in their hands and smiles on their faces. "Keep this up, and you'll be a shoo-in for Homecoming Queen."

"That's not why I made them." I scoffed. "It took me three batches to get over the stress of listening to my mom call literally everyone on her contacts list. She even told the dentist! Also, let's be real. I have about as much chance of being Homecoming Queen as I do at fitting into your skinny jeans."

Toni looked me up and down. "I think you could if you really wanted to."

Was she serious?

Gah, my best friend was clearly losing it.

"No, Toni, I couldn't." I gestured from my curvy frame to her much slimmer silhouette. "Unless those have some kind of magical *Sisterhood of the Traveling Pants* deal I don't know about."

She rolled her eyes. "Not the jeans, silly. I was talking about Homecoming. You have as good of a chance as anybody."

A girl and guy I didn't know came up to me just as I was about to argue.

"Hey," the guy said, "we heard someone named Cupcake was giving out free food."

"Yep, that's me," I said, handing him and the girl two cookies. "Hope you enjoy."

She smiled. "Thanks, that's so nice of you."

"No problem," I said.

"It is nice. Isn't it?" Toni put in. "This is Ariel Duncan aka Cupcake, and she's running for Homecoming Queen. We'd appreciate your vote."

I blushed. "No, I—"

"That's awesome. Congrats," the girl said and took a bite of her cookie. Her eyes went wide. "Oh, you've definitely got my vote."

"Mine, too," her boyfriend mumbled through a mouthful. "Thanks again for the sweets."

"Welcome," Toni said and waved them away.

Once they were out of earshot, I turned on her with a frown.

"What?" she said, all innocent.

"Toni, why did you do that?" I asked. "I'd never use food or anything else as some kind of bribe to get votes. That would just be sad, not to mention unethical."

Toni finished chewing, then jerked her head at something behind me.

"Tell that to her," she said.

I looked over my shoulder. Lana and a couple of her friends were currently coming toward us down the hall, each carrying a tray filled with little cups. There was a sign hanging from each tray. As they got closer, I could finally make out what it said.

Take a shot and make good choices! Vote Lana Leavengood for Homecoming Queen!

Lana stopped by my locker, giving Toni and me a smile.

"Would you like a royal shot?" she asked, and I noticed there were gold crowns on the cups. Wow, she had really gone all out.

"Sure," I said, reaching forward, "these look great, Lana."

Toni slapped my hand away. "We'll pass, but thanks."

"I see you brought something as well," she said. "Sweets aren't really as good for you as espresso, but to each her own."

"Oh, these don't have anything to do with Homecoming," I said, then had to correct myself. "Actually, they're the result of stress that was brought about by Homecoming. But that's all."

A few girls from the varsity basketball team came over.

Toni handed them cookies, saying, "Enjoy, and make sure you vote Ariel Duncan for queen."

"Sure," one of them said while I sputtered.

"You always make the best stuff, Cupcake." Heather Newsome smiled at me. We'd sat next to each other and survived Mr. Baxter's Econ class last year. In the end, I'd only learned one thing: I never wanted a career in economics. Ever. "These cookies are awesome."

"Thanks, girl," I said. "How are you doing?"

Heather shrugged. "Eh, not bad, just waiting for the season to start. You?"

I considered telling her the truth—that it was weird to be nominated for something I hadn't even known I was in the running for—but decided against it. We were friendly, but not that close.

"I'm okay," I said. "Just hoping for a calm, uneventful senior year."

"You and me both," she said. "See you around. Good luck on the Homecoming thing."

Before I could tell her I wouldn't need luck, I wasn't planning on winning, she'd already walked away. Tank came over next, taking the cookie Toni handed him. Before he could say anything, Lana stepped between us with a big smile.

"Hi Teddy," she said. "Would you like a shot of espresso?"

"Nah," Tank said, "I better not."

"Ah come on. You look like someone who has good taste. Espresso is the healthy choice."

He shrugged. "Cupcake's cookies always taste healthy to me. Plus"—he patted his stomach—"too much caffeine can make you gassy."

Lana's face turned red at that.

Tank nodded to me and then was off. When I glanced

at Toni, she was smiling, and I didn't realize why until I looked to my left. Lana was currently giving my cookies the stank eye.

"Would you like one?" I asked, but she was already shaking her head before I could finish.

"All that sugar would go straight to my waistline," she said.

"I actually used maple syrup as a sugar substitute. It's supposed to be better for you."

Lana sniffed. "I'll pass."

"Oh okay." Throwing Toni a stern glance, using telepathy to tell her not to smack my hand again, I took two cups off of Lana's tray. "This was really clever and kind of you. Thanks."

"Hmm," she said. "Ladies, we still have more cups to hand out, more votes to secure."

Lana and the girls in her posse came to attention. They headed down the hall, passing people cups along the way, Lana smiling all the while. It didn't even look the least bit strained. I definitely couldn't have pulled that off, I thought. My jaw hurt just from looking at her.

After handing one of the cups to Toni, I took a drink.

"Ooh, that's good," I said with a nod. "And just look at these cute little cups."

Toni drank hers in one go then shrugged. "It's okay, kind of leaves a bitter aftertaste, though. Unlike your delicious choco chips."

I rolled my eyes. "This isn't some sort of competition."

"Actually"—she put a hand on my shoulder—"that's exactly what it is."

"But I always bake things at home and bring them to school," I said. "It's a common thing. There's no ulterior motive. I just want to give people a pick-me-up."

"You don't have to tell me that. I know." Toni shook her head. "And so do a whole bunch of the students here. I think it's one of the reasons they voted for you."

"Huh?"

"You're so sweet, A—some might say too sweet for your own good. Heck, you were nice to Lana just now, even though she was being her usual snobby self."

I crossed my arms, taking a bite out of one of the cookies.

Fresh and sweet with just a little bit of softness in the center.

Delicious.

"That's exactly why you'd make the perfect queen," she finished.

"I don't know what you're talking about," I said after swallowing. Geez, this was a good batch. "I'd be terrible."

"No, you'd be wonderful," she countered.

Great. Now she sounded like Mom.

"Someone probably did it as a joke," I muttered.

The more I'd thought about it, the more it made sense. Just because there hadn't been a *Carrie* moment at the time of the announcement didn't mean there wasn't one coming. Kids could be cruel; Toni and I knew that better than most. But I also knew there were good people in the world.

"Pssh, whatever. I, for one, cannot wait to hear about all of your awesome adventures."

Glancing at her out of the corner of my eye, I finished the rest of my cookie. "I can't believe you're actually asking people to vote for me. Could you stop, by the way? I love you, but that's totally unnecessary."

Toni thought it over, then nodded. "You're right. We'll attract more people if they just think you're bringing the cookies out of the kindness of your heart."

"Toni."

"Which I know you are," she added. "I was just saying."

I sighed. "Seriously, why do you care so much about this anyway?"

"Well…you know I can't stand to see people like Lana win. They always get everything they've ever wanted. Does she really need a crown, too?"

She already has a few, I thought. Lana had won Miss Honeycomb High School as a sophomore, the first underclassman to ever do that if I wasn't mistaken. And she was also the reigning Miss Sweet Northern Plains—whatever that meant. There was even a billboard in town with her smiling face on it.

"And I love a good underdog story," Toni added.

I nodded. "We both do."

There had to be more to it than that, though. Toni seemed to be deeply invested in the Homecoming outcome. I wanted to know why.

"Plus," she said brightly, "you're my best friend, so of course I have to root for you."

I lifted a brow, waiting.

"Annnd I may or may not have been the one to nominate you."

My jaw dropped as I looked at my bestie with new eyes.

"Oh goodness, please tell me you're kidding," I said.

It shouldn't have surprised me, but it did. Toni loved me like I loved her. She knew I hated the spotlight—and yet, she'd entered me into an event that put me smack-dab in the center of it? Good grief.

Toni shrugged. "I have no regrets. This is your destiny, A."

I groaned. "Ugh, Toni, why? Why would you subject me to something like this?"

"Whining doesn't suit you, my friend. And I told you already. You're going to be wonderful. I can picture it now: Queen Cupcake," she said, spreading her hands as if the words were on a marquee or something. Oh, the horror. "Doesn't that sound nice?"

I was literally speechless.

"And hey, now you get to spend time after school with Rhys Castle. It was an unintentional side effect, but you can thank me later."

As the bell rang, she skipped away, leaving me with my jaw on the floor and two empty cookie platters. Toni, my own best friend, was the one who set this whole thing in motion.

I didn't know whether to laugh or cry.

Chapter 7

*C*rying was a very real possibility.

Hours later, after the final bell rang, I met up with the rest of the court. Ms. Weaver told us we'd be going outside and proceeded to lead us into the forest behind the school. The trees were tall, the overgrown grass came up to my thighs, and the worst part was I kept hearing little *things* buzzing in the air around me.

I was going to kill Toni.

Best friend or not, she'd put me here.

Outside.

With the bugs.

Don't get me wrong—I had a lot of respect for Mother Nature, recycled every chance I got, turned off the water when I brushed my teeth, always made sure to put my gum in the trash and not just throw it out the window. But Toni was the reason I was tripping over weeds, breathing in strange forest-y scents, surrounded by unknown insects and creepy crawlies.

"Ah, here we are," Ms. Weaver said.

Suddenly the trees receded, and we emerged into a clearing. The grass was still tall, but there were wildflowers everywhere, dotting the space with yellow, purple, and pink blossoms like something out of a fairy tale. It was beautiful.

"Wow," I breathed, taking in the large expanse of blue sky.

Everyone grew quiet, waiting to see what our first task would be. On the event calendar for today, it had just said TRUST in big bold letters. Not that that was mysterious or anything.

"I'm sure a lot of you are wondering why we're here," Ms. Weaver began. "I wanted to do something a little unorthodox so we can bond as a group. Homecoming Court is special, and you're a part of that now! This"—she gestured at the space around us—"is sacred ground."

"You mean there are dead people here?" one of the freshman nominees asked, looking a little freaked out. "Gross!"

"Cool," someone else said while Zander shook his head.

"No offense, Ms. Weaver"—the big football player held up his hands—"but I don't mess around when it comes to the dead."

"Same here," Tessandra said and quickly crossed herself.

"Um, no," Ms. Weaver said slowly. "I only meant this is an important part of Honeycomb history. We're here, where it all began. Before they built the new stadium, the first ever Homecoming King and Queen were crowned in this very field! It's full of tradition…not dead bodies."

I could've sworn I heard Zander sigh in relief.

"Remember how you were divided into pairs yesterday? Please go to your prince or princess now."

Rhys Castle slowly walked over, settling himself at my side, but he didn't say a word. That was fine. We were one of the only pairs who hadn't talked on the way over, but whatever. My prince seemed even less eager about all of this than I was. In fact, he looked absolutely miserable to be paired with me. So why did he refuse to switch when he had the chance?

This guy was a mystery, but not one I was interested in solving.

Once everyone was in place, Ms. Weaver went on.

"Good, good," she said. "In order to get to know one another, I thought we could do a few trust exercises. I—"

Lana raised her hand.

"Yes, Lana," Ms. Weaver said.

"I didn't realize we'd be exercising," she said. "Are we going to be getting sweaty? Because I don't have the right clothes for that and may need to sit out."

Ms. Weaver eyed her for a moment then said, "You'll be fine, Miss Leavengood."

"But—"

"A little sweat never hurt anyone!" Her voice brooked no argument. "Everyone will be participating, and by the end of this first activity, hopefully we'll have broken the ice between you and your partner. Ready?"

As she surveyed the group, something flew straight at my head, and unable to help myself, I ducked, biting back a squeal of panic.

"Ariel?" Ms. Weaver said. "Did you have a question?"

"Oh, no," I said, realizing I was crouched over in a defensive position. But dang, that kamikaze fly or whatever-it-was had come at me out of nowhere. "I was just…tying my shoe. It must've come undone on the walk over."

As I bent down, pretending to fiddle with my shoelaces, Lana rolled her eyes, and everyone in the circle looked back to Ms. Weaver—except Rhys. His eyes seemed to track my movements, but for the life of me, I couldn't tell what he was thinking. I straightened, trying not to notice how his gaze affected me. I felt too warm and unsettled all at once.

"As I was saying, our first awesome exercise is called 'What's in a name?'" Ms. Weaver explained. "Turn to your partner, say 'Hi, my name is,' fill in the blank, and then tell them the origin of your name. That's it! We'll take a few minutes to complete this task. Start whenever you'd like."

Taking a deep breath, I pivoted to face my partner. Rhys did the same.

"Hi, my name is Ariel," I said, feeling so embarrassed. "Because my mom loves Disney, I was named after a mermaid who collects forks and talks to fish." Rhys's lips twitched at that, but I forged ahead. "Surprisingly, I don't hate it. I just wish the name fit me better."

I nodded for him to go.

He crossed his arms. "Hi, my name is Rhys. My parents named me. The end."

I blinked. Was this guy serious right now?

"And?" I prompted.

He lifted a brow. "And what?"

"Oh, come on." I smiled. "That can't be all. You don't

hear that one every day. Rhys isn't a typical name."

"Neither is 'Cupcake.' Wonder where that comes from."

I ignored his attempt to put the spotlight back on me. "Is it a family thing? Were you named after your dad or a grandfather or something?"

Rhys lifted a brow. "No, my dad's name is Glenn, the same as his dad. Pretty sure Glenn the third wouldn't have fit *my* personality."

Nope, I thought, looking him over. This guy was definitely an original.

"So, where did Rhys come from?" I asked.

I thought he would brush it off again, but surprisingly, he sighed.

"My mom used to get these cravings when she was pregnant." Running a hand down his face, he mumbled, "I can't believe this. It's not like we're superheroes. We don't need an origin story."

I bit back a laugh. "You're not a superhero—noted. Though I think a ton of Honeycomb football fans might disagree."

Rhys's intense eyes shot to mine. "I've never seen you at a game."

"There are a lot of people in the stands," I pointed out. "You might've just missed me."

"Yeah, I guess."

Okay, I thought. This was progress. Rhys had spoken actual words, and he wasn't scowling at me quite as much as before. Better keep him talking. Plus, I actually *hadn't* been to any games, so he had me there—not that I'd admit to it.

"You were saying something about cravings," I said. All

this talk of names was making me think of my father—who I usually tried my best *not* to think about. I could still hear him calling me "Cupcake" in his derisive tone. Refusing to let the memory get me down, I focused on Rhys.

"My dad told me Mom loved pickles and Reese's peanut butter cups," he said. "The combo was one of the only things she'd eat. They've never confirmed it, but I think that's where the name comes from. Either that or she found it in a book. She's always reading."

He looked at me, his eyes daring me to laugh, but I didn't.

"That's awesome," I said.

Rhys's lips did that thing again, just a slight movement, a tilt up on one side. "You think so?"

"Yeah, definitely. I love to read, too. And isn't it funny how many names come from food? I mean, based on that story, you could've been named Pickle." I shrugged. "With Homecoming and all, you'd now be Prince Pickle. I think Rhys suits you much better."

Rhys seemed to be choking, and I grew concerned.

"Hey, are you okay?"

"Yeah," he managed. His face was red. "You just surprised me."

"Sorry," I muttered.

"Don't be." Rhys gave me a real half smile, the first I'd seen from him, and my breath caught. "Prince Pickle, that's a good one."

I couldn't respond, was too taken aback by the bright expression on his usually surly face.

Seriously, Rhys. Who are you?

Chapter 8

*L*uckily, right then Ms. Weaver announced our next assignment. Her voice broke me out of my Rhys-induced daze before I could do something silly like swoon.

"Okay, kids," she said. "Now that we all know a little about each other, it's time for our next fun activity! This one requires your phones."

"Sweet. If it's a photo contest"—Zander shot Lana a wink—"we are definitely winning this one."

"For once, I agree," she said.

Ms. Weaver's smile grew. "Sorry to disappoint, but it's actually not a photo challenge."

Lana and the others looked deflated at that, but I only felt relief. Pictures were so not my thing. And after seeing his almost smile, I didn't relish the idea of taking one next to Rhys. He was too pretty for words.

"Though I do plan on taking pictures of each couple at some point for the school's website," she added, and I winced. "But today, like I said, is about bonding and trust. Please unlock your phones."

I pulled mine out and waited.

"Now, hand it over to your partner."

Protests went up all around. Geez, I thought, they're just phones. It's not like she suggested we do something ridiculous like strip naked.

Ms. Weaver silenced everyone with a raised hand.

"Come on, guys!" She glanced over the group. "It's not that serious. You'll have exactly five minutes to look around. Notice I only said *look*. You will not text, email, message, or delete anything. This is simply meant to give you insight into the prince or princess the Honeycomb chalices paired you with."

Bryleigh raised her hand. "And if we refuse?"

Daniel, who was her partner, frowned. "Why would you?" he said. "It's just five minutes."

"I know," she said, "but a phone is super personal. It's kind of like a diary. I don't know how I feel about someone digging through my stuff."

"Yeah, Ms. Weaver," Tessandra added. "No offense, but I think this is a clear invasion of privacy."

Zander's cheeks were red. "I don't want anybody looking at my phone. You're with me on that, right, Rhys?"

Rhys shrugged. "I'm cool with it."

He was? My eyes moved to the guy standing at my side. After how reluctant he'd been to reveal how he got his name, I would've thought he'd be a firm no on the phone issue.

"I didn't think it would be a big deal," Ms. Weaver muttered to herself. "How about this," she said after a moment, "if you want to do the phone exchange, do it. If not, check out the other person's social media account instead. Will that work?"

The majority of the court seemed to sigh in relief.

Ms. Weaver nodded. "Awesome! Talk it over with your partner, choose your option, and let's get to know each other! I'm setting my watch to five minutes now."

Rhys was the first to speak this time.

"What do you want to do?" he said.

I shrugged. "I don't really have social media—unless you include my baking vlog. So, I guess the phone exchange?"

"Sounds good," he said and gave me his phone.

For some reason, I was suddenly too shy to do the same. *Deep breath, Ariel.* I had nothing to hide, right?

I placed my phone in his palm, and Rhys started looking through the thing immediately. I was eager to look at his phone, too. But the way he was so focused, how his intense eyes roved over the contents of my device, held my attention. I knew what I had in there: wallpaper of me and my mom at Disney with us wearing the ears (classic Minnie Mouse for her and cupcake-inspired for me), way too many pictures of baked goods, some class notes, and other things. I didn't think there was anything incriminating. But what did he see?

"This is making me hungry, Cupcake," he finally said, and I grinned.

"Yeah, good food pics will do that," I said.

"I'm serious. My stomach just growled."

With only a couple minutes left, my eyes went to his phone. I wouldn't lie to myself—I was curious. Who was

Rhys Castle really? Would his phone reveal any secrets? His wallpaper was a picture of him and three other guys from the team facing the back in their football jerseys. Yeah, it was kind of cliché, but still, I couldn't help but appreciate his broad shoulders.

Shaking myself out of it, I kept searching. There were a handful of apps. The camera roll had several pictures of his family and a surprising number of his dog. *Ah, what a cutie*, I thought. And then…

"Oh my gosh," I breathed.

A Rhys selfie. Shirtless. With muscles upon muscles on display.

Holy wow, Batman.

I knew I should look away but couldn't. Worse, the shirtless pics had me blushing all the way to the tips of my ears.

"Something wrong?" Rhys asked.

My eyes shot to his as I tried desperately to close the app. "Nope. It's all good."

He lifted his chin. "You sure? Do you like that picture or something? You've been staring at it for a while."

"Wha—*oh my gosh*," I said again as my cheeks flared. Unfortunately, instead of closing, I'd somehow managed to zoom in, and now Rhys's incredible torso and abs were the only things visible. "I wasn't—I mean—"

Rhys chuckled. "It's okay, Cupcake. I was joking."

I wanted to die.

"Had to take those and send them to some college coaches along with my health stats. They like to know we're in shape."

"Well, that you definitely are," I mumbled.

"Excuse me?"

"Nothing, nothing." I waved him off. "I just thought it might be something you did. Take shirtless pics of yourself to send to a girlfriend, post online, or hang on your wall at home."

His brows drew together. "Do I look like a total asshole to you?"

"No, that's not what I meant. You're just…really fit." I bit my lip.

Rhys lifted a brow. "Thanks."

In a bid to leave the awkward behind and change the subject, I said, "You know, I just realized. Rhys and Azriel are characters from this epic fantasy series I love. Isn't that hilarious? Our names are almost identical. Az and Rhys are both male, though."

"You mean SJM?" he said.

My eyes shot to his. "Seriously? You've read *A Court of Thorns and Roses*?"

Rhys shrugged. "Sarah J. Maas is a goddess. I've read all the books. Rhysand is my favorite, although Azriel and his shadows are a close second."

Shut the front door. Tight-lipped, frowny-face, super-jock Rhys had actually read one of my favorite series of all time—and *liked* it?

Was this some kind of alternate universe?

"What's your favorite part in the books?" I asked just to test him.

"Love all the battle scenes," he said, "especially the one in Velaris where everyone and their mother gets in on the action. Yours?"

"Oh my gosh, there are so many! The romance is my favorite part, of course. Feyre and Rhys for life. But another fave has to be at the end of *Mist & Fury* with the cauldron, where Nesta points at the King of Hybern before she gets forced under."

"Oh yeah, that was epic."

"Totally epic," I breathed. "I kind of hated Nesta at first, and then I loved her. And I don't know why, but I love how SJM can toy with my emotions like that."

Rhys nodded. "I hear you."

"Maybe we should do a buddy-read sometime."

"No thanks. I like to read alone."

Message received, I thought.

Just like that, our little bonding moment was officially over. But the fact that it happened at all… My head was spinning.

Lowering my gaze and hiding from the confusion addling my mind, I opened his music app. It was filled with songs, some current, some old. There were quite a few rap songs but surprisingly mixed in with those were a few I liked as well.

"Wouldn't have taken you as someone who listens to Fleetwood Mac," I commented.

"Wouldn't have taken you as someone who likes looking at half-naked pics of me," he said, causing my blush to deepen. "But I guess you can't judge a book by its cover."

Huffing, I rolled my eyes as Ms. Weaver called time, pushing his phone back at him.

"Do you enjoy embarrassing me?" I asked.

Rhys pretended to think about it as he handed back my phone. "Honestly? I don't hate it," he said with a smirk.

Jerk.

Chapter 9

"All right, kids, I hope you had a good time with that," Ms. Weaver said. "Our third activity requires the most trust and is by far the most fun. This will be our last exercise for today."

Thank goodness, I thought. It's nearly over.

"We'll be doing a trust fall."

I waited for her to say she was kidding, that we'd be doing something simple like telling our partner our deepest fears or our dreams for the future. But she didn't.

"One person will close their eyes, hold their arms out to the side, and fall backward. The other person stands behind them and catches. Sounds easy, right? All you need to do is decide who will fall and who will catch." Ms. Weaver checked her watch. "We're running a little short on time, so let's take ten minutes for this one."

I watched as the other pairs got into position. People were already falling and laughing. It seemed like there was very little discussion necessary.

I glanced sidelong at my prince.

"Cupcake," he said.

"Rhys," I said back.

"I can feel you staring at me."

Dang it.

"Yeah well." I sighed. "I'm ready to do this whenever you are."

Rhys nodded then came up behind me. I could feel my brow furrow as I spun to face him. He met my frown with one of his own.

"What are you doing?" he said.

I rolled up my sleeves then held out my hands. "What does it look like? You heard Ms. Weaver. I'm getting ready to catch you." Rhys blinked, and I twirled my finger in a circular motion. "Now, if you could just turn around…"

He was silent a moment.

"Are you serious?" Rhys said.

"Yes."

He just stared.

"Something wrong?" I asked. "You understood the instructions, right?"

"Yeah, I did," Rhys said. "She wants us to do a trust fall."

I gave him a half smile. "I know it's weird, but that's the assignment. Don't worry. I saw this in a movie once. All you have to do is fall backward into my arms. Easy."

His lips were still in a firm line, and he didn't budge.

"Rhys," I said, getting a little impatient now, "is it something else? Almost all the other couples are done.

We've only got a few minutes left."

Rhys cocked his head to the side. "I thought you were messing around, but I guess you're serious. Cupcake, you realize I'm a football player, right?"

I rolled my eyes. "I think we've established that. So?"

"*You* should fall, and I'll catch."

My laugh couldn't be contained. "No way. I may not be a sports expert, Rhys, but I know the quarterback is the one who *throws* the ball, not catches it. This exercise is about trust. I'll be doing the catching."

"I'm bigger than you," he explained patiently. "I lift weights every day. As you so eloquently put it, I'm fit."

I crossed my arms and stood my ground.

"Come on. This makes no sense. I could crush you, Cupcake. Why won't you just let me catch you?"

I knew he liked to tease me, but I couldn't believe he didn't get it.

I mean, Rhys had eyes.

The reason was clear.

"Listen, Rhys, I'm not like the other girls on Homecoming Court, okay?" I said, uncomfortable, but if he needed me to spell it out, so be it. "I'm a big girl. My mom calls me voluptuous, and I love her for it. But I've always struggled with my weight. There's no way I'm going to make some guy 'catch' me."

He shook his head. "You're not *making* me do anything. And your reasoning is ridiculous. I could literally pick you up and spin you around."

"I don't— What's that?" I said, suddenly thrown offtrack by a loud buzzing.

"The sound of my teeth grinding because you're so stubborn?"

"No, no," I hissed, "that noise."

My heart started to pick up speed as Rhys shrugged.

"Oh, there's a ladybug or wasp or something behind you," he said all nonchalant like I wasn't in mortal peril. My eyes went wide. "It's been there a minute. Don't worry; it'll probably go away on its own."

But it didn't go away.

If anything, the ladybug/wasp/killer insect only got closer.

And it sounded angry.

I tried to hold still, but it was useless. With a squeak, I jerked away, ducking to the right. But the bug followed. I weaved again to the left—but it seemed to anticipate the move.

"What are you doing?" Rhys said, and I swear there was amusement in his voice.

"What's it look like?" I yipped again as the insect zoomed by my ear. "It's chasing me. I'm trying to escape."

"It's probably just a ladybug," he said. "They can't hurt you, you know."

"Says who?"

I was close to tears. Why wouldn't it just go away?

"Ahhh!" I ran in the opposite direction of the bug—and straight into Rhys.

Cringing, I watched as the bug came toward me again, but there was nowhere to run. It got closer and closer. I'd accepted the fact that I was a goner—when Rhys suddenly acted. Lifting his hand and waiting until just the right moment, he swatted at the bug, making direct contact. As it lay there on the ground, I didn't know who was more stunned, me or the insect.

It recovered a second later and finally flew off.

"You...made it go away."

"Yeah. You okay there?" Rhys asked. "I think it was a wasp, but it's gone now."

"You could've been stung," I said.

"It would only hurt for a second." He shrugged like it wasn't a big deal. "Again, are you all right? You seemed really scared."

I swallowed, realizing I was pressed against his side.

When the heck did that happen?

Clearing my throat, I moved away and crossed my arms. "Yeah, I'm good. Thank you."

"No problem," he said. "Maybe now you trust me enough to let me catch you? Since I saved your life and all?"

"I just hate bugs." A shudder of disgust shot through me. "They're so gross. Ugh, I just hate them *so* much."

"Really? I couldn't tell."

I looked to Rhys and saw him wearing that half smile once more. Jeez, he was annoying—but I couldn't deny I was impressed with his bug-swatting skills. Because of our face-off with the evil wasp, we only had a little time to complete the final exercise. With a deep breath, I turned around.

"Okay," I said. "You can catch, and I'll fall. But Rhys?"

"Yeah, Cupcake?"

"Just don't blame me if I break you."

"I'm not scared." By the sound of his voice, I knew he was amused.

"I can't believe I'm doing this," I mumbled. Then to him, I said, "You ready?"

"Whenever you are, Cupcake."

With a deep breath, I closed my eyes, imagining all the possible things that could go wrong: me flattening Rhys like a pancake, Rhys crumpling under my substantial weight and the earthquake that would follow, the other princes and princesses laughing and their horrified gasps, me somehow breaking Rhys's throwing arm, thus damaging any chance he might have at a future in football, the fall going perfectly and Rhys commenting after the fact on how heavy I was.

Ugh, I never thought about my weight like this. Why, oh why was this so incredibly hard?

"Cupcake?" Rhys said. "Don't overthink it. Just fall."

Easy for him to say.

Right. Here we go.

Oh God, please don't let me crush the quarterback.

I held my arms out and leaned backward, secretly trying to hold on to my equilibrium as long as I could. There was a moment of falling. Then Rhys was there, catching me beneath both arms like it was nothing, his hands wrapping around my waist.

"Got you," he said, the words hitting my ear and making me gasp.

Rhys gently set me back on my feet.

I turned to check him for injuries, but none were visible.

"You're okay," I said in wonder.

"Yeah," he said. "Told you I'd catch you."

"You lied before," I said, and Rhys frowned. "Stopping killer bugs with your bare hands, catching girls without breaking a sweat—you are totally a superhero, Rhys Castle."

He shook his head. "For a second I thought you were talking about those pics."

And just like that, my mind went back to his bare chest and torso.

I shrugged, trying to play it cool. "People send pics to their significant others all the time. It's not unheard of."

"Well, I don't," he said as Ms. Weaver called us to huddle up. Rhys began to turn but then stopped. "Also, if that's your way of asking if I have a 'significant other'—"

My jaw dropped.

"I don't have one of those, either."

Rhys turned and walked away, leaving me there staring after him. What the heck? Why would he say something like that? There was only one reason I could think of, and it made me frown. Awesome, now Rhys thought I had a crush on him. As if a few trust exercises, including one trust fall, would literally make me fall for him.

I gave a mental laugh. Yeah, right.

I was too smart for that.

If I couldn't stop thinking about the feeling of his arms around me, that was only natural. It would pass.

Rhys had probably already forgotten about it.

And I would, too.

Chapter 10

Forgetting should've been easy.

First, everything that happened after school, including the walk to and from the field, took less than an hour. Second, I was not one of Rhys Castle's fangirls. Far from it. I didn't care if he had a girlfriend or not; that was completely TMI. He didn't even stick around after we got back to the school, just rushed off to football practice without another word. Third, I had a new entry to record for my vlog, which usually helped me unwind.

So, why was I still thinking about Rhys?

He must've cast a spell on me or something because, even hours after we'd parted, I couldn't stop replaying how he'd protected me from that wasp.

Ugh.

It wasn't like he meant it as some big, gallant gesture. Rhys was a football player, for goodness sake—he liked hitting things. Even though, as quarterback, that wasn't actually his job, I knew. *Snap out of it, Ariel.*

Time to focus and get these cupcakes finished.

The trust fall was actually my inspiration. Right when Ms. Weaver mentioned it, my mind immediately went to *Mean Girls*, which I'd watched way too many times. There was this scene near the end where the girls do a group trust fall. Not even one character hesitated. Obviously, none of the people in the movie had any qualms about their weight. I'd always thought that part was unrealistic.

But the movie was still awesome.

I decided to do a dozen cupcakes. For the cake itself, I chose chocolate mixed with real strawberries. The frosting would be petal pink, and each cupcake would be topped with a sugar disc, featuring a different quote or character from the movie painted on it. Recording my baking videos was pretty par for the course, so even with my inattention, I knew the cupcakes would turn out gorgeous.

Almost as gorgeous as Rhys's half smile, I thought… then gave myself a mental head slap.

I got down to business and took my time. One of the beautiful things about baking was how precise it was. I'd decided long ago that I loved it more than traditional cooking. I mean, yes, you could add a little more of this or that, but for the most part, when it came to baking, if you followed a recipe to the letter, you were ensured a great result.

That really appealed to me for some reason.

With all the uncertainty in the world, it was nice having something I could count on. Something I could control.

"What smells so amazing?" Mom asked, walking into the kitchen and stopping to hug me.

"*Mean Girls*-inspired cupcakes," I said.

"Ooh." Mom gave me a wink. "So fetch," she said. "I assume I'll be able to take these to work for the kids?"

I nodded. "Of course! I'll make another batch now that will have only frosting. I just need to save one for Toni. If she sees the vlog and I don't bring her one, there'll be heck to pay."

"Which one are you thinking?"

"I'm between the 'On Wednesdays, we wear pink' and Damien in the blue hoodie. It's my personal fave, but…"

Mom grinned. "Well then, you take Damien, give Toni the other one, and I'll take the rest. Also, thank you for making extra. You know how hangry those five-year-olds can be."

I faked a shiver. "Yeah Mom, I still don't know how you do it."

"I've always loved kids," she said simply.

I knew that. Mom was a kindergarten teacher who not only loved her job but was amazing at it. Unlike me, she didn't freak out when her students had to go to the bathroom or started crying or tried to eat crayons. My cluelessness when it came to anyone younger than ten was probably a side effect of being an only child. But I had so much respect for her and everyone in her profession.

God bless teachers, I thought, especially the ones who love their students.

"And," Mom put in as she swiped a strawberry, "I think that's why I got blessed with such an amazing daughter."

"Ugh." I laughed. "You're so cheesy."

"Nope," she said, "I'm a cool mom."

"I think that was another *Mean Girls* reference, but you really are," I said, checking the time on the oven. "Hey, you want to watch the movie with me? They've only got about ten more minutes."

Mom nodded, throwing an arm around my waist. "You know it. And then I want to hear all about Homecoming and school." She patted my cheek as she walked by. "But mostly Homecoming."

I held back a sigh.

Her words brought me right back to that field with the bugs, too-happy Ms. Weaver, and Rhys aka Prince Pickle aka Bug-Swatting Superhero.

Once the cupcakes were out, I filmed a clip with the finished product, arranged the cupcakes on a tray (setting one aside for Toni), walked into the living room, and plopped onto the couch to watch the movie with Mom. It turned out I didn't need to set one aside. After I sent her a text, Toni came over to join us.

"These are so awesome, A," she said, reaching for a cupcake, the very one I'd put in a special container for her. Then she gave my outfit a once-over. "By the way, you can't sit with us. It's Wednesday. We wear pink."

"Okay, okay," I said, hopping off the couch and snatching her cupcake away. The look on her face was priceless. "I guess I'll just have to take my desserts back, then."

"Wait," she said quickly. "You can stay, I guess, since you come bearing gifts."

I scoffed. "And because I live here."

"That, too," she said then took the cupcake back and dug in.

Both she and Mom wanted a recap of what happened after school, so I gave them the rundown. By the time I was done, they were grinning. I thought it might've been because Tina Fey was a comedy genius, but it turned out that wasn't the reason.

"I'm impressed," Mom said. "I can't believe you stayed so calm with that bug."

My eyes narrowed. "Are you making fun of me?"

"God no!" She held up her hands. "I meant that. Remember the time there was a spider in your car? You nearly got in an accident."

"Yeah," Toni muttered, "she swerved pretty good though, gave me whiplash."

I shivered at the memory. "It dropped down from the ceiling, Toni. The ceiling! Like a spider ninja assassin."

My best friend tried to cover it up, but I could still hear her muffled laughter.

Mom smiled. "See? This was definitely an improvement over that. You're getting better at combatting your fear."

I couldn't disagree with the first part of her statement, but I still had major issues with insects. Rhys had been the difference today. He'd been so brave and awesome in that moment. As if she could read my mind, Mom lifted a brow.

"I think I like that prince of yours," she said. "He sounds like a good kid."

I shrugged. "He's all right, I guess. If you like the grouchy, intense type."

"Ariel, please," Toni sniffed. "Rhys is one hundred percent swoon material, and he saved you from being stung. Don't pretend you aren't totally curious. You probably haven't been able to stop thinking about it."

Gah, she knew me too well.

But I could still hear Rhys's rejection in my ears. When I'd suggested the buddy read, he shot me down. Hard. We were being forced to spend time together, I reminded myself. Now, if I could only make Toni understand...

Mom saved me from having to respond. Bless her.

"We need to start thinking about your dress," Mom said. "Homecoming will be here before you know it."

I nodded, thankful for the change of subject. "I'll look online and see what I can find."

Her face fell. "Online? Don't you want to go shopping, try a bunch on? It would be so much fun!"

Trying on clothes? Fun? *Yeah right.* Buying off the rack was a luxury my wide hips, big chest, and butt did not enjoy.

"Sorry, Ms. D, but who cares about clothes?" Toni said, and then she turned to me. "Rhys Castle, football hottie, touched you. Voluntarily."

I pursed my lips. "Actually, it wasn't completely voluntary. Ms. Weaver assigned us the trust fall, remember?"

She waved that away. "Eh, a very small detail."

Mom bit back a laugh this time. "This Rhys must be something."

"You have no idea, Ms. D." Toni sighed. "Here, I'll show you a pic."

I watched in amusement as she pulled up something on her phone—it was Rhys's social media account. There were only a few pictures, less than ten; it looked like he wasn't that active online either. But apparently it was enough.

Mom tilted her head. "*This* is the guy they paired you

with?" she asked me.

"It is," I said.

"Hmm," she murmured, and I had no idea what that meant.

The two kept looking over the pictures, and unable to help myself, I gave in. With a roll of my eyes, I leaned over to see what all the fuss was about. There was no harm in looking, right?

"I think half the students at Honeycomb High have a crush on him," Toni said.

"Are you one of them?" Mom asked.

"Oh no. I grew out of my Rhys phase years ago. I just like him for Ariel."

"And does she like him?" Mom said.

I threw her a look. "Real subtle, Mom."

Toni pretended like I hadn't spoken. "She hasn't confirmed it yet. But he seems decent and smart—in addition to being hot—and I think he's dedicated to football like Ariel is to baking. That's why I think they'd be good together."

My jaw dropped. "Toni, be serious. Rhys Castle?"

"I am serious," she said. "And hey, don't give me that face. You two would make beautiful babies."

My cheeks went red, and I was speechless.

"He *is* pretty," Mom commented.

I shook my head. "You guys, I have to see him tomorrow. It's going to be awkward enough as it is. Try not to say anything else over-the-top, okay?"

"Ooh, and the plot thickens," Toni said in delight. "What will you and Rhys be doing tomorrow?"

"I'm curious about that, too," Mom said.

I had studied it so many times, I could picture the homecoming itinerary from memory.

"Dance lessons," I said, wincing as their smiles turned brighter. "In the packet there's an address where we're supposed to meet Ms. Weaver. I'm a little nervous, to be honest."

"Don't be nervous, baby," Mom said, patting my thigh. "It'll be fine. You have great rhythm—you get that from my side of the family, by the way. And I know you love to dance."

"Yeah, Mom," I said. "Up in my room. By myself. Where no one can see me."

She wasn't having it. "You're going to be amazing, and I can't wait to hear all about it."

"Plus," Toni said, "look on the bright side, A. You'll get to touch Rhys again."

If she was trying to put me at ease, it didn't work. Those words echoed through my mind as we watched the rest of the movie. And as my head hit the pillow that night, I had trouble getting to sleep because my nerves were turned up to a fever pitch.

But I couldn't decide if that was because I was anxious or excited.

Chapter 11

*S*chool helped me get out of my head…somewhat.
Still. There were reminders of Homecoming every-where.

The student council had picked a theme. It was Vintage Hollywood—which I had to admit sounded pretty awesome. There were so many ways you could go with that. Tickets went on sale today for the dance. Posters had been placed here and there along the halls. Everyone seemed excited.

But that also might've been because our first football game of the year was this Friday. There were just as many posters and decorations for that if not more.

I had a pop quiz in second period, a test in fourth, and in my next-to-last class, Mrs. Weebly let us work on a paper that was due in a couple weeks. The paper was for Lit, which was one of my favorite subjects. We were in the library the whole period—again, one of my favorite places—so by the time the final bell rang, I was feeling refreshed, ready for anything.

Or so I thought.

Even though I'd seen him multiple times in the halls—Rhys was a hard guy to miss—we hadn't spoken since the other day. We'd never talked much before, so it wasn't like that was some big surprise. But as I was on my way to my locker, he stopped in front of me.

I was startled but managed not to bump into him this time.

"Hey, I may be late today," he said. "For the dance thing."

"Oh," I said.

"We've got football, and then I have…something else. It's important. After I'm done with that, I'll drive to the studio."

I waited for more, but he stayed silent.

"So you're just going to leave it there and be all mysterious?" I asked.

"Yep." Rhys's jaw ticked as he nodded. "Just didn't want you to think I was bailing on you or anything."

"It's cool. Thanks for letting me know," I said. "That was…actually thoughtful of you."

Rhys shrugged. "No big deal. See you later, Cupcake."

And then he was gone.

I stood there, trying to wrap my mind around the strange conversation. Rhys obviously had a secret he didn't want to share—that much was clear. Still, I had no idea what it might be. Looking around, I saw a few sets of eyes on me, but for the most part, they followed Rhys's back as he walked away. I was right there with them.

That was such a decent thing to do, letting me know he'd be late. How many teenage guys would think of that?

Not many, I figured.

I was proven right a little over an hour later. Our dance rehearsal was about to begin. The studio was a big space with a wooden floor and lots of mirrors. Everyone from Homecoming Court was here—well, almost everyone. Ms. Weaver must have known about football practice and the other secret thing Rhys had going on because she didn't look upset that two of the princes were MIA.

Lana, however, was a whole different story.

Her arms were crossed, and she kept glancing down at her watch, then to the door with this stressed look on her face.

"Well," Ms. Weaver said, "I guess we should begin. I've only rented the studio for three and a half hours. And I'm sure you're all eager to dance, dance, dance!"

"Ms. Weaver," Lana said, "my prince isn't here yet. What am I supposed to do?"

She nodded. "I know. Coach Feinnes told me Rhys and Zander would be arriving late. Why don't you and Ariel work together until they get here?"

Lana muttered something that sounded like, "Zander, the big oaf, he should've told me." But to Ms. Weaver, she smiled and said, "Sure, that would be awesome."

When she turned back to me, the smile dropped a little.

"Just so we're clear," she said, "I'm the girl in this scenario."

My brows furrowed. "Can't we both be?"

Lana simply shook her head. "We could, but we won't. I'm the girl. You're the guy. That's just how it is, Cupcake."

"Okay," I said, "but I don't think it really matters."

"I'm glad you see it my way," she said.

It wasn't worth arguing over. Whether I was the girl or the guy, I'd do my best.

Ms. Weaver stepped to the center of the floor along with the man who had opened the studio for us. His hair was black and so were his clothes, the top buttons of his shirt undone, revealing a small *V* of skin. The guy had a natural tan and the whitest teeth I'd ever seen.

"I wonder if he does toothpaste commercials," I said.

Lana shushed me.

But I just couldn't help it. "I'm just saying he should. I'd buy what he was selling if it made my teeth sparkle like that."

"Oh my gosh, Cupcake," she hissed. "Will you shut up?"

"Jeez, okay," I said.

A second later, Lana added, "Besides, he probably goes for whitening appointments. It's common in the pageant world."

"Really?" I asked, and she nodded. Well, that made more sense.

"Princesses and princes," Ms. Weaver said, "may I present to you, Mr. Dominic Patachoui! He's an expert in all things ballroom, and he has graciously agreed to help us prepare for Homecoming. Each year, the winning king and queen share a first dance, and the other students clear the floor while we spotlight the royal couple."

Lana was nodding along with several others, but this was news to me.

Dancing while everyone watched...

It sounded like my worst nightmare.

"All the nominees will be a part of the second dance, and everyone else can join in after. The reason we're here today is to learn how to dance. *Properly*," she emphasized. "There will be no twerking here. This is a booty-popping-free zone. If you want to grind, do it on your own time."

I wasn't the only one who laughed.

"These are choreographed ballroom dances, ladies and gentlemen!" she went on. "Without further ado, I'll hand things over to Mr. Patachoui."

We clapped as the man stepped forward.

"Thank you very much, Juliana," he said with a slight accent. "I'm so glad I could help and work with you kids. I will teach you much today. But here is what I want you to keep in mind…" There was a pause, and then, *"Tradition!"*

The word came out more like a shout. Even Ms. Weaver jumped.

"Tradition," he repeated more softly, "is why we are here today. Grace is what I'm going to teach you. And as we all know, grace and glory go hand in hand. If you want that crown, you're going to have to work for it. Are you ready to work?"

No one said anything.

"Well, are you?" he raised his voice again.

"Yes," came the response. Honestly, I thought everyone was too afraid not to answer. Mr. Patachoui was a little intense.

"Then let's go, people." Mr. Patachoui's white teeth made another appearance. "We'll start with the basics: walking arm in arm. This shouldn't be too hard."

He was right. It shouldn't have been.

But for whatever reason, Lana and I couldn't get our walk together. When I stumbled for the third time, she huffed.

"Come on, Cupcake," she said. "It's just walking. You do it every day. What is the problem?"

"The problem," I said, "is you keep trying to take off without me."

Lana lifted a brow. "You're walking too slow."

"But that's what we're supposed to do," I said. "Mr. Patachoui called it a 'slow glide.' You're going too fast."

"Whatever," she said. "At this rate, we'll never make it to the other end of the room. A snail moves quicker than you."

"I'm just following the instructions."

"No, you're holding us up."

I looked at her a moment then nodded. "Okay, I'll try it your way."

Lana seemed happy to have won the argument. I did as she asked, and we made it to the other side of the room where Mr. Patachoui was standing.

"Very good, girls," he said with a nod, "but next time, try moving a bit slower."

As he walked away, I bit back a smile, and Lana held up a hand.

"Don't you dare say it," she warned.

"Who, me? I wasn't going to say anything." After all, Mr. Patachoui had already said it for me. "Want to try again?"

Lana nodded begrudgingly, but before we could lock arms, Rhys and Zander sauntered into the room. Lana's hands went to her hips.

"Well, it's about time," she said to Zander.

"Yeah, sorry I'm late," he said, running a hand down his neck. "Coach had the defense stay extra-long to discuss strategy and watch game videos."

"I'd appreciate a warning next time if you're not going to show up."

I saw Zander nod sheepishly out of the corner of my eye, but I was looking at Rhys.

"How did practice go?" I asked, taking him in. "And the other thing?"

"Fine," Rhys said.

What I really wanted to say was: Please tell me more. What happened at your secret rendezvous? But I didn't want to pry. So instead, I went with—

"Make any good shots?"

His eyes sparked at that. "Nah, but I threw some good passes."

"Ah."

"You really don't know much about football, huh?"

"No, but I'm glad to hear it went well. It's been kinda rough here."

"Oh yeah? Did you miss me, Cupcake?" Rhys asked.

I looked over to Lana, who was currently ignoring Zander's awkward apology. Turning back to Rhys, I gave a solemn nod.

"You have no idea," I said.

Chapter 12

"*S*o, you ready to dance?" I asked.

"No, and I should warn you." Rhys tucked his hands into his pockets. "I'm not the best at this."

"Yeah right, stop being modest. A lot of football players are great dancers. Just look at *Dancing With the Stars*."

"No seriously. I can't dance. It's like the only thing I suck at."

How he managed to make that sound both arrogant and charming at the same time, I'd never know. Maybe it was because of how uncomfortable he looked admitting one of his weaknesses.

I lifted a brow. "Everyone can dance. And with a last name like yours, you have to be amazing."

Rhys frowned. "What do you mean?"

"Castle," I said like it was obvious. But Rhys still looked confused. "Oh come on, *Dirty Dancing*? It's a cinematic classic."

"Never seen it," he said.

I gaped at him. "You've never seen...wow, Rhys. Just wow. You are blowing my mind right now with your lack of movie education."

"Are there castles in it or something? Because fairy tales aren't my thing, Cupcake."

"It's set at a resort," I said. "No actual castles. The main guy is named Johnny Castle. He's this awesome dance instructor."

Rhys shrugged. "Doesn't sound like we have much in common."

"I'll be the judge of that."

Before he could respond, Ms. Weaver came over with that signature pep in her step.

"Ah good!" she said, looking from Rhys to Zander. "The two wayward princes have arrived. I hope you came ready to dance! We were just about to start the choreography."

Zander rolled his shoulders and neck around. "Awesome, dancing is my thing. I've been looking forward to this."

I nodded. "I've seen you at the pep rallies. You're really good."

"Thanks, Cupcake," Zander beamed.

As Zander popped into a squat, Rhys said, "Man, what are you doing?"

"What does it look like?" he said. "I'm stretching, duh. You're supposed to stretch before any physical activity— wouldn't want to pull anything."

Lana, who looked horrified, spoke up then. "Ms. Weaver, are these partnerships really set in stone?"

"I've already told you," Ms. Weaver said. "The chalices

have chosen."

"But Rhys and I—"

"Aren't together anymore," Rhys finished. "We haven't been for a while."

"That's not what I meant," she mumbled under her breath.

Lana's dismay was obvious. Without even thinking, I heard myself say, "Again, if Lana wants to trade, I would be fine with that."

Rhys's brows drew together. He said nothing, but there was clearly something going on in that head of his. Too bad reading guys had never been my specialty.

Ms. Weaver shook her head at me and patted Lana's shoulder.

"The partners remain intact," she said. "I'm sorry, Miss Leavengood, but Homecoming Court has a long-standing tradition of picking via chalice. You can't just choose your partner."

"It's not that," Lana said. "If we traded, it would be more aesthetically pleasing and make more sense, but whatever." Her eyes went from Rhys's to mine. "I just hope there aren't any lifts. For both your sakes."

Ouch. So that's what I got for trying to help. Awesome. I knew one thing: Lana would definitely not be getting the title for Miss Warm and Fuzzy.

Zander followed Lana to the other side of the room. Ms. Weaver gave us a tense smile, moving on to check in with the others. And Rhys…laughed.

He actually had the audacity to laugh.

What an asshat.

Far as I was concerned, he and Lana were made for

each other. Every time one of them did something semi-decent, they followed it up with a heaping dose of jerkish behavior.

"Are you laughing?" I asked.

Rhys nodded, totally unrepentant. "Yeah, I am."

His answer made me see red.

"Oh, I hope you go to sleep and wake up with spiders in your bed," I said then walked off in a huff.

Unfortunately, Rhys followed.

I ignored him until I couldn't stand it anymore.

"What?" I said finally.

"I don't get why people call you sweet all the time," he said. "You're really not."

Was he serious right now?

"Excuse me?" I rounded on him with a frown. "Are you calling me rude? Because you were the one being a jerk."

Rhys shook his head. "No, not rude. You are sweet, but a little spicy, too. You got spunk, Cupcake. Who knew?"

A blush rose to my cheeks unbidden.

"And I wasn't laughing at *you*," he added. "I was laughing at Lana. She's got issues."

Don't we all?

"Well, thanks…I guess," I said, some of the anger leaving me. "Also, I take it back. I'm sorry about the spiders thing."

"Yeah, that was gross." Rhys faked a shudder.

I laughed. "You act like you're the one afraid of bugs or something."

"Nah. But considering how much you hate them, it was a good insult."

"I was pretty upset," I said.

Rhys shrugged. "You know, you shouldn't let Lana get to you. She's just jealous."

That brought me up short. Lana Leavengood, the queen of Honeycomb High, jealous of me? I couldn't believe it. Although...

My eyes gave Rhys a once-over, and I began to understand.

"You mean because I get to partner with you," I said.

"I guess. Among other things."

What things? I thought. The way Rhys was looking at me, the tone of his voice... Oh, I was curious. Before I could ask what he meant, though, his next words sidetracked me.

"Also, I'd appreciate it if you'd stop trying to get rid of me," he said.

"I wasn't—"

"Listen, I get it. If you like Zander, that's cool. He's a good guy."

Were we seriously having this discussion right now?

"But you're mine."

I nearly choked at that.

Mine?

Rhys's voice was steady, his gaze unflinching.

"I'm yours?" I repeated.

"Yeah, and I'm yours," he said. "At least until Homecoming. Glad you agree, Cupcake."

Mr. Patachoui clapped his hands twice to get everyone's attention. I was grateful for the distraction. It was just what I needed to take my mind off Rhys's words that kept echoing in my mind.

"Time to learn the official Homecoming choreography,

kids," he said, flashing a smile. "We'll be working on two dances, one for the group and one specific to the king and queen. This first dance is my original choreo. It was inspired by couples' dances seen back in the old Regency days. Please, face your partner."

All the students did so.

"Gentlemen, bow while the ladies curtsy." He seemed to notice the same-sex couples then and added, "If you have two ladies or two gentlemen paired together, you must talk and decide which one of you will lead. Ms. Weaver, would you assist me?"

"Of course," Ms. Weaver said.

"Those who are leading, keep your backs straight as you bend at the waist. Those who are following, place one foot slightly behind the other and smoothly bend both knees. Eyes should remain on your partner."

That part should've been easy.

But wow, those eyes.

I felt warmth rush through me as Rhys's gaze met mine. His blue eyes weren't like a storm today, more like the ocean, deep and intense. I couldn't tell what he was thinking. But having all that focus on me? It made my knees weak. I only prayed Rhys couldn't read my mind.

Aside from the weak knees, Rhys and I—and the other couples—got through that first part without much trouble.

I was feeling good about my curtsy as Mr. Patachoui gave me a nod.

"Very nice," he said. "Now, one step forward and across, then two back to the starting position. We'll do that first to the right, then left," he said. "Your arm will rise to cup your partner's cheek. However—and this is very important—your skin will not touch."

Mr. Patachoui waggled his finger.

"Part of the beauty of this piece and of the Regency era was how innocent it was. There was very little touching yet so much quiet yearning."

I thought I heard Zander mumble, "That's no fun," which made me grin.

But my amusement only lasted until we had to try it ourselves. After watching Mr. Patachoui and Ms. Weaver, we performed the steps. They added a few other movements, and then we put them all together.

Or at least…we tried.

The first step went okay. At that point, I thought Rhys was pulling my leg earlier when he said he couldn't dance. Sure, he was a bit stiff, obviously uncomfortable, but he wasn't terrible.

Then came the moment when he went the wrong way, and we bumped heads.

"Sorry," he muttered as I rubbed my temple.

"No problem," I said back.

On the next try, Rhys somehow managed to step on my feet…both of them in quick succession. I could tell he felt bad about it, and I tried not to wince. But man, that hurt.

"Told you I was bad," he said.

"You're doing fine," I retorted.

But it was obvious as the minutes went by that Rhys wasn't fine. A light sheen of sweat broke out on his brow. Every time he messed up, he seemed to concentrate even harder, but that only made it worse, causing him to hesitate, make more mistakes, and be off beat. I didn't know how many times he'd stepped on my feet. By the fifth time it happened, I stopped counting.

One thing was for sure: my tennis shoes were not cut out for this. But I tried my best to make Rhys feel more confident, take it slow, and be patient. He was struggling but trying.

Rhys's frustration was real when Lana breezed past us. She and her partner didn't seem to be having any problems.

"How's it going?" Zander asked while Lana smirked.

"Fantastic," Rhys deadpanned. "Can't you tell? Cupcake's toes will probably fall off after this, but other than that, it's all good."

I almost laughed but winced instead as Rhys's heel accidentally caught my pinky toe.

"Sorry," he said.

"It's okay," I repeated.

"You don't look too bad to me," Zander put in.

Rhys gave him a look. "Don't lie, Z. I suck. And I know part of you is loving this."

The other boy suddenly smiled. "Not gonna lie—it is nice to see there's something you're *not* good at, QB."

"Thanks a lot," Rhys muttered.

"But you'll get it. No worries," Zander added.

"Yeah, you two shouldn't worry at all," Lana said. "Just because this is our only practice, and there are only a couple hours left, doesn't mean you'll fail."

Zander bit his lip as Rhys and I accidentally bumped chests.

"I'm guessing," Zander said to Lana, "right about now,

you're glad we got paired together, huh?"

Lana blinked innocently. "Well, of course I am! Why would you think any differently?" She waved to Rhys and me. "Good luck, you two. Just a friendly reminder: the clock is ticking."

Lovely.

Chapter 13

*I*t was finally time for the second dance.

Thank goodness, I thought. There was no way it could be worse than the first.

Right?

Rhys seemed relieved as well—or at least, he wasn't gritting his teeth as much as he had been a moment ago. His frustration might've been funny, but again, it was clear that he was trying and just couldn't get it. That made me want him to succeed that much more.

Mr. Patachoui and Ms. Weaver stepped forward again.

"For our second piece, we'll be performing a traditional waltz," the man said. "It's one hundred percent elegance, perfect for a king and queen. The position we're standing in now is called closed hold. Try it with your partner."

Although I'd never done it before, I recognized the pose immediately. I'd watched way too many Regency-era movies not to. Scenes from *Bridgerton* ran rampant through my mind.

Elegant, Mr. Patachoui had said.

Romantic, my mind whispered.

My prince stepped toward me, and I felt myself freeze.

"Cupcake?" Rhys asked. "You good with this?"

Was I? I wondered. It struck me now that throughout the couple's dance we hadn't had any skin-to-skin contact. There was a certain safety in that. This was different.

With a thick swallow, I gave him a nod.

"Sure," I said, cursing my voice as it squeaked a bit. "I'm awesome. Are you good? You look good."

Rhys's lips tilted up on one side, and my eyes widened as I realized what I'd just said.

"I meant you look ready," I said quickly, wanting to die.

"I got what you meant." He lifted a brow. After another beat, he said, "Are you going to put your hand on my shoulder or what?"

I scoffed. "Of course. I was just about to do that."

It was clear Rhys was laughing internally. His eyes dared me to make the first move. In what seemed to be slow motion, I watched my hand rise and then rest gently on his shoulder. In answer, his hand moved to my waist.

My breath hitched.

It was pathetic, but no other person had ever touched me like this. I was aware of every one of his fingers and the slight warmth that went from his hand to my body. Speaking of, I was aware of that, too: my body. I'd never been more intensely aware of my curves.

I'd always loved the slight dip of my waist, the roundness of my hips. It made me feel womanly. But now, as Rhys touched me, I wondered what he thought—and was afraid that I might not like the answer. Before I could overthink it, Rhys locked his other hand with mine and brought it up to the side, completing the starting pose.

Mr. Patachoui's voice filtered through the haze in my mind.

"There are three steps to the waltz. The gentlemen step forward as the ladies step back," he said, doing just that with Ms. Weaver. "That's followed by a step to the side and step together. Then we go back with the opposite foot, side, together, always using a nice rise and fall motion. Once you feel comfortable, you'll try a quarter turn. Try to stay on beat, and remember, it's about elegance. Okay, kids, and... one, two, three. One, two, three."

I met Rhys's eyes and found him already staring at me.

"Three steps." He shrugged. "Sounds easy enough."

His breath didn't seem elevated. He was acting completely normal. I forced myself to match his cool.

"Yeah," I said. "Pretty simple."

Rhys's brows lowered. "But I think..."

I'd almost succeeded in getting my heart rate back to normal when I felt a pressure at my waist. Rhys's hand tightened as he drew me closer, keeping his eyes on my face.

"There," he said. "That's better."

I was glad he thought so. My cheeks were flaming, my heart once again going haywire.

"You good?"

I nodded, and we began the waltz. Even with my weird reaction, Rhys did much better with the second dance. Granted, it wasn't a lot to remember, and he was still stiff.

But I thought we were doing all right.

Until Mr. Patachoui came over.

As he stopped near us, he watched only a few moments before shaking his head.

"No, no, no," he said. "The steps are correct, but it's too robotic. You need more ease, more grace. Young man, you need to lower those shoulders and relax. Enjoy your partner."

Rhys muttered something under his breath that I didn't catch.

"Smooth out those steps," Mr. Patachoui said. "Think of gliding across the floor. The waltz is art. Make it beautiful."

After a minute, he left.

Rhys and I used the rest of the time to try to perfect our "art." Even though his steps were somewhat clumsy, and he kept whispering the counts aloud, I couldn't help but like Rhys better. He hadn't given up. He hadn't stomped off or thrown a temper tantrum (like one of the juniors on the Court did). Rhys was right, he wasn't the best dancer, but the fact that he tried anyway endeared him to me.

The way his touch lit me up helped, too.

But I couldn't forget how evasive he'd been this morning. What was he hiding? And who was the real Rhys? My charmingly awkward dance partner...or the rude jerk who came out at the most random of times? I wasn't sure.

"Oh, you all did so well!" Ms. Weaver said, addressing the group and pulling me from my thoughts. "I know for several of you this was out of your comfort zones"—was I imagining it or did her eyes move to Rhys as she said that?—"but you pushed through. The numbers you learned today will be performed at the Homecoming dance, so please practice. And don't forget to thank Mr. Patachoui for his excellent instruction!"

We'd been dismissed and were headed to the door like everyone else, but before Rhys and I could walk by him, the dance teacher stopped us.

"You two," Mr. Patachoui said, looking from me to Rhys. He seemed to be sucking on his teeth. "It needs work."

"Thank you for teaching us," I said.

"A lot of work," he repeated. "You, young lady, move very well. But your partner…" He shook his head. "It's rough, but I actually believe you have potential. I like this pairing."

Rhys nodded. "Thanks again."

"You're welcome." Mr. Patachoui shooed us away. "Keep working."

As we walked outside, I stopped and turned to Rhys.

"Well, we did it," I said. "And see? You didn't do so bad."

"No need to sugarcoat it," Rhys said. "I'm very competitive, Cupcake. I know I was the worst one in there."

I shook my head. "No, the worst was that kid who walked away and quit, leaving his partner stranded. Even Mr. Patachoui said we have potential."

Rhys didn't agree or disagree. I wanted to ask him something but wasn't sure if I should. Anxiety rose in my chest. He'd probably turn me down, but I decided to push forward anyway.

"Do you want to get together sometime and practice?" I said.

Rhys frowned. "Honestly? I'd rather be sacked by Michael Strahan."

"Who?"

"Strahan," he said. "He's a former pro football player, defensive end for the New York Giants, holds the record for most sacks in a season. Come on, Cupcake. You have to know who Michael Strahan is."

I scrunched my brows in thought, then shrugged. "Sorry, I don't. It's not really that surprising, since I've never been to a game."

"Never been to a Giants game or…?"

I bit my lip instead of answering.

Rhys got the message loud and clear. "Wait, really?" he said, his eyebrows rising to his hairline.

"Nope," I said. "I've never seen a football game. But it's not a big deal. You've never seen *Dirty Dancing*, which is just cuckoo. So…"

Rhys just kept looking at me like I was the cuckoo one.

"So dance practice," I said to get us back on track. "If we spend some time on the routines, it might make us both more comfortable. How about Mondays after school?"

"Can't," he said. "I have football every day except Tuesday."

"Hmm, that's when I usually film videos for my vlog. How about this Friday?"

Rhys blinked. "We have our first game this Friday."

"Oh, I didn't realize," I said.

"You know," he said, a glint in his eye, "there *are* posters all over school. And they mention it every day in the morning announcements."

"Guess I just forgot."

Rhys shook his head, but he was smiling.

"Saturday then?" I asked. "How's that sound?"

"I can do Saturday."

I smiled, thinking we'd finally found a day that worked.

"But," he added, "only if you come to the game on Friday night."

"Why? I'm going to the Homecoming one in a few weeks anyway."

"If I have to dance and embarrass myself in front of you, you at least have to give me a chance to redeem myself on the field." Rhys began walking backward. "That's the deal, Cupcake. You come see me play Friday. I come to your house to practice on Saturday. Take it or leave it."

I thought about how Mom might react to having Rhys over and winced.

"Can we meet at your house?" I asked.

"Sure," he said. "So, it's a deal? I'll see you at the game?"

I nodded. "Yeah okay. I'll be there."

Rhys grinned. "See you then, Cupcake."

On the drive home, I couldn't stop seeing that grin. I tried not to overthink it. Despite what Rhys Castle said, he wasn't mine. And I wasn't his.

Still…it took a couple hours of stress baking to get him off my mind.

Chapter 14

"*W*ho knew there was so much nudity in football?" My eyes went wide as I looked from the field of fully clothed football players to my best friend.

"Toni," I said, "what the heck? Where'd that come from?"

She shrugged, gesturing down a few rows to the student section of the bleachers. "Just look at them. They've got to be freezing their butts off."

I followed her gaze. Sure enough, there were several shirtless guys and girls with flesh-colored tank tops huddled together. Each had a dark green letter outlined in white painted on their chest, and together the message spelled Let's Go Trojans! I had to admit, Toni had a point. A lot of the students were wearing shorts. The wind tonight wasn't playing around. And it really did look like most of them were naked from the waist up.

But that was the point.

"Ah," I said, burrowing deeper into my sweater. "Yeah,

apparently they're called the naked boys—and girls. Kind of a cross between a super fan and cheerleader. It's about school spirit."

Toni scoffed, giving me side-eye. "How do you know that?"

I squirmed in my seat. "I may have done some research before the game."

The shrewd look on her face made me blush.

"What exactly did this research entail?"

"Googling what to expect at a football game and binge-watching the first two seasons of *Friday Night Lights*," I mumbled. Toni's jaw dropped, but before she could say anything, I added, "Don't look at me like that—it was addictive. And don't even get me started on the movie. That was even better."

Toni shook her head. "I'm going to have to check for myself, but if the guys look anything like your boy Rhys, I may have to do some bingeing of my own."

I frowned. "He's not *my* anything."

"Whatever," Toni said. "Tell me again how your super-hot prince begged you to come see him play."

"Ugh, it wasn't like that. He just asked me so he could make up for the dancing."

She lifted a brow. "It couldn't have been that bad."

"Oh yeah?" I retorted. "I iced my feet through *FNL* season one. By the end, they were still throbbing."

Toni winced, but my eyes narrowed on the smirk that followed a second later.

"What?" I asked.

"I bet you were nice about it," she said.

"Of course I was." I shrugged. "I didn't want to hurt his feelings. It's not Rhys's fault he has two left feet."

"Okaaay," she said, "true or false: he asked you to come tonight."

I tilted my head in thought. "It was more like a trade. But yeah, I guess."

"And you're going to his house tomorrow? To *practice*?"

The way she said "practice" made me roll my eyes.

"Yeah, but that was my idea," I said.

"I bet it was, you saucy thing," she tittered.

"We're only going to his place because I've never had a guy come over." I shook my head. "You know my mom. I love her to death, but there's no telling how she'd react."

"I bet she'd be pleased as punch."

"She would," I confirmed. "She'd also probably read a lot into it—kind of like someone else I know."

My BFF just raised a brow.

"It's only to work on the dance," I said. "Seriously. Rhys runs as hot and cold as my shower."

"Sure, sure."

Toni pointed, bringing my attention back to the game.

"Let's not argue," she said. "Offense is taking the field. Your boy is up."

I sighed but didn't correct her again. Toni had decided Rhys and I were a thing (or that we soon would be). She read into every one of our interactions, dissecting them, turning every word into something romantic. To be honest, I couldn't really blame her; my mind did that sometimes, too. I blamed movies, books, and TV for setting my expectations way higher than they should've been.

But this wasn't a teen rom-com, and Rhys Castle was so out of my league we weren't even in the same galaxy.

As the team got set for the play, I couldn't take my eyes off Rhys. It was hard to believe this was the same guy who'd struggled through our dance choreography, unsure and awkward. He certainly had all the right moves tonight. Rhys's voice was strong as he called out the plays. When the ball was snapped, he was in full control, his movements fluid, finding his man and throwing the ball straight to his target.

Down after down, they got closer to the other team's goal.

On the next play, Rhys was almost sacked—a term I now knew from watching all those hours of *Friday Night Lights*—but he spun away. No one was open, so he took his chance and ran. The cheers from the crowd grew louder as he passed the twenty...the fifteen...the ten...and...

"Touchdown!" the announcer said over the speakers.

The crowd went wild. Toni and I cheered right along with them as the marching band started up a song. The energy was infectious.

Okay, maybe I could get into this organized sports thing after all.

"Rhys Castle, starting quarterback for the Trojans, has just run the ball in for a twenty-five-yard touchdown. He's a senior with a very bright future, ladies and gentlemen. Let's give it up for Rhys!"

As he jogged back to the sidelines, getting pats on the back and high fives, I had to shake my head.

Was this even the same guy?

I mean, his footwork out there was crazy, his arm like a

cannon. Confidence was in every movement he made.

Rhys removed his helmet to get water, and that confirmed it. Yep. Same dark hair you'd love to run your hands through, same large hands that had actually been on my waist not too long ago.

A shiver raced up my spine.

And yup, same strong jaw that got tighter when he frowned. There was the Rhys I knew.

"Ariel," Toni said, breaking me out of my daze. "I know you say the guy can't dance, but…"

"Yeah?"

"Honest to God, Rhys Castle doesn't look like he'd be bad at *anything*."

I couldn't help but agree.

The game ended with Honeycomb winning 42-13. It wasn't a surprise. The momentum seemed to be on our team's side the whole time, and with Rhys's stellar performance and the defense holding the line, it was no contest. As the stands started to clear out, Toni and I made our way down the stairs.

"Do you have a dress for Homecoming yet?" Toni asked.

"Nope," I grimaced. "I was thinking of doing some online shopping this weekend."

"Well, don't wait too long."

"Yeah, yeah, thanks, Mom." I nudged her with my elbow. "What about you? Any plans for Homecoming?"

Toni sighed. "To die single while you dance the night away with your quarterback."

She was so dramatic I had to laugh. "Toni, be real."

"I am," she said. "No one's asked me, and there's only

like two more weeks left."

"That's plenty of time. Besides, what about Ben Schultz?"

"What about him?"

"I noticed him gazing at you in homeroom. I think he's got it bad."

She fluffed her bob. "Ben was probably just checking out your awesome rack again."

My lips curved up in a smile. "No, his eyes were definitely on you."

"As if I'd be interested," she said and crossed her arms. "Did you see him tonight? I think he was one of those naked boys."

"No," I said, "but I find it interesting that you picked him out."

She rolled her eyes. "Please, A. I mean, yes okay, he has a bit of a nerdy-cute thing going on. And okay, yes, I've seen him staring. But who goes out in these temperatures half naked? Only polar bears and people trying to catch the flu, my friend."

"Hey, Toni." It was none other than Ben himself, sounding out of breath, almost tripping on his way over to us. It was impossible to miss the big O on his chest. "I thought that was you."

"Hey," Toni said back.

After a moment, Ben turned to me. "Ariel. How's it going?"

"Going all right," I said, smiling as his eyes immediately moved back to my friend.

"Good, that's good. Did you two enjoy the game?"

"Yeah, it was okay. Football's not really our thing." Toni

gestured to his chest. "But…aren't you cold?"

Ben's face reddened, and he looked down as if only now realizing he was still sans shirt.

"Uh, yeah," he said, quickly pulling his T-shirt out of his pocket and over his head. "That'll teach me not to listen to my mom when she says sign up for spirit club. It'll be fun. Haha."

His laugh was awkward, but I saw Toni bite back a smile.

"For the record, I wasn't complaining about the no-shirt thing," she said. "I mean, you look good, Ben. There's nothing to be ashamed of."

"Great. I mean, thank y-you," Ben sputtered and then took a deep breath, giving her a genuine smile. "Hey Toni, can we talk for a sec?"

I widened my eyes as my best friend looked to me.

"Yeah sure," she said. "As long as Ariel says it's okay…"

I nodded. "It's more than okay. It's wonderful," I said, waving them both away. "Have an awesome talk, you guys. I'll just go wait by the car. Take all the time you need."

Toni and Ben looked at me like I had a few screws loose, but I didn't even care. I had a feeling I knew what he was going to say, and despite her protests, I knew Toni wasn't completely immune to Ben. And he was obviously smitten with my best friend, which showed good judgment. I gave a mental sigh as I watched them go.

I was just about to leave when…Rhys called out to me.

"Hey, Cupcake!"

My eyes cut to the right, and holy wow. This had to be a hallucination, because there was no way Rhys Castle was jogging toward me, still in his football uniform, his helmet held in one hand by his side.

He stopped about a foot away, only the fence separating us.

"Thanks for waiting," he said, looking like something out of a dream.

I swallowed. "No problem."

"Glad I caught you before you left. I wanted to tell you I can't meet up tomorrow."

"Oh."

Why the heck did I sound so disappointed?

Rhys ran a hand over the back of his neck. "Yeah, I forgot I have the SATs in the morning. Then there's this paper I still have to write for Mr. Simmons's class. Pretty sure I'm going to be dead after that."

"I thought you might have another mystery appointment," I said.

His jaw tightened. "No, not this time."

"Okay. Did you want to pick a different day?" I asked.

"I was thinking I'd try working by myself," he said. "See what I can do. Take some of the pressure off."

"Sounds like a good idea." My brow furrowed as I thought over his words. "But what do you mean by pressure?"

"I mean, you," Rhys said, causing a surprised laugh to burst from my lips.

"Me?"

"Yeah, I thought it might be easier without you watching."

"Please, you just performed in front of a stadium full of people," I pointed out. "One of whom was me, I might add."

He shook his head. "That's different."

"How?"

"Not sure if you know this, Cupcake, but you're…kind of intimidating."

This was news to me.

"And no guy likes to fumble in front of a pretty girl," he finished with an endearing shrug.

My heart leaped at the word, but I squashed it down hard. Rhys was obviously joking around. Just because he used the word *pretty* didn't mean I had to start doodling his name in my notebook and planning the freaking wedding.

And his reaction when I'd mentioned his mystery appointment was the same as the other day: 100 percent cagey. Who knew? Maybe he had a secret girlfriend—or boyfriend—he didn't want anyone finding out about. Oh my gosh, that could totally be it. What if Rhys thought I was hitting on him, and every time I mentioned his "appointment," it made him uncomfortable? Ugh. Time to make sure he understood I'd be good with just friendship.

"Talk about intimidating," I said. "You were impressive as heck out there, completed all your passes, no sacks, and that touchdown? Wow."

"Thanks." The corner of Rhys's lips rose. "One game, and you already sound like an expert."

I shrugged. "Clear eyes, full hearts, can't lose."

"Ah, I see," he said. His eyes were laughing, but thankfully he didn't make fun of me. "You know, back in middle school I went through a phase when all I wanted to do was watch reruns of *Friday Night Lights*."

"No way."

"Oh yeah, I even asked my parents if we could move to Texas."

My smile grew as I pictured it.

He lifted his chin as he noticed the bag in my hands. "What do you have there?"

"It's nothing," I said quickly, hiding it behind my back.

Rhys frowned. "Huh? Doesn't sound like nothing."

Rolling my eyes at myself, I brought the bag back out and handed it over to him.

"These are for you," I said, trying to ignore the nervous hitch in my voice.

"For me?" he said, unable to mask his surprise.

"It's no big deal. My grandma always taught me to never go to an event empty-handed."

Rhys reached into the bag as I kept rambling.

"They're cake pops," I said as he studied the little football-shaped cake on a stick. "I didn't know what you like, so there are vanilla and chocolate ones. Fewer of the chocolate, since Toni and I ate a couple. But yeah, there's dark chocolate covering, and the laces are white almond bark."

During my rambling, Rhys had removed the clear wrapper. He bit into his pop, his eyes getting wider as he chewed.

"They're good," he said. "Really good."

My cheeks warmed as he took another bite. "Thanks."

"No, thank you, Cupcake. I'm always hungry after a game." Rhys gave me a nod. "And this is a million times better than a protein bar."

"Hey Castle," someone on the team called. "Coach is looking for you."

"Be right there," Rhys said, then turned back to me and

held up the bag. "This was thoughtful. Thanks again."

I shrugged. "Good luck on your SATs—and the dancing."

"Thanks," he said with a small smile, and I felt my breath catch. "I'll need it."

Rhys jogged away, and the minute he was gone, Toni took his place. She told me how Ben had asked her to Homecoming (as I knew he would), how she'd said yes and couldn't wait to go. My bestie was so excited, and I loved hearing all the details. She'd already found the perfect dress and put it on hold months ago. Ben was a total sweetheart (Toni's words not mine). And she was so glad we both had dates now.

But…that wasn't entirely accurate.

Toni was so happy. I didn't want to interrupt and bring her down, so I kept my thoughts to myself, but the difference was clear. Rhys hadn't asked me. He wasn't officially my date and was only meant to escort me for a few minutes during the Court ceremony. I mean, the guy probably hadn't even known I was alive before fate, Toni, and the Honeycomb chalices threw us together. For all I knew, we'd make our Court appearance, dance our two dances, and he'd go off with his real date.

There had to be a ton of girls who'd love to go with him.

And if my theory was correct about the secret girlfriend or boyfriend, he'd already be spoken for, anyway.

I still couldn't stop thinking of what Rhys said. How he wanted to work on his own, how there'd be less pressure—but was that the real reason? Maybe he thought *I* was the problem? Maybe without me, behind closed doors, Rhys was a regular Fred Astaire? Though he definitely seemed to like the cake pops, my mind added. Or maybe I was overthinking this like I did everything else...

Ugh.

Being a girl was hard enough.

Why couldn't guys come with step-by-step instructions like the recipes I loved so much?

Chapter 15

Mom always let me do the grocery shopping. It made sense, since I used the kitchen way more than she did. Plus, it meant she could sleep in on the weekend, saved her a trip, and she knew how much I loved coming here. What she didn't know was how much it irked me when people put items back in the wrong place.

I spent at least ten minutes every Saturday moving things back to where they belonged on the shelves.

I stuck to the baked products aisle. It was my happy place, and I knew exactly where everything should be. Did I get weird looks from the store employees? Yeah, sometimes. But did they try to stop me? Heck no, I was basically doing their job for no pay.

"You're welcome," I'd said the one time I was approached by a manager. He had watched me a few minutes, nodded, then let me be.

Like I said. The situation was win-win. I was basically

providing free labor while I shopped.

The spices were a mess today, so I spent most of my time on those. But it wasn't until I was sorting the semi-sweet, dark, and milk chocolate chips into the appropriate boxes that something interesting happened. I was nearly finished when I heard a groan from the next aisle over.

I knew this place like the back of my hand, so it wasn't a surprise to look down aisle fourteen and see the usual frozen meals, vegetables, and pizza.

What was a surprise?

The first thing I noticed was a person, a very male person, leaning into an open door. The groan came again as I walked closer. Curiosity—it would do me in one of these days, I thought. But the closer I got, the more familiar the figure became. I knew those forearms, those broad shoulders...

"Rhys?" I said. "Is that you?"

My voice must've startled him because he jerked back. Rhys emerged from the freezer, wearing a black ball cap, white tee, and gray sweatpants. His eyes were tired when they met mine. Strangely, it didn't make him any less attractive.

"Cupcake," he said. "How are you today?"

"Better than you, I think."

Rhys yawned.

"I take it the SATs were just as boring and soul-sucking as usual," I said.

"That"—he pointed to my face—"is a perfect description."

"I try."

He looked at the cart in front of me while I checked out the items in his arms. He had a few frozen dinners, a bag of bacon, carton of eggs, loaf of bread, and a huge six-pack of Powerade. Compared to Rhys, it looked like I was buying out the whole store.

"I cook a lot," I said by way of explanation.

"I can see that," Rhys replied. "At least someone in your house does. My parents usually get takeout, and the only things I can make are toast, scrambled eggs, and spaghetti." He lifted his arm. "Hence the frozen meals."

"Hmm."

He nodded. "Yeah, they're gross. Unlike those cake pops you gave me—they were delicious. When I got back to the locker room, all the guys on the team were asking for one."

I smiled. "Did you share?"

"Hell no," he said. "I could lie, say it's because I didn't have enough for everyone. But the truth is I wanted them for myself."

"Because you were so hungry," I put in.

Rhys shook his head. "Because you made them for me."

I blinked.

"Looks like you're going to be doing more baking," he said.

Shaking off his last remark, I nodded. "Yeah, I have a lot of different dishes to make. I release at least one video a week, so I have to plan ahead."

"If you ever need a taste tester, I'm your guy."

Gah, as sweet as that was, I wished he hadn't said it.

I'm your guy.

My inner hopeless romantic wanted to hear his words a different way, but I forced myself to be real. Rhys was just offering to try my food, nothing more.

"I'll keep that in mind," I said, then gestured to the freezer. "What were you doing in there? When I walked up, I could've sworn your eyes were closed. Kind of looked like you were taking a nap."

"Nah, just getting a little R & R."

I bit back a grin. "With your head next to the frozen peas?"

"It's refreshing, Cupcake. Like having your head on a cloud or something. Haven't you ever done it before?"

"That would be a definite no," I said.

"Well come here and try it," he said, waving me over. "Trust me—you won't regret it."

Rhys held the door open to the refrigerated section and waited for me to step closer.

"This is silly," I said, feeling a cool blast emit from the fridge. "It's also probably not energy efficient, having the door open like that, letting out the cold."

That earned me an eye roll. "Just try it, Cupcake. The sooner you do, the sooner I close the door."

With a sigh, I took a few more steps and, feeling like everyone's eyes were on me, put my cheek on the sack of peas inside. The cool wafts of air hitting my face were actually soothing, the chill traveling along my skin not altogether unpleasant. Rhys's eyes were on me the whole time.

I exhaled a sigh, settling farther into the peas.

He cocked his chin as I pulled my head back a few

moments later. The smile on my face wasn't forced at all.

"That was nice," I said.

"Told you. Next time you're stressed, you know where to go."

I scoffed. "As good as it felt, I probably won't do it again. I'd be too self-conscious."

Something struck me then.

"Hey…does that mean you were stressed?" I asked.

"No more than usual," Rhys said.

I shot him a questioning look. Did that mean he was okay—or that he was always stressed? It could've been either, really. Before I could get an answer, Rhys changed the subject, his eyes moving to my cart.

"You mentioned some dishes," he said. "Can you tell me what they are? Or is it a secret?"

"Sure," I said, "though I don't know if it's that interesting."

"This is for your vlog, right?"

My brows rose in surprise. "Yes… You know about Sugar & Spice Movie Reviews?"

Rhys gave a small shrug. "I may have checked it out, watched a few videos."

What? When? I wanted to say. *Exactly how many videos did you watch? Did you follow, like, or comment on any of them?* Wow, even in my head, I sounded over-the-top. *Simmer down, Ariel. The guy asked you a question and mentioned your vlog.*

I had like twelve thousand followers. Rhys potentially becoming twelve thousand one wasn't a big deal. *But it feels like one*, a voice in my mind whispered. *Because it's Rhys.*

"Cupcake?" Rhys said, breaking me out of my thoughts.

"Sorry, I spaced out for a second," I said and forced a laugh. "I'm actually doing a series of desserts based on movies around the world. My favorites are always romance and rom-coms, so yeah." My cheeks flushed, but I forged ahead. "Each dessert will go with one of them."

His eyes were bright. "That sounds cool."

I pointed over my shoulder. "I actually have to grab a few more things, so…"

"Mind if I tag along?" Rhys readjusted the items in his arms. "I'm procrastinating, since I've got to write that paper when I get home."

"And practice the dances," I added.

His jaw ticked. "Yeah, and that. Lord help me."

I gave a mental laugh.

"Okay," I said. "It's just a few more items."

"Any almond bark?" he asked, sounding hopeful.

"Nope, sorry. It's not on the list."

"Aw, I was looking forward to more of those cake pops."

His words made me smile. I was so glad he'd liked the treat.

Before continuing on, I grabbed the frozen peas, some corn, and broccoli. I had to buy frozen pizza, too—Mom loved those things. But they were a little farther down. Rhys and I said nothing as we walked side by side, but it wasn't awkward. The silence felt comfortable. When I got to the place where they usually kept Mom's favorite pizza, there was only one left, and it was on the highest shelf.

Wonderful, I thought.

Stepping forward, I reached up, rose to my fullest height. My fingertips barely touched the box—but it fell over, making it even harder to reach. I growled internally. My eyes searched the row for one of those stepladders, but there wasn't one in sight. Okay then. Hyping myself up, I took a deep breath, bent my knees, and was just about to try again when a hand touched my waist.

"I got it," Rhys said.

He was so close, I felt each of his words caress the skin of my ear. Goose bumps rose in reaction, and I prayed he wouldn't notice. Rhys used the hand on my waist to steady himself as I held my breath. His other arm went around me, past my head, plucking the pizza off the shelf and bringing it back down. That was the first time I ever thought of a guy's hands as attractive.

"Here you go," he said, holding the box out to me, still standing too close.

I swallowed as I took it from him.

"Thanks," I mumbled.

"No problem."

It wasn't until Rhys stepped back that I realized just how warm I was.

Ducking my head, I dropped the pizza into the cart and walked away, gathering the other items as fast as I could. I didn't understand it. When we learned the waltz, Rhys had touched me for hours in the exact same spot. And yes, okay, I'd reacted. But this? This was ridiculous. You'd think I would've gotten used to his touch by now. But nope, my body still went up like fireworks.

And that was a problem.

I needed to get the heck out of there before I did something ridiculous like fall for Rhys Castle and his beautiful hands.

Friends, I reminded myself. *You are trying to be his friend.* And there was still his possibly-real possibly-fictional secret girlfriend or boyfriend to think about. If she or he, in fact, existed.

"So, what movies and what desserts?" he said, looking amused at my confusion. "For the around-the-world thing."

All right, this was good, I thought. Desserts I could talk about all day.

"A whole bunch of different ones," I said. "Right now, I know I'm doing molten lava cake with chocolate-covered strawberries for *Strictly Ballroom*, one of my all-time favorites. Seriously, it's so underrated. Tiramisu for *A Room with a View*—the best and most romantic version with Helena Bonham Carter, of course. Crème brûlée for *Amelie*. I mean, what else would you make for that movie? And beignets and berries for *French Kiss*. It's laugh-out-loud hilarious and so swoony."

He gave a small grin. "Okay, I gotta admit, I've never even heard of any of those movies. But the food part sounded really good."

My jaw dropped. "You've never seen *any* of them?"

I thought he had to be joking, but he shook his head as we joined the checkout line.

"I don't have a ton of free time," Rhys said quietly. "Are they on Netflix?"

"I don't know," I said. "But I'm sure they must be streaming somewhere. If not, they're definitely worth a search."

As we went through the line, I kept talking about the movies, trying to convince Rhys that he should watch them.

Partly because I really believed anyone with a beating heart would enjoy those films and partly because when I got to talking about desserts or movies, sometimes it was hard to stop.

Everything Rhys bought fit into one bag. My purchases were divided into at least ten. As we walked to the exit, I was still rambling on about movies and why the recipes were so perfect for them when he stopped my cart with a hand.

My voice cut out as he loaded his arms with the bags containing my groceries.

"What are you doing?" I asked.

Rhys gave me a look. "What do you think? I'm carrying your bags to your car."

I blinked. "You don't have to. I can handle it."

"I know," he said, then turned his eyes to the parking lot. "Where's your ride?"

"Over there," I muttered, shaking my head as we walked across the lot to my Subaru. Rhys made carrying everything look easy when I knew it was anything but. "Seriously, I could've gotten those. I do groceries every Saturday."

Rhys moved his gaze to mine. "It's no problem. Think of it as payback for the pops."

After I opened the trunk, he placed the bags in and then faced me.

"Can I ask you something?" he said.

"As long as it's not too personal," I joked.

"Why Cupcake?"

My brow scrunched. "I don't understand. Why what?"

"I meant why do people call you that?" he said. "You make all these desserts, a ton of them more interesting than cupcakes. So where does the name come from? Are cupcakes your favorite or something?"

I drew in a breath, trying to ignore the pang in my chest.

Rhys couldn't have known, but that question cut deeper than he could've imagined.

"My dad used to call me that," I said.

He nodded but misunderstood. "Ah, kind of like my uncle calls me Hot Shot—though I've asked him a thousand times not to."

"I guess." I shrugged. "Dad left when I was seven. He liked to flip between names: Chubby Wubby, Miss Piggy, Cupcake. Sometimes, when he'd been drinking or was feeling extra mean, he called Mom and me 'worthless.' But yeah," I said with a laugh, "Cupcake was the least offensive."

"He sounds like a real jackass," Rhys said.

The seriousness in his voice made my heart clench.

"What kind of parent says that stuff to his kid?"

"Mine, apparently," I said.

Rhys shook his head. "You must hate it when people call you that."

"Not really. The good news is I turned it into a positive. I love to bake, and my mom says even as a baby I had the sweetest disposition. The name fits. I own it. Now when people say it, I hardly even think of him anymore."

I shot Rhys a smile and tried to lighten the mood.

"Plus, my cupcakes *are* to die for," I added. "So there's that."

Rhys kept studying me, and after a minute, I began to fidget.

"What's up?" I asked.

"Nothing," he said. "Just trying to think of a new nick-name for you."

I lifted a brow. "Why? I said it doesn't bother me."

"Yeah, I know." Rhys waved my words aside. "But I can't keep calling you Cupcake, not now that I know the full story. For the record, your dad sucks."

"No argument here," I mumbled.

"Don't worry," Rhys said. "I'll figure something out."

"Or"—I lifted my hands—"you could just call me Ariel? It is my name, you know."

"Yeah, but everyone deserves a cool nickname. The process can't be rushed, though. It takes time."

I blinked. "You're taking this really seriously, huh?"

"Shh," Rhys said and held up a hand, "I'm thinking."

What a weirdo.

A very cute, sweet, and charming weirdo, I thought as Rhys narrowed his eyes, trying to come up with the perfect nickname.

Shifting back on my feet, I lifted a shoulder. "Well, I know you have a lot to do, and I should get these groceries home before they melt. Thanks again for your help. That was really decent of you."

"No problem," Rhys said. "After all, I am your prince."

See what I mean? Totally cute.

"You should check out those movies I mentioned," I said.

"I will," he mumbled.

"After you practice the dances, of course."

His brows lowered as I threw him a grin.

"You teasing me?"

"I would never," I said and got into my car to start the

engine. Rolling my window down, I threw him a wave. "I'll see you later, Rhys."

He stood there, watching me a moment.

"I *will* practice," he said.

"I know," I said back.

"Next time we meet, I'll be able to dance circles around anyone on Homecoming Court."

I nodded, speaking without a trace of sarcasm this time. "I know, Rhys," I said. "I believe in you."

"Glad to hear it." Rhys's lips lifted in a slow smile. "Drive safe, Princess."

A little thrill went through me at that.

As far as nicknames went, I thought as he walked away, it wasn't the worst. And when Rhys said it, there was so much warmth in his eyes that…yeah. Princess.

I didn't hate it. I didn't hate it at all.

Chapter 16

*M*om was awake when I got home, and she helped me bring in the groceries. When she asked why I was later than usual, I mentioned running into Rhys.

"Wait, so he carried the bags to your car?" she said then sighed. "How romantic."

My cheeks heated. "Not really, Mom. He was just being nice."

"I like him," she declared.

I...think I might like him, too, I thought but didn't say.

"Hey, what's this?" Mom lifted the frozen peas with a frown. "How'd these get in here? I thought you hated peas."

I swiped the bag as a blush stole up my cheeks.

"I do...usually," I said. "But these are special peas."

Mom squinted at the bag in my hands. "They look normal to me."

"They can be used to make tons of things," I said quickly. "Chicken pot pie, shepherd's pie, peas and carrots."

"Hmm," she said, "but again, all of those involve peas, which you said have a weird, mushy texture and taste like sadness in your mouth."

I forced a laugh. "Did I say that? I don't remember."

Mom nodded. "You absolutely did."

"Well…maybe I've had a change of heart."

Mom hummed again, studying my pink cheeks and no-doubt-guilty expression. I turned away before she could ask more questions. Opening the freezer, I placed the peas inside with care, pushing them to the back corner so Mom wouldn't wonder why I wasn't eating them. She was right, of course—I still didn't like peas. But these were special because they reminded me of a certain someone who I seriously needed to stop thinking about.

"That Rhys seems like a great guy," Mom said as if she'd read my mind. "It's pretty cool that you got paired up with him for Homecoming."

She was quiet for a moment, then…

"Speaking of," she tacked on, "if you wanted to look at dresses, I've got the whole day free."

"Smooth, Mom," I said. "Real smooth."

"What? I thought it would be fun." Her voice was all innocence. "You know how much I love to shop, and I can't think of a better thing to search for than the perfect Homecoming gown for my baby."

I sighed, giving in. "Okay."

She whooped as I pulled out my phone, and she opened hers.

"Awesome!" she said as I typed. "There are so many great choices. I've already found a few."

Glancing over and seeing all of the open windows on her phone, I blanched.

"A few?" I repeated weakly.

"Well, only like twelve." Mom kept flipping through the pictures. "There are so many possibilities. I remember you saying the theme is Vintage Hollywood. Kudos to whoever came up with that one."

"I think it was voted on by the student council," I said.

"Well, there's so many ways you can go with that. And my baby deserves the best, so don't worry about price. I—"

"There, all done," I said.

Mom blinked. "Excuse me?"

I shrugged. "I found a dress."

"You…you already found one? That fast?"

"Yeah," I said, "it wasn't hard. I just typed in Homecoming dresses and gowns, skimmed the page and picked one that looked nice. It's black, classic, affordable. And it's my size. You know how I hate to shop, so I one-clicked. It should be here in a couple days."

Mom shook her head. "Did you read the reviews at least? Sometimes ordering on the internet can be tricky. The pictures aren't always accurate. Quality matters."

"I'm sure it'll be fine."

"But don't you want to research all your options?"

"A dress is a dress, right?" I said.

"Yes," she replied, "but is it *the* dress? Ariel, I'm really not trying to be a pain. But this is a special occasion, and you're a special girl. I just want you to be happy."

I smiled, patting her hand. "I'm good, Mom. Now that that's done, do you want to watch a movie?"

"Fine." Mom gave a gusty sigh. "But we better make it a funny, romantic one. I need cheering up, since my daughter stole all my shopping joy."

"Rom-com it is," I said.

She nodded and, though I knew she was a bit crestfallen that we hadn't shopped till we dropped, I felt like a weight had been lifted from my shoulders. I could finally cross "find a Homecoming dress" off my mental list. And I hadn't even had to try on a stitch of clothing.

That was a win in my book.

As Mom and I watched *French Kiss* for the millionth time, I couldn't stop thinking about a certain boy with stormy blue eyes. Those eyes followed me into my dreams as well. That should've been my first clue that something was wrong.

Actually, no.

The peas were definitely a warning sign.

But sometimes when you see the cliff, it's too late.

You're already falling.

Chapter 17

*B*reakfast was one of my favorite meals. On my list of faves, it came right after dessert and brunch. With school starting so early, I usually settled for yogurt and berries or a bowl of cereal. Every time I got to have a hot breakfast, though, it was a treat.

But I could've done without the running commentary.

"Are you seriously going to eat all that?" Lana asked.

The horror in her voice was clear, but as I turned, I noticed that both her and Bryleigh looked hungry. They stared at the omelets on my plate, eyes flaring as I added a dollop of sour cream.

"No," I said, "I'm making one for Toni, too. She loves these things."

Lana crossed her arms. "This is supposed to be Homecoming breakfast, Cupcake. It's an exclusive event. You know, for members of the court only."

"There's more than enough food for everyone."

"Yeah, because most of the girls are too embarrassed to eat, but what if the guys want seconds?" She shrugged. "And besides, that's not the point. It's a perk of being on the court. That food is for us—whether we eat it or not."

My brow scrunched as I thought over her statement. "That's just silly. Why would they be embarrassed? The guys are stuffing their faces; why can't we? Plus, food is fuel to get us through the day. And I *could* eat both." *If I wanted to be sick all day*, I mentally added. "But I'm choosing to share instead."

"How nice of you," Lana snarked.

"What's in it?" Bryleigh asked, her eyes going a bit wider.

I shrugged. "Just eggs, tomato, peppers, cheese, sour cream, and salsa."

The head cheerleader licked her lips. "That sounds… really good."

"No," Lana said, "it sounds like a heart attack waiting to happen."

"They're all fresh ingredients," I said. "Ms. Weaver put out a good spread. If you want, I could make you one, too."

"Well, we're not interested. Right, Bry?"

When the other girl didn't immediately agree, Lana nudged her with a sharp elbow.

"Right," Bryleigh said, then reached past me. "But I will grab a banana."

Lana gave her a look, and she threw up her hands.

"What?" she said. "I'm hungry."

Zander came up behind us then. He placed his hands on Lana's shoulders and said, "Hey, my lady, you're looking extra good today. How's it going?"

"Fine." She shrugged him off. "And I asked you not to call me that. It's embarrassing."

"But it's what I call you in my heart," he said with a pout, causing Bryleigh and me to laugh. Zander's gaze landed on my plate, and he lifted his chin. "What you got there, Cupcake? Looks good."

"Just an omelet," I said.

"Ooh, can I get one of those—or possibly two? I'm starving."

I smiled at his enthusiasm. "Sure, no problem. You can have these actually. I'll just make some more."

"Awesome," he said.

Lana walked away in a huff, and I rolled my eyes.

Zander took a bite of his omelet, watching her go with a frown. "What's her problem?" he said around a mouthful of food.

"I have no idea," I said. "Maybe she missed breakfast."

We all stopped to look at the barely touched spread in front of us. "Yeah...maybe that's it," Zander said with a slight grin. "I'll bring her a little something," he added, snagging a muffin and plastic fork. "Thanks again."

When I came out of the staff room, which indeed had a sign on the door stating, Homecoming Court ONLY, Toni was waiting for me in the hall.

"I can't believe they reserved a room for you guys," she said. "Or that there's something called Homecoming breakfast. How ridiculous."

I shrugged. "Eh, don't knock it. If there wasn't, you wouldn't have this omelet, my friend."

"Good point," Toni said and took a bite.

We walked the halls, enjoying our breakfast.

"So, did you do anything else interesting this weekend?" she asked. "Besides spend time with a certain quarterback, I mean?"

Rhys's face passed through my mind, but I shook my head.

"Not really," I said. "I think I told you everything on the phone. But ooh, hey, I did get a Homecoming dress."

It took me a second to realize Toni had stopped walking. Looking over my shoulder, I lifted my brows.

"Something wrong?" I asked.

"Oh no," she said, walking forward, "my bestie got her dress for the big day without consulting me first. There's no problem at all."

"You got yours ages ago," I pointed out, "and didn't tell me until last Friday."

She rolled her eyes. "Yeah, but that was just because I was embarrassed. I had a dress, but no one had asked me—I didn't want to jinx anything. What's your excuse?"

"Hm, let's see. Shopping is the bane of my existence. In the mall, I'm surrounded by advertisements of girls with zero acne, zero body fat, and seemingly zero real-life problems. Not to mention, the clothes never fit right. It's like they don't even know curvy girls exist—which is why it took me ten seconds to search and find a dress—which is also probably the reason I forgot to mention it," I said and gave her a shrug. "But it's coming tomorrow if you want to stop by. You and Mom will be the first to see it."

"I accept your invitation," Toni said, locking her arm with mine. "Besides, I'm sure you were distracted after your

Saturday tryst with Rhys at the grocery store."

I sighed. "Oh my God, it was nothing. Just a few minutes in the frozen food aisle."

Toni's smile grew. "Sounds fun to me."

"Listen, for the hundredth time, there's nothing going on," I said. "Rhys and I are just partners for a project, that's all."

"Sure…but the boy stuck with you to shop for groceries."

I lifted a shoulder. "He was avoiding homework."

"You said he checked out your vlog. That's interesting."

I waved that away. "So do a lot of people."

"Okay," Toni said, "I'm loving the confidence. You should be proud of your vlog following. But I thought the majority of your viewers were females between the ages of twenty-five and fifty."

"It's oddly impressive how you remember these things," I muttered.

"Which," she added, "would make a male teenager an outlier."

"I guess," I conceded. "But don't make it into more than it is, Toni. I'm begging you."

"He also carried your bags," she put in.

"He did, because it turns out Rhys is actually a nice guy. I'm sure he would've done that for anyone."

Toni nodded as if she'd finally figured something out.

"You like him," she said.

I blinked, not having expected that. "N-no, I don't."

"And she stutters on the denial." Toni stared at my face then shook her head. "You must like him a lot, huh?"

My tongue felt paralyzed for a moment. I was so surprised.

"I—why would you even say something like that?" I asked.

She held up a hand. "Please. As your best friend, I know these things."

"Well, you're wrong," I said while crossing my arms.

Her brow scrunched. "It's not like it's a big deal, Ariel. I've liked a ton of people. Everyone gets crushes, all the time—especially on guys like Rhys. He's a good-looking jock, who's also apparently nice."

"Yeah," I said, "but you know I'm more interested in baking than boys. I have goals, Toni. Those do not include getting my heart broken by some guy I met in high school. No thank you."

"Why do you think he'd break your heart?" she asked.

I shrugged. "You know my romantic history—or lack thereof. My crushes literally end up crushing me. And not in a good way."

Toni's eyes softened a bit. "If you're talking about Darryl—"

I winced at hearing the name again.

"—he was a rotten little weasel who never deserved your love. We've been over this a million times."

"Yeah, but I should've known better than to fall for his charming BS."

Darryl had been my biggest crush. There were others before him, sure. But he was the first guy to ever like me for me—or so I'd thought.

Darryl was my lab partner in eighth grade. We'd talked a lot during class, gotten to know each other. I thought we had a real connection. But it turned out he'd only been using me, both so he could copy my homework and for the sweets. I brought him something almost every day. At the end of the semester, I'd finally worked up the courage to tell him how I felt—but he was surrounded by his friends when I approached him at his locker. Darryl, my sweet, charming lab partner, pretended like he didn't know me. He laughed in my face when I asked if he wanted to hang out later—though during class, he'd been the one who kept saying "we should hang out sometime." When I suggested we go somewhere more private to talk, one of his friends had called me a derogatory name. More laughter. And that was that.

My thoughts about relationships had shifted.

I was still a hopeless romantic.

I still believed in love—just not for me.

"Rhys seems like he's capable of major damage," I told my best friend.

"You'd have to like him a little for that to happen, though, right?" Toni said.

I rolled my eyes. "Okay, even if I did have a small, miniscule, teeny tiny crush, it wouldn't matter anyway."

"Why not?"

"Because Rhys Castle is an enigma. His moods are unpredictable—offensive and arrogant one moment, nice and thoughtful the next. There's definitely something going on with him, something he's hiding. Plus, he would never be into someone like me," I said.

"Ah," Toni said, "because he's into guys? Sorry I didn't realize."

"He's not gay," I said, "at least as far as I know. He used

to date Lana."

"Okay, then he's into mean girls, so he could never appreciate my best friend's kind, sweet soul. I get it now." She tilted her head. "But didn't they break up?"

I shook my head with a grin. "Rhys and I only hang out for Homecoming stuff. He wouldn't even talk to me if it weren't for that."

Before Toni could say anything, another voice spoke over her.

"Hey Princess," Rhys called out.

"You forgot to mention the pet name," she whispered as we watched the crowd part for him.

I spoke through a forced smile. "That's because it wasn't relevant."

"Oh, I definitely think it is."

Rhys's long legs ate up the distance between us. No one got in his way, and soon he was standing right in front of me.

"Hey," he said and threw a thumb over his shoulder. "I just passed Zander in the hall with these amazing-looking omelets. You responsible for those?"

"Yeah, I am," I said.

"I knew it." Rhys nodded. "There was no way he did that by himself. They looked too good."

I held up my empty plate. "I would offer you some, but we already ate ours."

"It's cool," he said. "I was kind of bummed about you making food for someone else, though. I thought that was our thing."

"Sorry," I said, "I didn't realize we had a thing."

Rhys gave me a half smile. "I was joking, Princess."

I narrowed my eyes at him. "Funny. I didn't know you did that, either."

"I'm full of surprises," he said. "But that's not why I'm here."

"What's up?"

"Got a question for you. Do you want to come over to my house later?" he said.

It was a good thing I was done with that omelet, I thought. Otherwise, someone probably would've had to perform the Heimlich. As it was, I choked on air.

"You okay there?" he asked.

"She's fine," Toni said and patted my back. "This happens sometimes. It's nothing."

Rhys was quiet, but when I looked up, I noticed him staring at me with concern.

"I thought you had football," I said when I got my hacking under control.

"I do," he said. "But I figured we could meet up after."

Toni's face was smug as she took our plates and chucked them in a nearby bin.

"Shoot, I should get going," she said. "Wouldn't want to be late to homeroom."

"But—"

Toni shot me a grin as she walked away. "Don't worry, *Princess*. We'll talk later."

Once she was gone, I turned back to Rhys.

"That was Toni," I said unnecessarily. "She's my best friend."

"Yeah, I think we might've had some classes together," he said. "Are you really okay? That cough didn't sound good."

Gah, just kill me now.

"Yeah, I'm fine." I ran a hand over my cheek. "You just surprised me, that's all."

Rhys cocked his head. "I asked if you want to come over. Why would it cause that kind of reaction?"

Because for a second I thought you were asking me out.

Ugh. It was so embarrassing. My conversation with Toni was the only explanation for my bizarre thoughts, but there was no way I'd admit the truth. Rhys would laugh till he was blue in the face.

"I don't know," I lied.

"Okay," Rhys said slowly. "But do you want to come? To my house? I practiced the dances over the weekend."

"Oh yeah?" I said. "How'd it go?"

He shrugged. "It went well. My brother says I suck way less than when I first started."

The warning bell rang as I was still trying to take in the realization that Rhys was not in fact an only child like me. Why this surprised me, I didn't know. But it did.

"So will you come?" he asked.

I lifted a brow. "You want me to come so you can show me your sweet dance moves? Sure, I'll be there. What time?"

"Five o'clock work for you?" His throat bobbed, and there was this guarded look in his eyes as he added, "I also have an appointment. You know, one of those mystery ones you like to tease me about. So, it can't be earlier than that."

"Yeah, I have to go by my mom's work, but I'll come after."

"See you then, Princess."

With that, Rhys disappeared back into the thinning

crowd. My eyes lingered on him far longer than they should have, my pulse pounding harder than necessary. The guy was definitely not good for my heart, I decided.

Now, if I could only stop staring, it would all be fine.

After last period, I drove home to pick up a few things before heading across town to Mom's school, Blue Skies Elementary.

"Ashley, take that finger out of your nose right now," Mom said. "That goes for you, too, George. Young ladies and gentlemen do not pick their noses. They use a tissue."

Mom was having this talk with the kids in her after-school class when I walked through the door.

"And is Clarence back from the bathroom yet?" she asked.

"Not yet, Ms. Duncan," a little girl with black hair said. "He's been in there for a long, long time."

"I know, sweetheart," she said.

"A looong time," she repeated.

"I'll go check on him in a second."

"What do you think he's doing in there?"

"Heaven only knows," Mom mumbled. Her eyes went to me, and she smiled. "Oh hey, Cupcake. I hope you haven't been standing there long."

"No, just got here," I said. A glance at her face let me know she was happy among the chaos. Her classroom was colorful yet organized, the perfect place for kindergarteners to learn and play. "How are you? Can I help with anything?"

"I'm good," she said. "These little ones are testing me today, but we're about to settle down for a movie. Then we get to have some yummy cake to celebrate a very special someone's birthday."

The little girl's eyes widened. "Is it me, Ms. Duncan? It's my birthday today!"

"Why yes, Shamika, it is," Mom said. She gestured with her head as the girl jumped, then went over to another girl and started talking. "She's so sweet. Baby, could you put the cake down and watch the little ones while I go check on Clarence? He's been gone a minute. There's no telling what's happening."

I winced. "Yeah, you go ahead. We'll be fine."

"Thank you so much," she said then hurried past me to the bathrooms. A few seconds later, I heard her saying, "Now Clarence, what did we say about soap? It's for cleaning, sweetheart, not painting the walls."

Setting the cake down on her desk, I straightened up and saw a little boy staring at me.

"Who are you?" he asked.

"Hi," I said, "I'm Ariel. What's your name?"

"George." The boy's finger started to travel up to his nose, and I quickly grabbed a Kleenex. "I'm five," he said.

"Oh, that's nice," I said. "Do you want to hear a joke, George?"

His hand paused. "Sure, I like jokes."

"How do you make a tissue dance?" I asked.

The boy tilted his head.

"You put a little boogie in it."

George smiled, and as I held up my tissue-covered hand, instead of picking his nose, he blew it—thank goodness. Then he laughed.

"Look, look," he said. "I made it dance. With my boogies!"

I chuckled, too.

"I know, George. Good job."

"You're funny and nice," he said then grabbed a clean tissue to show his friends his new trick.

Mom's voice came from behind me as I was sanitizing my hands.

"I saw that," she said. "Well done."

I shrugged. "It was nothing."

"That boy has been picking his nose on and off since the last bell rang," she said. "I'd say it's something."

"Maybe," I said. "But my talents lie in baked goods. Little kids scare me, as you know."

"And yet, you're good with them."

I smiled at her. "It must be in the genes."

"Darn right it is," she said. Grabbing a plastic cake cutter, Mom went to the desk and removed the cover. "And this cake is gorgeous."

"Thanks," I said. "Here. I brought the plates, napkins, and party hats as well."

Mom shook her head, her eyes a little glassy. "This is going to make Shamika feel so special, and I know the other kids are going to love it, too."

I stared down at the cake. It was a simple, round chocolate cake with yellow, pink, green, and white frosting. Mom had told me Shamika loved flowers, so I'd added a bunch of them. The daisy chains framing the cake looked good, but the roses really tied it all together.

A lot of the kids in the after-school program weren't well-off. Mom had confided in me once that often the families couldn't afford to celebrate birthdays, and she just wanted to give them something. The kids didn't always stay in the program; some moved, and new ones came in all the time. And yes, a few wealthier kids were in the mix. But rich or poor, it didn't matter. I'd made a cake for each of their birthdays ever since.

"You did well, baby," Mom said.

I shook my head. "You got this program started. You buy them coloring books, crayons, snacks, and who knows what else. These kids are lucky to have you, Mom."

She smiled. "Thanks for that. Are you staying for the movie?"

"No, I actually have to go in a few minutes," I said.

"Well then, let's sing and give you a piece for the road."

Mom clapped her hands, calling all the kids over.

"Today we're celebrating a very special young lady," Mom said. Shamika was smiling as she bounced up and down. "She is turning six, and we all get to celebrate together. Isn't that wonderful? Happy birthday, Shamika!"

"Thank you, Ms. Duncan," she said.

"And now we get to eat this beautiful cake my daughter made."

The kids cheered.

"And then we'll watch Shamika's favorite movie, *Tangled*."

After singing the birthday song, the kids all lined up for cake, and I helped Mom pass out the pieces. Shamika, of course, got to go first. Her eyes widened as she gazed at the cake, and then she looked at me.

"You made this?" she asked.

"Yes," I said. "I hope you like it."

"Oh, I do! It's beautiful. Thank you so, so much."

"Happy birthday, Shamika." I gave her a wink. "Also, good choice. I love *Tangled*."

"You do?" she asked. "It's my favorite."

Mom threw an arm over my shoulders. "My daughter loves it, too. And guess what else? She is actually a princess! Isn't that awesome?"

"Mom," I mumbled.

Another little girl stepped up then. "No she's not."

"Actually, Ashley, she is," Mom said with a laugh. "Her school picked her to be one."

"Well, where's her crown?"

Shamika rolled her eyes. "Maybe she left it at home."

Ashley shook her head, her lips set in a mulish frown. "No she's not. She can't be."

"And why do you think that?" Mom said.

"Everyone knows there are no fat princesses."

Shamika, who had a little pudge, put her hands on her hips. "There are, too. Girls and boys can be anything they want to be."

"That's right," Mom said. "Beauty comes in all shapes and sizes."

"Name one," Ashley said. "Go on, name one fat princess."

Shamika and my mom blinked but didn't respond.

"See? Told you so."

The little girl shrugged, took a plate of cake from my

stiff hand, and walked away. My jaw was still on the floor, but maybe it shouldn't have been. A lot of times kids spoke without thinking. Her words shouldn't have felt like a punch to the gut.

But they did.

Chapter 18

As much as I tried, I couldn't forget or shake how much Ashley's words bothered me. Sure, she was young, but she spoke the truth. It was a sad fact. None of us could think of even one plus-sized princess.

What the heck was up with that?

Needing something to take my mind off everything, I said bye to Mom and the kids, got in my car, started the engine, then…just sat there.

I frowned. My mood was kind of crappy. I would've loved nothing more than to drive home, but I'd promised Rhys I would meet him.

There were only two problems with that.

1) I didn't know his address.

2) I didn't have his phone number to call and ask.

Maybe it was for the best, I thought, as I sent a text to Toni, telling her my situation and asking if she wanted to come watch a movie with me, since I probably wouldn't be able to meet Rhys. If he had gotten so much better, then what was the point of us meeting anyway?

Toni sent me a response immediately.

Toni: The point is he invited you to his house, Ariel!!! A boy, a real boy!

Me: As opposed to a fake one LOL?

Toni: Haha, you're so not funny :/. But seriously, don't worry. I'll handle it.

Me: What do you mean?

Toni: Just answer when the guy contacts you.

I rolled my eyes.

Me: Pretty sure he'd need my number for that—which he doesn't have.

Toni: Are you sure???

Me: Unless he has some secret stalker-ish tendencies I don't know about, then yeah. I'm sure.

Toni: LOL! You crack me up! Say hi to Prince Rhys for me :P

I was still looking at her last text when a moment later, my phone rang. The call was from an unknown number. Though I'd usually hit ignore or let it ring, I was curious. The phone had been ringing for about a minute when I answered.

"Hello?" I said hesitantly.

"Princess," Rhys's voice said on the other end. "Your friend tells me you need my address."

My eyes widened, and I felt myself smiling. Amazing. Toni could do anything when she put her mind to it. "Only if you still want to go over the dances."

"You know it," he said, and there was a ping on my

phone. "Just sent you the info. Did you get it?"

"Yeah, I did," I said.

"Need anything else?"

"No…but hey, I was wondering. How did Toni already have your number? I didn't realize you two knew each other that well."

"We don't," he said. "She messaged me on social media. I got a notification."

For some reason, that made me sigh in relief.

"So I'll see you in a few?" he asked. "I've been dying to show you my 'sweet dance moves,' as you called them."

"Sounds good, Napoleon," I said. "I'll see you soon."

Rhys sounded confused. "Who's that?"

"Uh, *Napoleon Dynamite*? It's this quirky movie with a cult following. Hilarious one-liners, a llama named Tina, big dance solo at the end. Ring any bells?"

"Nope, sorry."

Figures, I thought. It's even more obscure than the other ones he hasn't seen.

"You really should watch more movies, Rhys," I said. "There are so many awesome ones out there."

He grunted. "Maybe. Are you on your way yet?"

"About to pull out of the parking lot," I replied. "My GPS says I should get to your house in ten minutes."

"Okay, well, I'll hang up so you can focus on the road," Rhys said. "See you in a few."

"Yep, bye."

"Bye, Princess."

I wasn't sure whether it was the nickname or his concern about my safety, but my heart warmed as I hung up the phone. The GPS was wrong—the trip took fifteen minutes with traffic, but I pulled up to Rhys's house and parked on the street so I wouldn't block anyone in. His one-story house was light blue with white trim. The lawn was small but well-kept, and Rhys's car was in the driveway. Even if it wasn't, though, I would've known it was his house based on the lawn sign that had his name and football number on it along with Go Trojans!

I knocked, and a few seconds later, Rhys answered the door.

"Hey," he said.

"Hey," I said back. "Your house is really nice."

"Thanks, I'll let my parents know."

Smart aleck.

"I'm also digging the sign." I smiled, pointing to the lawn. "It's very *Friday Night Lights*."

"It's embarrassing. I've asked my folks to take it down, but they won't."

"That's because they're proud of you," I said.

"Yeah, yeah. Come on in, Princess." Rhys gestured me inside. "I promise not to step on your feet this time."

I nodded. "I'll hold you to that."

He placed a hand over his heart as I walked past him. "If it happens, I vow to help you to your car."

"Okay, now I'm kinda scared."

Two steps inside the house, I heard distant thumping—it sounded a bit like thunder. The noise got louder, and a second later, I was almost tackled to the ground by Rhys's dog, who came zooming out of nowhere, throwing himself at me paws first, colliding with my chest.

"Oof," I said as the dog planted big sloppy kisses all over my face.

"Hercules," Rhys said in a stern voice. "Down boy."

Amazingly, the dog responded.

"Sit."

Again, the dog sat, looking between Rhys and me, his long tail wagging fiercely back and forth. But he didn't jump up again. Considering his excitement from before, I was impressed by his restraint. What really won me over, though, were those chocolate brown eyes.

"Incredible," I said in awe. "How did you get him to do that?"

Rhys gave a shrug. "We've worked on his training since he was a puppy. Hercules was always a quick study. He's smarter than most humans."

"I can see that," I said, bending down to greet the big guy properly. I was no dog expert, but he looked like a German shepherd with a mixture of black and tan fur. Those eyes of his stared right back into mine with clear intelligence. "Very nice to meet you, Hercules. You are such a beautiful boy, and I hear you're smart, too."

"Hercules, shake hands," Rhys said.

The dog lifted his paw, and I gave it a gentle shake.

"Good boy." The fondness was clear in Rhys's tone.

"And a gentleman, too," I remarked. While I was petting his ears, the dog closed his eyes with a sigh. "Ah, what a wonder you are. Hey, is Hercules a *Sandlot* reference?"

"What's *Sandlot*?"

Instead of answering, I just shook my head. "You're killin' me, Smalls."

"I...have no idea what that means," Rhys said. "But I think he likes you."

"He seems like a sweetheart to me," I said. "I bet he likes everybody."

Hercules rolled onto his back, and I gave him what he wanted, petting his tummy until one of his legs started going wild. The movement made me laugh in delight.

"Princess, I assure you," Rhys said, "he doesn't respond like this to everyone."

"Really?"

"Yeah, dogs can tell a lot about people. Hercules obviously sees you're a kind soul."

Rhys got down next to me to pet the dog, who looked like he was loving every second. Hercules's tongue was out now, and his eyes were closed like he might fall asleep. We petted him for another minute—and to be honest, I could've stayed there much longer; Hercules was so cute—but we had to get started on the dancing.

Rhys led me into the house through a large living room. The sectional in the shape of an *L* took up most of the space, but there was a recliner as well as a coffee table that had been pushed back, creating an open space in the middle of the floor. The big screen TV attached to the wall was gigantic.

"You have *that*, and you never watch movies on it?" I said.

"No, it's usually football for Dad and me, Hallmark for Mom, or games for my brother," Rhys said, running a hand over his neck. "I have a TV in my room, too."

He paused.

"But movies aren't really my thing."

Tilting my head, I said, "Yeah well, football isn't my thing. But I watched your game and enjoyed it."

"You did?" His lips lifted slightly. "Good to know."

"My point," I said, fighting down a blush, "is that movies are awesome if you give them a chance."

"Wow, you're really passionate about this."

"Of course I am! Films provide an escape, make people feel less alone, give them hope and joy. A great movie can do all that and more." I shrugged then continued, "It's why they're so fun to share. I love movies—almost as much as I love baking, and that's a lot."

Rhys stared at me a few seconds then said, "I guess I'll have to try some then."

I nodded, satisfied that he'd finally given in.

"So, is this where we're practicing?" I asked.

"Yeah," he said with a half smile. "We could use the kitchen, if you want, or go outside—but the ground's a little uneven in places. Or there's always my room if we need more privacy."

"Here's fine," I said.

"Okay." Rhys stepped forward as I faced him. "Try not to be too impressed. Compliments make me blush."

I rolled my eyes at that.

But as we got started, I couldn't deny there was definite improvement.

First, Rhys kept his promise. He didn't step on my feet once as we ran through Mr. Patachoui's choreography. Second, he wasn't counting out loud anymore. And third, he just seemed more confident. The music was playing on

Rhys's phone, and as we went through the movements, it was clear he had worked on this. At some point, Hercules had followed us and sat there, watching us dance with a content expression.

I smiled as the song came to an end.

"So, what did you think?" Rhys said, and I could tell he knew he'd done well.

I gave a shrug. "It was good."

"Good?" His voice was incredulous. "That's all I get? Come on, Princess. I was awful before, and I practiced my butt off. You've gotta give me more than that."

"I thought you didn't like compliments."

"Well," Rhys said, "I changed my mind."

A laugh escaped as I took in the stubborn set of his jaw. "You did awesome, and you know it."

"Now you're just saying that."

"Don't be silly. You were wonderful."

Rhys's muscles relaxed as he cocked his chin. "You think so?"

"Yeah," I said, "you must have practiced a lot. It looks so much better."

"Feels better," he admitted. "You want to go through it again? Dancing with someone is a little different."

"I'd love to."

As we restarted the dance, Rhys was even more confident, and though this was the one where we didn't touch, every time his eyes met mine, I felt it like a physical caress. My mouth started talking without my permission. It was my mind's sad attempt to fill the space between us with more than just tension.

"Did you know that some professional athletes take ballet to get better?" I asked.

Rhys's brow scrunched. "I hadn't heard that."

"It's true. Ballet is supposed to increase flexibility, help with footwork, improve balance. There are a ton of benefits."

"Sounds like it."

"Kobe Bryant even took tap," I added.

"Really?" he said.

I nodded. "Yeah, it helped strengthen his ankles and avoid injury."

"Well, *tap* I think I could handle," Rhys said. "But I don't see myself doing ballet. Not a big fan of tights."

"Pretty sure the guys wear black pants. And I can definitely see you rocking a leotard," I said then gave myself a mental slap.

Gah, why did I say that?

Because he's beautiful, and you know he would look good in anything.

Yeah…but did I actually have to say it out loud?

Argh.

"Nah, I couldn't pull it off," Rhys said, his eyes moving over my body. "But I bet *you'd* look good in one."

Although the music hadn't ended, I stopped dead in my tracks.

"That's not funny," I said.

Rhys stopped, too, and crossed his arms. "It wasn't meant to be."

I couldn't tell if he was serious. Rhys sounded sincere, but…

Okay, so I was good with my body. People had ideas

about the perfect figure, and I knew mine wasn't what others saw as perfect. That was fine. But leotards were like bathing suits, tight-fitting, rather revealing. The thought that Rhys might want to see me in one...

Was it hot in here or was that just my partner?

Chapter 19

"*Y*ou okay, Princess?" Rhys said.

I cleared my throat. "Yeah, I'm fine."

"You suddenly got this faraway look in your eyes."

"Hmm," I said, "sorry, I was distracted. We should probably run the dance a couple more times, since we didn't finish."

Rhys nodded. "Whatever you say."

Just as we were about to start again, the front door opened. A middle-aged couple walked in, carrying bags in their arms, followed by a boy who had to be Rhys's younger brother. They were like mirror images of each other—though his brother was shorter and looked all of twelve years old.

"So, Rhys gets the house to himself," the boy said, "and I'm forced to go to the mall with you two instead of staying home and playing Xbox? How is this fair?"

Rhys shook his head. "I'm older than you."

"Yeah, and more hormonal."

"Zachary David Castle!" the woman said. "You apologize to your brother and his guest right now."

"Why? It's true."

The woman didn't back down, and he rolled his eyes.

"Sorry," Zach said, then looked at me. "I guess you're the girl who has to dance with him?"

"I am," I said.

The kid shook his head. "Again, I'm sorry. He's been practicing for hours on end, but he still sucks."

"Hey," Rhys argued, "you said I got better."

"No, I said your level of suckage got better," Zach corrected, giving a shrug. "But could you really have gotten any worse?"

My dance partner's eyes lit on his brother, pinning him to the spot and promising retribution.

"I'm going to get you for that," Rhys said.

"Yeah, okay."

Before I could blink, Rhys had vaulted over the couch and pulled his brother into a headlock. The kid was wily, though. He slipped out of the hold, but Rhys quickly caught him again. It was obvious they'd done this a thousand times before.

"You'll have to disregard this little display of brotherly love," Rhys's dad said, coming over to me. "I'm Glenn Castle, Rhys and Zach's dad. And you are?"

"Ariel," I said. "Pleasure to meet you, Mr. Castle."

A groan sounded out, and I saw that Zach and Rhys were now wrestling on the floor.

"Does this happen often?" I asked.

"Only every day and twice on weekends." Mrs. Castle walked over to me, holding out a dainty hand. "I'm Jennifer, the mom—though I maintain they get this unruliness from their father."

A loud crash came from behind. But she ignored it, and so did I.

"It's nice to meet you," I said.

"In all seriousness, I hope this isn't bothering you, Ariel."

"Oh no."

Mr. Castle leaned over and whisper-shouted, "She has to say that. Unlike our two hooligans, the girl obviously has manners."

I laughed at that. "It's fine, seriously," I said. "My mom and I hate it when the house is too quiet. Plus, as an only child, I always wanted a brother or sister. So this is nice."

Mr. Castle smiled then took his and his wife's bags into another room. The boys' fight seemed to be winding down. Mrs. Castle, though, I noticed was looking at me.

"Rhys was right about you," she said.

"What do you mean?" I asked.

"You're just as pretty as he said you'd be."

My cheeks went up in flames. She must've gotten me confused with someone else, I thought. Before I could correct her—or question her relentlessly—Rhys joined us.

"Mom," he said, "I hope you haven't been over here embarrassing me."

"Of course not." She lightly hit his arm. "I was just getting to know her a little, that's all. What's embarrassing about that?"

Rhys narrowed his eyes. "I'm not sure. But sometimes

you say things you shouldn't."

"*Moi*?" she said.

"Yes, you."

His mother gave him a frown. "You know, sometimes I wonder where did my kind, loving Reese's Pieces go?"

Zach snickered from the couch while Rhys released a sigh.

"Well, I need her back," he said. "We weren't finished practicing when you guys came home."

"I bet you weren't," Zach mumbled.

Mrs. Castle turned to Rhys then. "I'll let you go in a second, but first I want to check in, see how you're doing. You went to your appointment, right?" she asked.

Rhys's jaw tensed, but he nodded. "Yeah, of course."

"Everything go okay?"

"Yep."

"Do you think it helped?"

"It always does, Mom. Can we go now?"

Rhys shot me a glance, but I didn't know what to do, where to look. This was clearly something personal; I wasn't sure he'd want me hearing any of it. In fact, knowing him and how much he guarded his secret, this might provoke an emotional ice storm of epic proportions. And yet, I desperately wanted to know more. If his mom was aware of his appointments and was asking if they "helped," I was probably wrong about the whole secret girlfriend/boyfriend idea.

Whatever the truth was, this sounded serious.

"Is the weekly appointment enough, or do you think you need more?" Mrs. Castle said. "We could always add to the schedule if—"

"Mom," Rhys said. "It's fine."

She nodded. "Okay, if you say so, I believe you. You'd let me know if things weren't fine."

"I would."

"Because you know I love you and your brother more than anything," she said. "You only have to say the word and I'll get you whatever you need. More appointments, a different doctor, anything."

The second to last word made my heart clench. Why would Rhys need to see a doctor? I wondered. He looked super healthy to me, was in the prime of his life. Nothing could touch him. But, if doctors were involved…did that mean Rhys was sick? Oh gosh, I hoped not.

Rhys let out a sigh.

"Dr. Moorehouse is doing a great job, Mom. And yes, I'm feeling good," he said. "Thanks for making it awkward. Can we go now?"

"Sure." Mrs. Castle nodded and gave him a quick hug. "I love you."

"Love you, too," he said then turned to me. "You want to go to my room?"

I gulped. "Your room?"

"Yeah, we'll get more work done there," he said. "It's smaller, but at least we'll have some privacy."

"Okay." My voice sounded cool, but inside I was freaking out. "That sounds good."

Mrs. Castle said it was good meeting me. Zach made some other snarky remark, but I couldn't focus on it as Rhys led me to his room.

On the way, I made a real effort to put the conversation I'd just heard out of my mind. There was a lot to process, and it only left me with more questions—that I was sure Rhys would say were none of my business. And he'd be right. He didn't say anything, which let me know he was content to pretend like none of the stuff with his mom and doctors actually happened, and I decided to do the same. He'd confide in me if and when he wanted to.

Rhys's bedroom door was plain white. The inside of his space was clean if a bit sparse. The walls were painted a light gray, the carpet, cream like the rest of the house. A double bed with gray covers sat between two shelves. There were a ton of trophies, books, a football, several pictures of Rhys and his family, and a large, framed picture above his bed of a football field.

"What's that grin for, Princess?"

Rhys's voice startled me. "Oh, nothing," I said, but Rhys gave me a look. "It's just this is such a guy's room."

He lifted a brow. "So you approve?"

"Yeah," I said, "though I'm not sure that matters."

"It does."

I so didn't know what to do with that. For some reason, Ashely's words filtered through my mind then: *everyone knows there are no fat princesses.*

Don't read anything into it, Ariel. He's not a real prince. You're not a real princess. And this story won't have a happy ending.

Shaking it off, I stiffened my spine.

"Why don't we do Mr. Patachoui's piece one more time before we try the waltz?" I said.

"Sure," Rhys agreed, starting the music. "I have the most trouble with this one anyway."

I didn't tell him then, but whether he was struggling or not wasn't why I wanted to run that particular dance again. It was because we didn't have to touch in this one. Being in his room felt intimate. I needed a moment to adjust before the waltz.

Despite his words, Rhys didn't seem to have any issues. We made it through the first dance fine; it was actually our best run-through. His dancing from last week to now was like night and day.

"I know your brother was teasing you downstairs," I said, unable to hold back, "but I'm not when I say this, so please don't take offense."

Rhys shrugged. "That's just Zach. What's up?"

"You seriously *don't* suck!"

"I'm trying not to be offended by the tone of surprise, Princess."

I laughed. "No really, you haven't even stepped on my foot once. How awesome is that?"

He gave me a nod. "So the bar was set that low, huh? Good to know."

"Well," I said, "you did offer to help me to my car if things went badly."

Grabbing his heart, Rhys feigned hurt, but his eyes were bright. "And she goes for the jugular."

"Rhys, stop. What I'm trying to say is I can't believe you got so good this fast. It's amazing."

"Thanks, Princess. Ready to move on to the waltz?"

I nodded as he started the music. But even though I

was expecting it this time, his touch still made me tremble.

"You good?" he said.

"Yeah." I laughed at myself and then gave him a shrug. "I guess this one is more difficult for me."

"Oh, and why's that?"

You're touching me.

It was the thought that ran like wildfire through my mind.

Rhys is touching me.

Rhys is touching me.

Rhys is touching me.

His hand was on my waist, his pinky occasionally grazing my hip, his eyes on mine making it hard to think—did he even realize what that did to me?

Jeez, I hoped not.

"The counts," I fibbed. "The way it's in threes is a little confusing."

Rhys tilted his head. "But when we learned, you got it on the first try."

"Beginner's luck. It didn't last, apparently."

"You seem like you're doing fine."

To keep him off the trail, I faked a misstep—that turned into a real one when Rhys's hand flexed against my waist. I nearly went down, but Rhys caught me.

"Careful," he said.

"Sorry," I muttered. "Like I said, the waltz doesn't like me."

Goodness, I was such a dork. In an effort to save face, I diverted the attention back to him.

"You said the other dance is harder for you?" I asked.

"That's right."

"Is that because it's not as repetitive? Or because it's longer, so there's more to remember?"

"Neither of those."

"Really?" I said. "Then why?"

"You sure you want to know?" he asked.

Rhys and I finished the dance in an elegant dip. He brought me up out of it slowly, and the look in his eyes was as stormy as ever. I wasn't sure I did want to know his answer, but I nodded anyway.

"The other dance is more challenging because of the premise," he said.

I was about to ask how when he went on.

"I'm not allowed to touch you." Rhys's jaw tightened. "But I want to. It...grounds me, helps me focus."

My heart skipped a beat.

"And that, Princess, is the definition of frustrating."

My goodness, I thought as my pulse skyrocketed, my breaths coming shorter. Did he actually just say that? Was it my imagination or was he leaning closer? My nerves seemed to melt away, Ashley's words about who could and couldn't be a princess a distant memory. Somehow my hands were still resting on his shoulders, and his had circled my back. The space between us had definitely gotten smaller.

His voice was quiet as he repeated, "So frustrating."

Our lips were inches apart when there was a knock on the door. The sound had me jumping away, and Rhys took slow steps back.

"Hey guys," Rhys's dad said, sticking his head through the half-open door, "I just wanted to see if I could interest you in any snacks."

"No, we're good, Dad," he said.

"Are you sure? I could bring up some carrot sticks, pretzels with dip or hey, how about some cheese?"

"We don't need anything, but thanks."

Mr. Castle frowned. "Well, maybe Ariel wants something. Did you even ask? Ariel, would you like some cheese? I have a whole plethora of them to choose from, and I've even dabbled at making my own."

"Jeez, Dad. She doesn't want any of your cheese." Rhys looked to me a second later. "I mean, do you?"

I just shook my head, unsure whether to laugh, swoon, or bolt.

My phone pinged with a text. It was from my mom, and I'd never been more grateful. Maybe it was cowardly, but Rhys had just blown my mind. I needed a moment to think and get myself back together.

"Sorry, Mr. Castle," I said. "My mom just texted. I really should get going."

Rhys looked surprised. "You're leaving already? But we've only done the waltz once."

And it was more than enough, I thought. My fingertips could still feel the shape of his shoulders, for goodness sake.

"It's okay. You've obviously got it down," I said, walking to the door. "Besides, we'll only have to do that one if we win king and queen. And though you totally have a shot at it, I don't see that for me. This was fun. Thanks for having me over."

"No problem," Rhys said. "I'll walk you to your car."

"That's not necessary. I'll see you later."

Before I knew it, I was in my car on the way back to my house. I didn't remember the drive at all. Jesus must've taken the wheel, because I was in a total daze. Somehow I made it home without incident. But inside, I was a total wreck.

What was that back there?

Chapter 20

"So, did you and Rhys hook up?" Toni asked.

My jaw dropped. We were in the library, sitting at a table, doing research for an upcoming lit project. She gave no warning, just popped the question like it was no big deal.

"No," I said, glancing around to see if anyone had heard. Thankfully, no one was near us. "Jeez, where did that come from?"

"I wondered about it all Sunday." Toni gave a shrug. "I was going to call, but I wanted to see the look on your face when you answered."

"And?"

"Annnd judging by your wide eyes and the goldfish impression, I think maybe more happened than you're letting on," she said.

I scoffed. "Please, it was nothing like that."

"Well, what *was* it like?"

"We practiced in the living room until his family came

home." I smiled at the memory. "His parents were really nice, and though his brother was sarcastic, it was fun seeing Rhys with all of them. Then, since we needed to review more for Homecoming, we moved the dancing to Rhys's bedroom and—"

"Wait, wait." Toni held up a hand, halting my words. "You're saying you went up to his room, and the two of you just danced?"

"Yeah."

"Or did you, you know, *dance*?"

Toni bounced her eyebrows, did a little shimmy, and blew me a kiss.

"I have no idea what that move means," I laughed. "But there was no hooking up."

She pouted. "Ah, come on. Not even a kiss?"

Almost, I thought.

I could've sworn Rhys was about to kiss me before we were interrupted. But with the touching and the dancing and his closeness, I hadn't been thinking straight. Who knows? There was a chance I'd imagined the whole thing. I didn't want to give Toni false info.

"No kissing either," I said.

Unfortunately.

To distract her, I pointed to my head. "Hey, can you help me with this? My hair's been giving me grief since I woke up this morning."

"Sure." Toni sounded disappointed. "But next time could you please kiss the prince? If not for you, then for me?"

"I thought you had your hands full with Ben," I said and grinned when I heard her sigh. "How's it going with you guys?"

"He's a total goof," Toni said, the affection clear in her voice. "Ben says the sweetest things and even insists on carrying my books. I have to admit, A—I think the kid's growing on me."

That was as good as a declaration of love when it came to my best friend.

"You mean you like him," I said.

"Yeah," Toni said, "I do. And we actually have kissed a few times, in case you're interested."

I looked over my shoulder and smiled wide. "When did this happen? How was it? And where was my phone call?"

"I think it must've been when you were at the elementary school with your mom." She stuck out her tongue then gestured for me to spin back around. Running her hands through my hair, Toni added, "It was awesome. And I would've called, but...we were a little busy."

"I see," I said.

"Ben's a fantastic kisser, by the way. I'm still waiting to hear if a certain quarterback has any skills in that area."

I shrugged. "I wouldn't know."

"But you'd like to," Toni put in.

Did I want to kiss Rhys?

Yes. A hundred times yes.

Had I replayed that scene in his bedroom again and again and again?

You know it.

Was I confident enough to say it out loud?

Not so much.

"Your silence speaks volumes, my friend." Toni laughed.

"Just let me know how it is when it happens."

"Don't you mean *if*?" I said.

"When," she repeated then lifted a handful of my hair. "Now, should we go with a messy fishtail braid or the classic half-up, half-down Belle at the ball look?"

"Either sounds good."

"I'm feeling Belle," she said. "With all the talk of Homecoming, it seems appropriate. Plus, you are a princess."

I frowned, her words taking me back to the other day.

"Why do you think there aren't any fat princesses?" I asked.

Toni paused. "Do you really expect me to answer that?"

"It was just something one of my mom's students said." I thought it over. "Actually, add TV, movies, and books to that. There are hardly any plus-sized leading ladies. Do you realize there's not even one Disney heroine who's fat? The closest you get is that little Lilo chick, who's like six, and her story isn't even a romance. Stitch is a blue alien who's a friendly pet. I mean, are they trying to say girls who have a little pudge aren't worthy of love? Because that's what it feels like."

"Ariel," Toni said, "you are so weird, but I love it."

I looked over my shoulder. "But seriously, why? I mean, would it have killed them to have one chubby girl?"

"Turn back around before you ruin my work," she said. I did as she asked and felt her hands moving through my hair once again. "Well, if you really want to know, the answer's simple. Someone on the Disney team was obviously a fat-ist."

My brows furrowed. "Huh?"

"Fat-ist," she repeated. "It means people who have this

illogical but ingrained prejudice against fat people. Actually, the whole world's fat-ist."

I scoffed. "I don't think that's a real thing."

"Think about it, A. Forget Disney. Why aren't there tons of stories about big girls finding happily-ever-after? It happens every day in the real world."

"You're totally right. And for that matter, why does the plot have to center around weight when the girl *is* bigger?" I added. "I love a good makeover story as much as anyone, but can't a girl just happen to be larger than a size two? A lot of people are. Thin people are cast all the time, and their weight is hardly ever mentioned."

Toni hummed her agreement as another thought occurred to me.

"And more often than not, curvy girls are portrayed as miserable. Why is *that*?"

"Because," Toni said sarcastically, "Hollywood thinks skinny equals happiness—which I can tell you right now, it doesn't—and fat people should lose weight before they can be happy."

I shook my head. "Screw that. Love yourself at any size."

"Amen, sister."

Toni gave me a high five, and ten minutes later the bell rang. She had turned my hair into a masterpiece as usual. I had no idea how she did it without a brush or tons of tools and hairspray. But I wasn't complaining.

I ran through a list of movies in my head, trying to think of any that featured a happy, overweight girl. In the end, I only came up with a handful. What a sad commentary on our times.

Maybe Toni was right, I thought as I walked up to my locker and reached in to grab my books.

"Maybe the world is fat-ist," I muttered.

"What was that?" Rhys was suddenly there, standing over my shoulder with his hands in his pockets. "Were you just talking to yourself, Princess?"

Taking a deep breath, I turned to him with a smile. "Yep, I was."

He lifted a brow. "Was it a good conversation?"

"The best," I replied. "I find myself very amusing."

"Funny, I do, too."

You'd think I'd be used to him by now, but nope. The sight of Rhys, being near him, still caused a stir of excitement in my tummy. I wondered when that would stop.

"Ooh." I snapped my fingers, opened my locker again, and reached inside. "I'm actually glad you're here. I brought these yesterday but forgot to give them to you."

"Yeah, you left pretty fast."

I ignored that, shut my locker, and pushed the movies into his hand.

"The best dance flicks of all time," I announced. "At least in my opinion. I excluded musicals because that's a whole other thing."

Rhys looked down, studying the covers. "You mentioned these before, didn't you?"

I nodded. "Most of them. I'd start with *Dirty Dancing* or *Strictly Ballroom. Napoleon Dynamite* is really just in there for laughs. And then I threw in *10 Things I Hate About You* because, come on. Heath Ledger serenading Julia Stiles in a football stadium to win her heart? The hilarious way he dances out of the security guards' reach when they try to catch him? You just can't beat that!"

He didn't say anything, so I went on.

"You don't have to watch them if you don't want to. I just thought they were good, and that…well, you might like them."

The words sounded forced even to my own ears.

"You know what? It's okay. This was a bad idea—"

I went to take the movies back, feeling all kinds of foolish, but Rhys put a hand on my wrist.

"It's not a bad idea," he said.

Sparks traveled up and down my arm at the contact.

"You brought these for me. You say they're good, so I'll watch."

He released my hand to put the movies into his backpack, but his gaze held mine, which did nothing to help my racing heart.

"I actually need to ask you something," he said.

I shrugged. "Go ahead."

"Do you want to go out with me?"

The warning bell rang, and students began clearing the hall. Rhys didn't seem in any hurry, though, as I stood there baffled.

"Out?" I echoed. "Do you mean to your house so we can practice some more? I don't think you need it, but okay."

"Actually," he said, "I meant to the movies or a restaurant. Something like that."

My brows furrowed as I took in his words. "Rhys, I know this is silly. But it kind of sounds like you're asking me on a date."

Rhys cocked his head. "That's because I am. What do you say, Princess?"

A jolt of electricity ran through me, but I quickly tamped it down. Why would Rhys want to date me? There had to be a reason, but I couldn't figure it out. I had no life experience to draw from, so my mind immediately turned to the one thing I could count on: my vast amount of movie knowledge.

"Is this a joke? Or like some kind of prank?" I asked.

"No," Rhys said slowly. "But I'd love to know how you came to that conclusion."

I'm not sure, I thought. In movies, only jerks asked girls out to humiliate them. Rhys would never be that guy—I knew that now.

"Oh," I said, "did you make a bet with Zander that you could turn me into the Homecoming Queen? Because sorry, Rhys, I already told you that's not happening."

"There's no bet I'm aware of," he said and crossed his arms. "But this is strangely entertaining. I can't wait to hear what you'll say next."

"Okay, I think I've got it." I smiled. "Your grades are bad."

Rhys's brows lifted. "They are?"

I nodded. "Yes, like, really bad. You're failing and in danger of being thrown off the team. Which," I added before he could interrupt, on a roll now, "is why you need a tutor. Football is your life. But you don't want anyone to find out about the tutor thing, so you need me to be your fake girlfriend."

"That's incredible," Rhys said, sounding impressed.

"So I'm right?"

He shook his head. "Not even close. What's incredible is how wrong you are."

My lips turned down as I grasped what he was saying.

"Well, are you writing an article about how to lose a girl in ten days?" I asked.

"Nope."

"Did you accidentally send letters to all the girls you've loved before?"

"What?" He laughed. "Good grief, Princess. Where are these strange theories coming from?"

I gave him a shrug. "Watched one too many movies, I guess."

"I think it was more than just one." Rhys put his hands on my shoulders, dipped his chin, and looked into my eyes. "Listen Princess, I want to date you. No bets, no BS, no hidden agenda. I just…like you. It's that simple."

"But—"

He shook his head, cutting off my question with a look.

"Do you react this way to all the guys who ask you out, or am I just that special?" he said.

Swallowing my pride, I lifted my chin a bit higher.

"I wouldn't know," I replied. "This is new for me. Guys don't typically—I mean, no one's ever asked…"

Rhys looked confused for a second before his face filled with understanding.

"Well, *I'm* asking," he said gently. "Just so we're clear."

I gulped as I looked him over. My goodness, his sincere tone, how his eyes had gone soft, the way he was looking at me… I couldn't believe this was really happening. He'd completely blindsided me. I still didn't know what to say but knew I had to answer his question.

"I'll…think about it," I said—then immediately wanted to die.

For real, please Lord, take me now.

An amazing guy finally asks me out—and *that* was my brilliant response?

Total. Fail.

Rhys looked surprised for a beat, but then his lips tilted up into a half smile.

"All right," he said. "Take all the time you need. No rush."

As his hands fell away from my shoulders, my heart whispered, *No, come back. I didn't mean it. That was my brain talking. She sucks and overthinks everything. I'll go with you anywhere, anytime you'd like.*

"Honestly, I can't say I have much experience with this, either," Rhys added as my mind and heart battled it out.

"What do you mean?" I asked.

"I can't remember a girl ever turning me down." He folded his arms across his chest and sent me a grin.

I couldn't help but smile a little at that.

"So, this is a first for me, too."

"Technically, I didn't turn you down," I said. "I like you, too, Rhys. My mind just needs time to process."

He nodded. "I get it, and that's cool. I want you to be sure when you answer."

My eyes closed with a sigh, thankful that he was being so kind about what could've been (and was) a truly awkward moment. As I reopened them, though, I couldn't seem to look at him directly.

"Thanks for the movies," Rhys said.

"No problem," I mumbled. "I hope you like them."

"I'm sure I will. But hey, I forgot something last night, too."

"What was it?"

"This," he said.

His hand moved to my cheek, and as our eyes met, Rhys leaned in closer, giving me plenty of time to pull away. But I didn't. I wanted this more than I wanted my next breath.

Rhys kissed me like he'd been wanting to do it for a while. He took his time, too. His lips were warm, soft, and oh-so-talented. My mouth moved with his, and I could only hope it was as good for him as it was for me. Because gah. Kissing Rhys Castle was amazing.

Unable to stay still, my hands moved up to his shoulders and circled his neck. He kissed me deeper for a moment (or it could've been hours, who knew?) and then slowly pulled away.

"Something to think about," Rhys said, his voice sounding rough, "while you're deciding."

I nodded, still in a daze as he took a step back.

"Also, my grades are good, Princess. I'm number seven in our graduating class."

"Really?" I asked.

"Yep."

"But the SATs…" My brain was recovering, albeit slowly, from that kiss, but at least I was forming coherent sentences. "I thought you were struggling."

"I am," he said. "I can't seem to get past 1300."

My eyes widened at the number. It was even higher than my own score.

He shrugged. "I was already accepted to my top college, but it's a personal goal. Plus, I could really use a scholarship. To help offset costs."

So he was smart, surprisingly nice, liked SJM novels, *and* could kiss me into next week? Why the heck had I asked for more time again?

"Have a great day, Princess."

"You too," I breathed as he walked back down the hall. "Thank you."

Goodness, did that really just happen?

My pounding heart and kiss-swollen lips could attest to the fact that yes. Yes, it had.

I needed to get home fast and text Toni—or actually, no. News this big definitely required a phone call.

She was never going to believe this.

Chapter 21

Turned out I didn't have to call Toni—she was at my house when I parked in the driveway. With everything that went down, I'd completely forgotten about inviting her to come over and see my dress, which was supposed to be delivered today.

"So he surprised you at your locker and kissed the heck out of you?" she said after I told her what happened. At my nod, she smiled. "Was it any good?"

"Oh my gosh, Toni," I said. "How can you even ask that? It's been at least twenty minutes, and I can still feel his lips on mine."

She shook her head. "I can't believe it."

"Well, it's true. You asked before, and now I can tell you without a doubt: Rhys is a phenomenal kisser, possibly number one in the universe."

"That's not what I mean," she said, ignoring my gushing. "I just can't believe you rejected him."

"I didn't," I said, "I just asked for more time. That's not a no, and I really did want to say yes."

"Then why the hesitation?" Toni said. "You're into him, and he's obviously into you. I'm all for playing hard to get, Ariel—it makes the asker have to work a little, and I'm one hundred percent for that. But if you want Rhys, why put him off like this?"

My face fell. "I don't know."

"Well, what made you doubt his intentions in the first place?"

Her question brought me up short, and instead of feeling elated like I had a moment ago, I suddenly felt down. The worst part was that I didn't know why. I couldn't tell Toni my reasoning because I didn't completely understand it myself.

"Let's table this discussion for now," Toni said and threw an arm around my shoulders. "I'm here to see your dress, not talk about your make-out session with the hot quarterback. *But* I want to hear all about it, every little detail, whenever you're ready to talk."

I wrapped an arm around her as well. "Sounds good," I said.

"Plus, your mom is probably in there waiting for us."

Mom was indeed sitting on the couch with a package in her lap. At first glance, the box looked harmless enough. It seemed a little compact for the dress I had ordered, but what did I know about these things?

"Hey baby," she said, frowning as she took in my face. "Is something wrong?"

"No," I said. "It's all good."

"Did something happen at school?"

Just my first kiss.

"Not really," I said—then figured what the heck? Mom and I told each other everything, and Toni already knew. "Actually, Rhys kissed me today," I added.

"He did?" Mom's eyes went wide. "And?"

"Oh Mom, it was..." I sighed. "It was amazing, better than the best dessert and movie combined."

"Those are strong words," she said and then tilted her head. "But why do you look sad?"

Toni jumped in as I shot her a pleading look. "Yes, the kiss was awesome, the best ever, blah, blah, blah. He asked her out, she said she wanted to think about it, and she's having deep thoughts. It's a whole thing," she explained. "But right now, she's going to model this dress for us. Right, A?"

I gave her a nod of thanks then turned back to Mom. She was gazing at me with a question in her eyes. But thankfully, she didn't ask.

"If you don't feel like doing this, it's okay," she said, gesturing to the box in her hands.

I shrugged. "Let me just get a cake started. I'm making one to practice for the bake-off. It shouldn't take long, and then I'll move on to the dress."

It only took me seven minutes to get all the ingredients mixed and set up in the oven. That was pretty good. Timing was a big component of competitive baking, so I liked to stay fresh.

When I went back to take the dress from Mom, she gave me an encouraging smile.

"This will probably help get my mind off things anyway,"

I said, trying to convince myself it was true, "and I guess I have to try it on sooner or later."

"Sooner's always better," Toni put in.

"Especially when you're dealing with online stuff," Mom added.

"Well, there you go," I said. "I'll just take this into my room, put it on, and give the dress a test run."

Mom nodded and held out her phone. "I'm ready for pictures when you are."

Ugh.

Five minutes later, I had opened the box, and as it turned out, I was wrong. It wasn't just the box that was too small. It was the dress itself.

"Mom, Toni," I called, "can you guys come in here?"

Their footsteps sounded seconds before my door opened, and they walked into the room, stopping on either side of me.

"Do you need help with the zipper?" Mom asked, but her words trailed off as she stared at what lay on my bed. "What's that supposed to be?"

"My dress for Homecoming," I said.

Mom and Toni leaned in to have a closer look. Sure, it was black, and it vaguely resembled some form of clothing, maybe a petite shirt. But those were the only similarities to the dress I'd ordered and the scrap of whatever-it-was that was delivered.

After a beat, Toni said, "It looks like it's child-size."

"That's what I thought, too."

But Mom shook her head. "No...but it does look pretty small."

"Yeah," Toni agreed. "Who do they expect to wear that? An Oompa Loompa?"

"Not me." I bent down and held up the dress to my side. "I couldn't even get one arm in there, let alone my entire body."

We took another minute to frown at the so-called "dress."

"You checked the size before you ordered, right?" Mom said.

"Of course I did." I pulled up the receipt on my phone and showed it to Mom. "It said made in China, but I figured a lot of our cups and other things are made there, too. Plus, it was on sale and such a good deal."

"Oh baby. Lesson one of online shopping: Asian sizes are totally different from the ones in America. They're even smaller than in the UK."

"Apparently," I muttered.

Mom shrugged as she took the dress from my hands. "Well, the material seems stretchy. Maybe with some Spanx? Do you want to just try it and see?"

"Mom. If by some miracle I was able to squeeze this"—I gestured to my body—"into that dress, I'd burst out of it in two seconds like an overstuffed piñata. Only what popped out wouldn't be candy and would most likely get me suspended."

Toni tried to hold back her laugh, but she couldn't.

"I'm sorry," she giggled. "But the visual of cupcakes going everywhere just got to me."

I scoffed. "It's not funny, Toni."

"I know, I know," she said, biting her lip. "Sorry."

"That is fifty dollars I'll never get back," I pointed out.

"Maybe with Spanx," Mom muttered again.

I shook my head. "Give it up, Mom. It's a lost cause."

"I guess you'll have to go to Homecoming naked then," Toni commented and did the same weird wink/shimmy/kiss combo from earlier. "I'm sure Rhys would enjoy that."

"Toni, please," I said as my face flooded with heat.

Mom sniffed. "Well, this won't do. We'll just have to go shopping for another dress. My baby isn't showing her cupcakes to anyone, not if I have anything to say about it."

After her declaration, it was silent—but a beat later, the three of us burst out laughing. The tension in my shoulders eased. The laughter didn't stop for at least a few minutes, and it felt so good that I sighed.

"Don't worry." I gave Mom's shoulder a pat. "I'll keep my cupcakes to myself."

"You better," she said.

My smile dimmed a bit. "Ms. Weaver is supposed to take us to the mall this week anyway. In the itinerary, she calls it a shopping day with the girls. Most of them already have their outfits, so it's just for 'fun.' I was going to fake being sick, but I guess I'll go, see if I can find anything."

Mom clasped her hands together. "Oh, that sounds wonderful. I'm sure you'll find a dress. Send tons of pics, so I can pretend I'm there, too. Any other Homecoming activities on the horizon?"

"Well, tomorrow we have the parade," I said with a shrug.

"What's that?"

Toni smiled. "It's where the royal court walks the hallowed halls of HHS, and all of us plebeians stand there, gazing at them and cheering as they pass by. Usually, it's pretty boring, but I have a feeling it's going to be awesome this year."

"Or embarrassing," I said.

"I'm going to cheer so loud, A."

"I wish you wouldn't."

"You better prepare yourself."

Mom and Toni kept talking about the parade while I went to the kitchen. My upcoming vlog features would include some of the around-the-world movies and desserts I'd been planning, and that made me think of Rhys. He'd been there when I got most of these ingredients. Our conversation and kiss from today ran through my thoughts over and over. Part of me was nervous about seeing Rhys again. But the other part was so excited I nearly burned the cake I was baking.

I tried not to see that as a sign.

It was bound to happen.

I was actually surprised it took this long for me to hear something.

Right when they announced that I'd been nominated to court, I knew someone would have a problem with it. I just hadn't realized how much their words would affect me.

Standing next to my locker, trying to get my mind right about the parade and being stared at by everyone in school—something I'd had nightmares about if I were being honest—I was just about to go meet the others when voices floated to me from a nearby classroom.

"I can't understand how Cupcake was nominated," a feminine voice said. "I mean, she acts nice and all, but this has to be a prank. Right?"

Taking a few steps closer, I peered around the corner. The classroom door was wide open. Two girls and two guys were inside, standing in a little square, and one of them was Lana. She hadn't been the one who spoke, though— that was the girl standing next to her. I realized this as Kendall added, "The sad part is she thinks it's real. How pathetic."

Kendall and Lana were besties like Toni and me. The main difference: Kendall was catty and not in a harmless way. We'd gone to school together for years, and everyone knew Kendall always went for the jugular.

"You can't say that, Ken," Lana replied. "She's on the Court. People voted for her. It was legit."

Kendall studied her nails. "Who in their right mind would look at that girl and think Homecoming Queen?" She laughed. "Absolutely no one. She stole that spot from someone who deserves it."

Desmond Cox lifted one of his brows. "Like who, you?"

"Obviously," she said. "Or even your girlfriend, Des— though I think her big butt might've gotten in the way."

"Shut it, skank. My girl's assets are on point."

"But if Cupcake was nominated, I guess she could've been, too."

"She would be pretty," Carter Rollins, the other guy in

the room, said, "if she exercised and lost some weight."

Like I hadn't heard that one before.

I rolled my eyes, though none of them could see. It would probably shock them to know I walked on the treadmill four days a week and ate healthy despite all the baking. Some people were just bigger-boned and had lower metabolisms. It didn't make them unhealthy.

Lana sighed. "My only gripe is she gets to partner with Rhys—"

"Poor guy," Kendall put in.

"—and everyone knows he's the front-runner for king," Lana finished.

"I don't think you have anything to worry about," Desmond said. "Just because the prince wins doesn't mean his princess does. People don't vote for the couple."

"I know." Lana nodded. "But I'm still nervous."

"Why?" Kendall said. "You're running against two girls who aren't as pretty as you and a pig. Again, poor Rhys. No one's going to choose that over you."

I winced at her words.

"You're awful, Ken," Lana said and shook her head.

"Thanks, it takes effort. Can we go now?"

As the four of them moved to leave, I had only moments to decide what to do. Part of me wanted to confront them. In my head, I could see it so clearly. I'd step out, block their path, and say:

Hey, I didn't choose this. I didn't even want to be on Court. But life threw me a curveball, so you know what? There's going to be a curvy, plus-size princess. Get over it. And I don't *need to lose weight. You haters need to expand your definition of beauty and stop being so petty. Thank you, next.*

That was how things should've gone.

Instead, I scrambled to the side, standing with my back to the wall, partially obscured by the lockers. Their footsteps echoed as they walked down the hall. I closed my eyes and gritted my teeth, frustrated by my own reaction. This wasn't me, I thought. I didn't hide. I wasn't a coward.

Unable to stand it, I took a deep breath and pushed away from the wall.

"Hey," I called. The four of them stopped, turning to look back at me. "I heard what you said."

Kendall lifted a brow in challenge. "And?"

I gulped. "Well...there's no need to be nasty. I'm a person with feelings just like you. And size isn't everything, you know. Anyone can be a princess."

Okay, so I'd been better, more fierce in my head. What else was new? But I still didn't expect Kendall to scoff and roll her eyes.

Her tone was unrepentant as she said, "It's sad that you think I actually care about your feelings. Almost as sad as you calling yourself a princess."

I had no response.

"Get real, Cupcake."

After they'd gone, I waited several minutes before forcing my feet to follow. That...wasn't as satisfying as I'd thought it would be. I was no stranger to insults—they'd been flung at me since I was young, and I'd definitely heard worse. But no one should have to sit and listen to people bad-mouth them.

I shook my head.

Kendall hadn't felt any remorse, and I hadn't really expected her to.

But that was what I got for trying.

Note to self: stay away from jerks.

Chapter 22

The rest of the Homecoming Court, Lana included, was already in the front office when I arrived.

"Hey," Rhys said, "glad you made it. I was starting to get worried."

"Sorry," I said. "Got held up."

He studied my face a moment. "Are you all right?"

I didn't want to lie, so I deflected instead. "It is what it is. How are things with you?"

"Good," he said and pushed his hands into his pockets. "I watched that movie you gave me."

My ears perked at this. "Which one?"

He shrugged. "Actually…all of them."

"You already watched them?"

"Yeah, I liked all four. But my favorite was the ballroom one," Rhys said.

I was still trying to absorb the fact that he'd watched every one of the films I'd given him.

"Who was your favorite character?" I asked.

His face turned pensive. "Scott was a talented dancer but kind of dense when it came to seeing people's true nature. So, I'd have to say Fran. She was a cool chick, with or without the glasses."

My jaw dropped. "You seriously watched it?"

"Yeah, I about died at the end when the music cut out," he said. "That would be like getting to the final minutes of the championship game and having all the lights turn off or something. I had no idea what would happen, but it was great."

"You're…" I didn't know how to finish, and my eyes filled because wow. He'd actually watched all the chick flicks I gave him. "Did you like *Dirty Dancing*?"

"I did." Rhys lifted a brow. "If that was us, though, you'd be Johnny, and I'd be Baby, aka the one who carries a watermelon."

I laughed in delight.

"Or actually, I'm more like that Napoleon guy. Even at the end of the movie, he's still awkward and has zero rhythm."

"What about *10 Things*?"

"Hilarious," he said. "You were right about the scene on the field. Must've taken a lot of guts—though the guy was in love with that Kat girl, so I get it."

"You did watch them!" I said.

"Yeah, but I already told you that."

I nudged his arm. "And I think we've proven that you do have rhythm. It just took some practice."

"I'm ready for more practice whenever you are," he said.

I couldn't be sure, but I thought his eyes dipped to my lips on the word "practice." Goodness, I nearly swooned right there.

Ms. Weaver interrupted my staring when she stepped in front of us.

"Good afternoon, Princess Ariel and Prince Rhys!" she said, adjusting the box she carried on her hip. "I'm here to give you a Homecoming keepsake. Enjoy the parade, and remember, always make sure your tiara's on straight and smile for the crowd!"

She lifted a metal stick out of the box and handed it to Rhys. It was silver, topped with a tiny crown at one end, and sported green jewels. The next thing she pulled out was a dainty-looking circlet that she handed to me. It was silver as well, covered in rhinestones, and the metal was fashioned to look like vines that came to a point in the center. *Beautiful*, I thought. So beautiful, that despite the conversation I'd just heard, it made me feel like a true princess. Ms. Weaver walked back to the front of the line.

Feeling a bit funny about it, I placed the tiara on my head, then turned to Rhys.

"Well?" I said. "Is it straight?"

"Almost," he said. "Here, let me."

As he reached up, I held my breath. His hands were gentle as he adjusted the tiara. When his eyes met mine, he pushed a stray lock of hair behind my ear.

"You look perfect."

"Thanks," I said on an exhale.

Rhys nodded, and we walked forward. Did he even realize how romantic that move had been? Man, I was a mess, and he hadn't even touched anything but my hair.

I could hear the cheers from the crowd outside. It was the end of the school day, but all the students and teachers had let classes out a few minutes early for the parade. They'd lined up the Homecoming nominees by class, placing the seniors in the back. Rhys and I were the next-to-last couple. And wouldn't you know, we were put right in front of Lana and Zander.

"Stop twirling your scepter like that," she hissed at him. "You'll poke someone's eye out."

"Ah, you're no fun," he said back.

"Please, just behave."

"Whatever you say, my lady."

Lana's groan made me want to laugh, but I held it in check. Rhys and I were almost up as Ms. Weaver stood at the door and gestured us forward.

"Okay, wait until they're about five steps out, and then join the procession. Take your time. Remember the slow glide. Good luck, kids!"

Rhys gave her a nod and then offered me his arm. I looked up at him, took a deep breath, and rested my hand on the top of his forearm. It was solid, strong like the rest of him.

"You ready, Princess?" he said.

I nodded.

"Then let's walk this hall like we own it."

His confidence must've been contagious, because the nerves flew away.

When the couple in front of us was far enough ahead, we stepped out, and the cheers got noticeably louder. My cheeks went red, but I kept up with Rhys. His steps didn't falter once. People shouted out his name left and right, but Rhys's frown was set—unlike Zander, who I heard behind us throwing kisses at the crowd.

"Yeah! Go Cupcake! You look gorgeous! Work it girl! Work it!"

My eyes immediately picked Toni out of the crowd. And oh my God—she wasn't lying about being loud. As we got closer, her hoots rose, and Rhys quirked an eyebrow.

"Friend of yours?" he asked, but I could tell he was just teasing.

My smile grew. "Absolutely not. I've never seen her before."

"I love you, Cupcake!" Toni screamed at the top of her lungs, and I laughed.

"I love you, too," I said, reaching out to touch her hand as we passed.

Funnily enough, a few other people shouted my name, too—well, my nickname. Some of them even put Rhys's and my name together, cheering for both of us. "Go Rariel!" was said several times. My eyes widened in surprise.

Rhys's face, however, was a hard mask. I hadn't noticed it before and probably wouldn't have if we weren't so close. But the way he was clenching his fists, the tension in his shoulders, the sheen of sweat on his brow? He almost looked…nervous.

Or unwell.

"You feeling okay?" I asked.

"Yeah," he said. "Why?"

"It's just that you're kind of pale, and I remember your

mom saying something about doctors. So…"

Rhys brushed me off. "It's nothing."

As we kept walking, we were about halfway down the long hall when another face jumped out at me. Kendall was standing with a group of her friends, frowning as we approached. Our eyes connected as her lip curled.

"Pathetic," she said, but it might as well have been a shout.

I somehow lost my footing. My ankle rolled, and I knew I was about to fall. I'd humiliate myself and Rhys in the process, my nightmares realized.

But somehow, he caught me.

Grabbing my waist with one hand, the center of my back with the other, Rhys stopped my free fall.

"No worries. I've got you, Princess," he said.

It was almost like our dip at the end of the waltz, I thought. Except this fall was unplanned, Rhys had reacted with catlike reflexes, and I was currently wide-eyed, hovering mere inches above the ground. The crowd ate it up, loving every second, banging on lockers and cheering.

"Nice catch," I said.

He gave me that disarming half smile. "All that football has to count for something, right?"

"Guess so," I mumbled.

I could've stared at him for hours, but he helped me straighten up moments later.

"You good?" he asked.

"Yeah," I said. "Thanks for that."

Rhys nodded, offered me his arm again, and I took it. But as I went to step on my right foot, a twinge rang out in my ankle that I couldn't ignore. I hopped quickly back to the other foot with a gasp.

"Everything okay?" he asked again.

"Yeah, fine."

We took a couple more steps, but he was watching closely this time as I winced and hobbled along.

"You're not fine," he said, pointing to my leg. "What's going on there?"

"I rolled my ankle a little." I waved a hand through the air like it was nothing. "Just need to walk it off."

"We don't have to finish this parade, you know," he said. "You're hurt. Ms. Weaver will understand."

Yeah, but then it might ruin your chances of being king, I thought. And I wasn't about to let that happen.

"I'm okay, Rhys. Really."

"If you two are done chatting, can you please *move*?" Lana was smiling as she spoke through clenched teeth. "For goodness' sake, she's fine, Rhys. You're holding up the parade."

I nodded. "Yep, we're going."

As I met his gaze, Rhys looked concerned.

"Okay, Princess, if you say so."

He gave a decisive nod, but before I could say a word, he'd scooped me up into his arms bridal-style.

"Rhys!" I hissed. "What the heck are you doing?"

"I'm not letting you walk on a busted ankle," he said.

"Seriously, put me down."

I went to get out of his hold, but his next words stopped me.

"I didn't want to tell you this," he sighed, "but I also may have seen a spider near your foot."

I froze instantly. "What?"

"Yeah, and it looked like a big one. I know how freaked out you get about bugs. So I didn't want to worry you."

My eyes searched the ground as I clung to his shoulders.

"Still want me to put you down?" he asked.

I shook my head. "I guess this is okay. As long as I'm not too heavy... I wouldn't want to injure you or make you feel emasculated."

"I don't know; I'm feeling pretty masculine right now." He pulled me closer to him as I squeaked. "Let's go, Princess."

I ducked my head in the crook between his shoulder and neck as he carried me the rest of the way down the hall. If the cheers were loud before, they were deafening now. Rhys held me like it was effortless. It made me wonder if he wasn't a superhero after all.

Even when the parade was over, he insisted on taking me to my locker.

"That was completely unnecessary," I said, blushing as he carefully placed me back on my feet. "I could've walked."

He looked like he didn't believe it, so I amended.

"Okay, I would've hobbled, but I'd have made it."

"I know," he said, "but I was there and glad to be of assistance. Also, full disclosure, the spider thing was a lie."

My brow furrowed. "What do you mean?"

"I just said that so you'd let me help."

"Well...thanks for being honest about lying...I guess?"

"You're welcome. And come on, admit it: you liked me carrying you."

"I admit nothing."

Looking away, I couldn't contain my smile. He placed a hand under my chin and gently lifted.

"Have you made your decision yet?" he asked.

There was no mistaking that he meant the date.

"I'm still thinking," I said quietly.

"Okay."

I looked up at him. "Is it really?"

"Yeah." Rhys placed his hand on my cheek, the rough pads of his fingers feeling lovely against my skin. "You're worth the wait."

As he leaned closer, my eyes shut on their own, hoping for another earth-shattering kiss. But what came was even sweeter. Rhys's lips pressed against my forehead, and I felt the touch everywhere.

"You keep thinking. And ice that ankle when you get home, okay, Princess?"

With that, he left me, breathless, alone, and staring after him.

A throat cleared and brought my attention to Mrs. Reeves, who was standing in the door to her classroom with a yogurt in her hand. She was looking straight at me.

"I should've probably stopped that," Mrs. Reeves said. "I like you a lot, Cupcake. But as a teacher, it's my duty to write up students for PDA."

"Oh, please don't, Mrs. Reeves," I said. "We weren't—"

"But," she cut in, "as a hopeless romantic, I had no choice but to let it play out."

My mouth snapped shut, and she smiled.

"Rhys Castle?" she said. "Really, Ariel?"

"I know."

Mrs. Reeves shot me a wink. "Just make sure he deserves you."

The funny thing was I'd never even thought of it that way. I'd only ever seen Rhys as out of my league, on another planet altogether, in another galaxy.

But now he was real to me in a way he never had been before.

A real person and friend.

A real possibility.

Somehow that made it even scarier.

Chapter 23

My ankle felt much better after resting and icing it. That was both good and bad. Good because I knew it wasn't broken, no need for a boot. Bad because it meant I really had no excuse not to go shopping with Ms. Weaver and the girls that Thursday.

The trip wasn't school-sanctioned or anything. It only lasted an hour, two tops.

But that was more than enough to scar me for life.

As soon as I got home, I walked inside, carrying no bags (that should've been Mom's first clue things hadn't gone well), and threw myself onto the couch with a groan (clue number two).

"So? How did shopping go?" she asked.

"It was a total disaster," I muttered.

"Ah, come on." Mom sounded skeptical as she sat next to my sprawled-out form. "I'm sure it wasn't that bad."

"Not bad, Mom—horrific." I threw an arm over my

forehead at the memory. "First, we all meet up—the girls, Ms. Weaver, and me—at the school. Then we carpool over to this street with little shops that specialize in gowns for pageants, prom, homecoming. Makes sense, right?"

Mom nodded for me to go on.

"Then a sales lady comes out, says how beautiful we all are, and asks if we want some mint-flavored water. That was actually quite good."

"I'm not seeing the problem, Cupcake."

I held up a hand. "Oh, just wait. I'm getting there," I said. "Ms. Weaver tells us to peruse the racks, that we can try on anything we like. After a few minutes, though, I notice something strange. There's nothing in my size."

"Oh no," Mom said, covering her mouth with a hand.

"Oh yes. At first, I figured they probably just keep the bigger dresses somewhere else. But when Ms. Weaver asked, the lady told her they don't carry anything larger than an eight. That there's no market for plus-sized eveningwear—which hello. I was the proof, standing right in front of her, that there was. But it gets better."

"I think I detect a hint of sarcasm."

"You do," I agreed. "*None* of the shops carried my size."

"Oh baby, I'm so sorry," Mom said.

"So, there I am sitting on a bench, watching everyone else try on dresses and drinking a gallon of mint water to drown my sorrows."

"Ugh. That had to suck."

"It did," I said. "On top of everything, because of the water, I had to pee the whole time."

Mom smiled as my laugh turned into a sigh.

"The other girls threw me these pitying looks when they thought I couldn't see." I shook my head. "And Ms. Weaver kept apologizing to me like it was somehow her fault the world is fat-ist."

My mother's brow furrowed. "Fat-ist?"

"Yes, fat-ist," I declared—then groaned again. "Shopping is the worst."

Mom rubbed my arm in a soothing way. "It'll be okay."

I wished I could share her optimism, but… "I don't see how. What sucks most is that I still don't have a dress for Homecoming, and it's next week."

"Don't worry, baby." She gave my shoulder a pat. "I happen to know a few stores we can check out, ones I'm sure will have your size."

"You do?" I said hopefully.

She nodded, and I sat up, throwing my arms around her, pulling her into a hug.

"You're the best. I'm so sorry I blew you off before. I should've trusted you all along."

"Yes, you should have."

I laughed at that. "I love you, Mom."

"I love you more," she said, giving me a tight squeeze before sitting back a bit to see my face. "We'll find you the perfect dress. Never fear. Despite what that saleswoman said, places do sell dresses you'll love that will love your curves back. Trust me, your mother's a shopaholic. I feel like I've been training for this my whole life."

Maybe it was the stress of the day, but her words made my throat tight with emotion.

"You know, you're wrong. I love you more," I said.

"Not possible," she said simply. "I have to go to the store to pick up a few things. You going to be okay here?"

I nodded and flopped back on the couch. "Yeah, thanks, Mom. I think I'll watch a movie while you're gone."

After she left, I turned on the TV and pulled up one of the rom-coms I loved, but for whatever reason, the jokes didn't cheer me up like they usually did. I stopped it five minutes in and switched to a different movie. Or actually, it was a mini-series, but whatever. Period dramas always made me feel better.

This day required a mega-dose of romance. Luckily, I knew just where to turn.

My heart felt lighter even as the opening credits rolled.

Immediately, I was transported into a story that I knew would have a happy ending. I curled up on one side of the couch, wrapped myself in a blanket, and let my troubles drift away. My eyes were glued to the screen when the front door opened about two hours later.

"Hey Mom," I called. "Mr. Thornton is about to propose to Margaret, one of the swooniest scenes ever—number one being the kiss at the train station, of course. Do you want me to pause it?"

"Hey baby," Mom said. "No, that's okay."

I could hear her moving toward the living room even if I couldn't see her yet.

"Why is everything done by the BBC better than anything here in the States?" I asked.

"Not sure."

I hummed. "Maybe it's the English accents."

Mom cleared her throat. "Ariel, you have a visitor."

"Oh?" I asked without looking. "Is it Toni? I was just texting her. She loves *North & South* almost as much as we do."

"No, it's not Toni."

"Then who—?"

My words cut off the instant I turned around and saw Rhys standing next to my mother. I gave my head a shake, but he stayed right there. Not an illusion, then.

"Hey," he said.

"Hey," I said back. "Well…this is a surprise."

Chapter 24

*M*om coughed, shot me a look, and I got the message. "Rhys, this is my mom," I said, hopping up to make the introductions. "Mom, this is Rhys Castle. He's my partner for Homecoming."

Rhys nodded. "We met on the porch."

"We sure did." Mom's smile was bright. "When I got here, Rhys was standing there about to ring the doorbell. He says he's here to return some of the movies you loaned him. Isn't that nice?"

"It is nice." I turned my attention to Rhys. "But you know, you could've given them back at school, saved yourself the trip."

"I would have," he said, "but I haven't seen much of you the past couple days."

That was because I'd been avoiding him ever since the parade—which I hoped he hadn't noticed.

"I kind of thought you might be avoiding me."

Ugh.

"Why would I do that?" I forced a laugh. "Hey, how did you know where I live?"

"Your friend Toni," he said and ran a hand through his hair. "She said you'd had a bad day, that maybe I should stop by and check on you."

Good gravy on a cracker. I gave a mental sigh. I'd been texting Toni on and off, telling her about the dress debacle. Apparently, she'd seen that as an SOS, but instead of coming herself, she'd enlisted Rhys's help. Awesome.

"Well, that was nice of her," I said. "But as you can see, I'm fine."

Rhys nodded. "Your ankle doing okay?"

My mind leaped back to the day he'd carried me down the hall, and I couldn't stop the blush if I tried.

"It's much better," I said.

"Glad to hear it."

Mom spoke up then, pointing over her shoulder. "You'll both have to excuse me. I've got work to do, lesson plans to create, books to pick out for the kids. Nice to finally meet you, Rhys." She smiled. "I've heard *such* good things."

Thanks for that, Mom.

Rhys nodded. "Nice meeting you, Ms. Duncan."

"You two have fun," she said and threw me a wink.

I shook my head. "Bye, Mom."

Once she was gone, I looked back at Rhys, who gestured to the TV.

"What are you watching?" he asked.

I shrugged. "It's a British mini-series called *North & South*."

"Is this another one of your favorites?"

"No," I said. "It's *the* favorite. My number one of all-time. I could watch Margaret and Mr. Thornton fall in love forever and never get tired of it."

Rhys cocked his head. "What dessert would you pair it with?"

I smiled at the question. How was it this guy just got me? "Definitely a traditional afternoon tea."

"What's that?"

"It's this awesome thing the Brits do," I explained, quickly pulling it up on my phone to show him. "There's a tray with three tiers, and each one has something awesome. Little sandwiches, scones, cakes, and pastries, and you can pick your favorite tea, too."

"Sounds like something my mom would like," Rhys said as he skimmed the pictures. "She loves anything from England."

I laughed. "Who doesn't? And ooh, I knew I liked her."

Rhys met my eyes. "She liked you, too—my whole family did. Even Zach, and you saw what a little punk he can be."

Warmth filled my chest at his words.

"I liked them a lot, too," I said, leaving out the most important part about how it was him I liked best of all.

"That's the other reason I came actually," Rhys continued. "I need to ask a favor."

My eyebrows went up in surprise. "Okay, I'm listening."

"Can you teach me how to bake a cake?" he asked. "My mom's birthday is next week, and I want to do something special."

Be still my heart. This guy was something else.

"After I told my parents what an awesome baker you are," he added, "it just kind of clicked. Mom's sappy—she's loved everything we made her since preschool. But with your help, I thought this could be really good and unexpected."

"Of course I'll help!" I said. "What flavors does she like?"

He thought about it a second. "Chocolate. She definitely loves chocolate."

"You're in luck. I just happen to have a recipe for the best chocolate cake ever." I gestured for him to follow me into the kitchen. "It's my go-to for birthdays. My grandma made it the best, but mine is close."

"Let's hope I'm better at cooking than I am at dancing," Rhys said.

I reached up and pulled down my recipe book.

"Are you sure you don't want me to do it?" I asked, flipping to the right page and laying the book down on the counter. "I'd be more than happy to make this for you."

Rhys stared at me a moment.

"For your mom, I mean."

"Thanks Princess, but no." He held up a hand. "I'm sure you would do it better, but I want this to be from me, you know?"

I did.

And gah if I didn't feel a pang in my heart at his thought-fulness.

Rhys was going to make some girl very happy someday.

"So, we'll just do a trial bake," I said. "No problem."

"Okay, where do we start?" he said.

"Here." I handed him an extra apron. "Put this on."

His eyes traveled over the garment then to my face. "Do I have to? It looks like a dress."

I couldn't help but laugh at the wary look in his eyes. "If you don't want to get flour on your clothes, I highly recommend it," I said.

Rhys watched as I slipped my apron on, then he finally gave in. With a sigh, he put it over his head, tying the strings around his back. But it kept falling open because he didn't tie it tight enough. With an eye roll, I reached around him to grab the strings.

Unfortunately, I didn't realize how close that would bring us until it was too late.

I might as well have been hugging him. The scent of clean soap, sandalwood, and something uniquely Rhys filled up my senses. He smelled good, really good. I could feel his eyes on me as I tried to keep my distance while untying the strings then brought them around the front, quick to form the knot.

"There," I said, taking a step back, hoping I didn't sound as frazzled as I felt. "Now you're ready to cook."

"Kiss my Cupcake?" He read the slogan on his chest then looked up. "I like it. And is yours…" Rhys squinted as he took in my outfit.

"Little-Mermaid-inspired? Yes," I said, straightening the material. "Mom got it for me; she loves all things Disney. And I love her, so I wear it."

His mouth turned up in a half smile. "She told me she loved football. We talked about that a little on the porch."

My brows lowered. "Exactly how long were you two out there?"

"Not long," he said.

I wondered if they'd talked about me but was too chicken to ask.

"She told me some interesting things," he added. "Mentioned a kids baking challenge you were in? I'd love to see that sometime."

Over my dead body, I thought.

"Eh, it wasn't a big deal." Shaking myself, I went back into baker mode. "Okay, so the first thing you'll do is preheat the oven then get all the ingredients and tools you'll need: bowls, measuring cups, mixer, spoons, that sort of thing. You can grab the milk and eggs." I pointed to the fridge. "And I'll get the other stuff."

Rhys nodded, and in no time, we had everything we needed.

"Next step," I said, "is to measure out and put the flour, sugar, baking soda, and cocoa powder in a bowl. Then sift them together."

It was slightly more difficult to complete the task because I was aware of Rhys's eyes on me the whole time.

"What can I do?" he asked.

"You want to crack the eggs into a second bowl while I melt the butter? Maybe put on a pot of coffee?"

As soon as the words were out of my mouth, he jumped into action. I wasn't used to sharing the kitchen with someone else, but this was actually nice. Rhys watched as I added the softened butter to the eggs.

"Now add the vanilla extract," I said.

Maybe it was just me, but he looked so cute as he tried to measure just the right amount. I let him mix those together along with a cup of coffee until it was as smooth as possible. We slowly added our dry ingredients to the wet mixture, with Rhys pouring and me mixing.

"The batter gets poured into two circular pans, and then we're good," I said. "Be careful with this part, though. The bowl can be kind of heavy."

I'd started to lift the bowl when suddenly Rhys's hands were beside mine.

"Thanks," I said.

As the mixture went into the pans, it spread evenly like usual. We'd already lined them with Crisco and flour, so the cake wouldn't stick when it was time to come out. But I barely paid that any mind. My attention was focused on the way our fingers touched, just slightly, his thumb to my pinky. But that touch, plus having him right behind me, was enough to make my whole body warm.

"Princess," he said.

The feel of his breath hitting my neck made me weak in the knees.

"Hmm?" I asked.

"I think we need to stop, or it's going to overflow."

I looked down, saw that he was right, and with a gasp, we righted the bowl.

"Er, yeah," I said with a laugh, putting some space between us. "That's good. You should always pay attention when you bake. If not, bad things can happen."

Rhys put the pans in the oven then turned back to me.

"And now we wait," I said. "In thirty-five to forty minutes, it turns into a beautiful cake. I can give you the recipe for that and the frosting. The cake has to cool, and the frosting has to set up before you add it. Long as you follow the instructions, you should be good."

"Thanks," he said. "Want to dry while I wash?"

I blinked. "We have a dishwasher for that."

Rhys scoffed then gently pushed me aside. "If there's one thing I know, it's how to wash dishes. Come on, Princess. The dishwasher never gets them as clean as a little elbow grease."

I shrugged, and again, with both of us working, we quickly finished the task. Once we were settled in the living room, I wasn't sure what to do next. His presence, having a boy in my house, was a novelty. The fact that he'd asked me out…that felt like a freaking miracle.

So why was I hesitating to say *yes*?

Chapter 25

"So," Rhys said, "you want to keep watching *North & South*?"

I sighed in relief. "Sure—but only if you want to."

He tilted his head. "Sounds good. Though I've got to be honest, I'd rather watch that kids baking thing you were in. Too bad you don't have that."

Mom walked into the room at that moment, carrying a glass in her hand, presumably to get water, but she stopped in her tracks at Rhys's words.

"Oh my," she said with a wide smile. I knew it could only mean trouble. "Did someone just mention the kids baking challenge?"

I quickly shook my head. "Nope, you must be hearing things, Mom. Old age will do that, you know."

"I'm going to pretend like you didn't say that. And I know I heard something."

Rhys, the traitor, raised his hand. "I was just saying how

much I'd love to see it, Ms. Duncan."

"It was nothing," I said.

"Nothing?" Mom scoffed. She set down the glass and put her hands on her hips. "Ariel Duncan, I can't believe you'd say such a thing. You were incredible, and you had so much fun. Don't you remember?"

What I remembered was that I had been right on the cusp of my awkward stage. I had a gap between my two front teeth because I hadn't had braces yet for goodness' sake. Was I cute at nine? Heck yes. But I didn't exactly want Rhys picturing me like that.

"All right, it's settled," Mom said. "Now we *have* to watch."

She found the video and had it cued up before I could object.

"Rhys, prepare yourself for all the amazingness that is my daughter."

"Mom," I said. "Is this really necessary?"

"Yes, it is." She gave a curt nod then turned to Rhys as the opening credits rolled. "I'm not just saying this because I'm her mom. Ariel was such a little cutie, and so talented, too! Ooh, she could cook up a mean dessert even then."

Ugh. Lord save me from proud mamas who liked to brag on their kids and share embarrassing videos.

"Can't wait, Ms. Duncan," Rhys said, and I could tell he was amused.

Mom sat in the middle of the couch between Rhys and me. And as the three of us watched the thirty-minute-long pilot episode, she kept up a running commentary.

"See?" she said when I first appeared onscreen. "Ariel

was one of the youngest bakers there and, in my opinion, the best. It's no wonder they chose her. And who wouldn't love that face?"

Rhys's eyes were smiling. "She was very cute."

A blush stole up my cheeks.

"I know," Mom said. "The cupcakes she made are about to wow the judges. Look."

She was right, of course. I knocked that first challenge out of the park. The cupcakes were baked to perfection, tasted oh-so-yummy, and my decorations were on point. One judge even claimed it was one of the best she'd ever tasted.

"So talented," Mom said again.

The kitchen timer went off as we were in the middle of the second episode. Rhys looked completely into it, so I got up, removed the cake from the oven and set it on the counter to cool. As I walked back into the living room, I saw nine-year-old me frantically trying to finish her dish. I remembered this part, too. The end result was a gorgeous plate of sugar cookies and me with flour in my hair. The look on my face as I'd gotten eliminated was still as happy-go-lucky as ever—though I'd cried a ton afterward.

Mom shook her head. "Oh honey, you know I still think that little boy Ruben should have gone home. His brownies were undercooked!"

I sighed. "I know, you say that every time."

"And your dish was gorgeous," she continued. "You were as amazing then as you are now."

"Thanks, Mom."

"Well Rhys, what did you think?"

My mom and I looked at him, waiting for his answer.

"I agree with you, Ms. D," he said. "Your daughter is something else."

Mom patted my thigh and stood. "Yes, she is, Rhys. I'll leave you two alone now, since my work here is done."

With that, she went back to her room.

Rhys was looking at me, but it was hard to meet his gaze.

"Why didn't you want me to see that?" he asked. "You were awesome."

I rolled my eyes. "Yeah well, I was also about to hit my awkward stage. This is so embarrassing."

"How?"

"It's hard to explain," I said. "I'm proud of making it onto the show, I am. And Mom's right; I did love being a part of it. But…having you watch it is like letting you read my diary or something. Totally awkward, not to mention personal. You know?"

When I finally met his eyes, the intense look in them made me pause.

"Wow," he said. "I feel like I should share something with you now."

My head was shaking before he even finished. "No, that's okay, Rhys. You don't have to."

"It's only fair. You shared something personal with me, so I want to do the same."

After taking a deep breath and releasing it, Rhys nodded as if he'd come to a decision.

"You know the appointments I go to?"

"Rhys, seriously, you don't—"

"They're to see my therapist," he finished. He rubbed

a hand across his neck nervously. "No one except for my family even knows that I go to one. But I do."

I gaped at him. This was his big secret? The talk I'd witnessed between Rhys and his mom about doctors probably should've tipped me off, but for some reason, I hadn't put two and two together. Rhys was so well-adjusted. He played sports, was popular, and got awesome grades. I just…yeah, I hadn't seen it coming.

"Aren't you going to say anything?" he asked.

I realized then that Rhys was watching me. He had been all along, waiting for my reaction. Trying to lighten the mood, I shrugged.

"A therapist. That's awesome," I said. "A lot of people have those."

"You don't think it's weird?"

"No."

"Don't you want to know why I see one?"

"Only if you want to tell me," I said.

Rhys studied my face a moment then shook his head. "I thought you might freak out. Think I was crazy or weak—or both."

"Why?" I asked. "Seeing a therapist isn't a bad thing."

"Oh yeah? Tell that to the judgmental eyes and ears in our high school," he said.

Touché.

"I started going to therapy because I was bullied."

"*You* were bullied?" I asked.

He nodded. "Every day in middle school. The other guys used to tease me because I was small. They'd push me around, call me names, steal my books. I was a late bloomer, didn't hit a big growth spurt until I was almost in high school. So yeah, it was rough."

I wasn't going to lie; it was hard to picture Rhys as small. He was larger than life now, both on the field and as he sat next to me on the couch.

"The therapy helped," Rhys said. "And I still go now because in high school there's all this pressure. Make good grades, be the best at sports, get into a good college, get a scholarship so you can afford college, look like you have everything under control. It can be…a lot."

"I get that," I said. "I used to go to therapy, too."

Rhys's brows lifted. "Really?"

"Yeah. It was for a different reason, body issues mostly, but that's the thing you've got to remember: everyone is struggling. Some people are just better at hiding it."

A beat of silence passed before he gave me a half smile.

"I'm glad I told you," Rhys said.

"Me too," I replied.

"Seriously, it feels like a weight's been lifted." His face relaxed, and I could practically see the tension melting off him. "This is amazing. I didn't realize how much I needed to tell someone until now."

I sent him a smile. "Glad I could help."

"You really did, you know," he said. "Secrets can be heavy."

Trying to lighten the mood, I shrugged. "I honestly thought you had a secret girlfriend or boyfriend for a while there."

Rhys blinked. "You thought I had a secret girlfriend?"

"Or boyfriend," I said.

He smiled a real smile as he shook his head.

"Princess, only you would think something like that," he said.

"Yeah well, I blame it on the movies."

"I'm glad I got to see you in that baking challenge."

For some reason, I was, too, but I wasn't going to admit it.

"Whatever. We so should've watched *North & South*."

"Okay," Rhys said. "Let's do that now. I don't have anywhere to be — for once."

"Are you sure?"

He nodded. "It's your number one, so I'm curious. Who is this Mr. Thornton? Your voice got all mushy when you talked about him. It kind of made me jealous. I have to know more."

We started from the beginning, and by the time the cake was cooled and frosted, we were through the first two episodes. I cut the cake then had Rhys taste it. His eyes were wide as he swallowed. That was followed by a groan of pleasure.

"I know," I said.

"Princess, this is delicious," Rhys said. "My mom's going to love it — when I bake her the actual birthday cake, of course."

I blushed. "I hope so."

"And hey, I'm definitely coming back to watch more *North & South*," he said. "I need to see how it ends."

"The ending's the best part," I said.

"I would come tomorrow, but I have a game."

"I know," I said. "I was thinking about going."

"I'd love it if you did." He gave me a soft smile.

We were silent a beat, then…

"About the whole date thing," Rhys said, and I held my breath. "There's no pressure. You get that, right?"

"Yeah, I do," I said.

"I'm strong, Princess."

I knew that.

"You don't have to avoid me," Rhys said. "If the answer's no, then—"

"No," I said, grabbing his hand to stop him. "The answer's not no. I want to go out with you. It's just…"

Rhys stared at me while I searched for an answer.

"Just…what?" he said.

"I, well, I have this big competition coming up, and I have to get ready," I said in a rush.

Rhys looked surprised. "Really? What kind of competition?"

It wasn't totally a lie, so I decided to just run with it.

"It's a baking competition for charity." I lifted a shoulder. "Me and some other bakers will duke it out. We already know the theme, but they give us a time limit. At the end, we're judged on taste and decorating ability."

"Wow, that sounds cool," he said.

"It is. If you win, $1,000 goes to the charity or cause of your choice. I compete for Blue Skies Elementary, the school where my mom teaches."

"Can people come watch?"

I swallowed. "Yes, there's an audience. They sell tickets and use some of that money for the prize. It's televised by one of the local stations. Mom and Toni usually come to cheer me on."

Rhys gave me that half smile. "Maybe I could come this year."

"Maybe," I said, thinking it was unlikely.

The competition was weeks away. Homecoming would be done way before then, and I wasn't sure if Rhys's interest in me would last that long. The thought caused an ache somewhere deep in my chest.

"So, you're not avoiding me?" Rhys asked.

I shook my head.

"And you're not saying no to the date? You're just preparing for this competition?"

"Yep," I said.

What I didn't say was that I'd prepped for it all summer. I could do the bake-off with one hand tied behind my back; that was how ready I was. But Rhys didn't need to know that.

"Okay, that's good," he replied. "Especially since this was basically a pre-date."

A surprised laugh escaped. "A what?"

Rhys gave a shrug. "A pre-date. We cooked together, ate food, watched a movie."

"Mini-series," I cut in.

"Hm," he said. "So yeah, like a date without the kissing."

Without thought, I lifted to my toes and pressed a kiss against his cheek. It wasn't enough though. So when he turned, I brushed my mouth against his for another.

"I think I like pre-dates," I breathed.

He leaned down and said, "Just wait until the real thing."

After one last kiss that lingered a bit longer than it probably should've, Rhys left, and I couldn't stop wondering: if this was a pre-date, what would the real thing be like?

Chapter 26

*I*t was Saturday, but Mom was still talking about Friday night football.

Case in point:

"Wow, what a game," Mom said. "It's been too long since I've seen one from the stands."

"So you liked it?" I asked.

"Absolutely! Thanks, girls, for letting me tag along last night. Hope I didn't cramp your style too much."

Toni laughed. "As if. We're not exactly popular, Ms. Duncan."

"We prefer it that way," I added.

Mom bit her lip. "When it comes to football, I know I can get loud. I just hope I didn't embarrass you guys."

I nudged Mom with my elbow. "You didn't, Mom. It was fun to hang out."

"Hey Ariel, I meant to ask," Toni said suddenly. "What was in that bag you gave Rhys? You bring him more cake pops or something?"

"Yeah," I said with a shrug. "He seemed to like them a lot last time."

Toni lifted a knowing eyebrow. "Oh, he likes something all right."

"And Rhys!" Mom said, sailing right by Toni's insinuation, for which I was glad. "That boy has some arm. I can't wait to see what his college career is like. He's going to be a star."

"Yeah." I sighed. "I think he already is."

Toni rolled her eyes. "Okay, can we focus, please?" she said. "Today's not about football or hot guys. We're on a mission, ladies."

Mom and I nodded. She was right. Gushing over Rhys's game wouldn't solve the problem at hand: I was still dress-less, and this was the last weekend before Homecoming. We had work to do, and I was glad to have the two most important people in my life here with me.

"Right, girls," Mom said as we stopped on the sidewalk. "We're not going home until we find a dress."

"Or until the shops close," I muttered, but Mom shushed me.

"Stay positive, Cupcake. This is your day. Just remember: if you believe, you will achieve."

Toni's brow furrowed. "Isn't that something you teach in kindergarten?"

Mom sniffed. "Yes, and it's true, for them and for us today."

My bestie lifted her hands up high in feigned self-defense. "Hey, I'm not arguing. I am a fan of both believing *and* achieving. I'm all in."

I bit my lip as I looked up at the store in front of us, bad memories assaulting me.

"You ready for this?" Toni asked.

"I guess," I muttered.

"Hey, it won't be like last time, if that's what you're worried about."

"Yeah," Mom said and gave my hand a squeeze. "We're here for you, baby. If you don't like anything, there are other places we can go."

Taking a deep breath, I gave a nod.

"Okay, let's do this," I said.

From my first step in the door, I knew this trip would be different. The bell jingled in welcome, announcing our entrance, and a woman called out from the back.

"Be there in a sec," she said. "Go ahead and make yourselves at home! Have a look around!"

"Okay," Mom said. "Thank you, we will."

This was like the shops Ms. Weaver took us to but with more character. Pictures of fashion icons, actresses on the red carpet, and famous singers lined the walls, and the mannequins came in all shapes and sizes. I'd never seen that before, and it helped ease my nerves.

There were different colors and dresses everywhere. Eveningwear was on one side of the store, casual on the other. I made my way over to a dress on the evening side. It was gorgeous. What immediately caught my eye was the fuchsia pink material. It shimmered, looking light yet substantial with a deep V-neck, long sleeves and a long skirt. The material looked like it had been dusted with stars. My favorite part, though, was the cinched-in waist. That just made it so much more classic.

"You have good taste," a voice spoke from behind me.

Turning, I saw an older woman with dark braids smiling at me. She nodded toward the dress I realized I was still touching, and I dropped my hand away.

"Do you like that one?" she asked. "It would look brilliant on your figure."

"It's beautiful," I said. "But I'm not sure I could pull it off. This dress needs someone worthy of its awesomeness to wear it."

She made a noise in her throat. "You most definitely could."

I gave her a small smile. "I think it might draw too much attention."

"A little attention's never a bad thing."

Toni joined us then, her arms already filled with dresses.

"Ariel," she said, sounding a little out of breath, "there you are. I've been looking for you. I found you a few dresses to try on."

The woman looked happy. "Should I open up a changing room?"

"Please." I nodded. "Thank you so much."

"You're very welcome," she said, taking the dresses from Toni's arms. Before she walked away, she plucked the dress I'd been staring at from the rack. "I'll just take this one, too."

"Oh," I said, "but I'm not even sure it's my size."

The woman threw me a wink. "I've been doing this a long time, girl. Trust me. It's your size."

As she disappeared into a back hallway, I glanced around.

"I like this place," I said.

"Me, too," Toni agreed. "It's cool and so was that lady you were talking to. Did you really only find the one dress, though?"

I shrugged. "It called to me."

"Well, let's see what else speaks, shall we?" she said, tugging on my arm. "And I'm talking about for me, too."

"I thought you had a dress," I said.

"I do." Toni sniffed. "But it never hurts to look."

We ran into Mom moments later, and like Toni, it seemed like she'd found several items.

"Want to try some of these on?" she asked hopefully.

I nodded and off we went.

My main goal had been to find a dress that fit. If I was being honest, that was my only criteria. What I hadn't expected was to have a large selection to choose from. Toni and Mom had gathered a bunch of choices, and while yes, some of them didn't look right on me, shockingly, the majority of them did. I modeled each one, and I had to admit: with the music pumping through the store's sound system, my mother and BFF there rooting for me, it was a lot of fun.

"Ooh, I like that one, too," Mom said. "I don't know how you're going to choose."

"Same," Toni said, "but I liked the red dress better."

Mom's eyes widened. "I forgot about that one."

"What do you think, A?"

I tilted my head. "I've liked most of them. But I still don't think I've found the one yet."

"Well, keep trying, then," she said. "Having too many

options is definitely a good thing."

"I agree," Mom said and shooed me back into the dressing room.

After a couple more tries, I got to a black dress. It fit the Hollywood Vintage theme perfectly. It was something I never would've pictured myself in, but I had to admit the way it hugged my body, the hourglass silhouette…I loved it. Mom and Toni did, too.

But I still had one last dress to try.

The fuchsia pink evening gown that seemed to draw me from the moment I walked in was on the last hanger. The black dress had been dramatic. But this one… Goodness, when I put it on and looked in the mirror, I felt beautiful.

"Oh my gosh," Toni said. "Ariel! You look amazing!"

Mom nodded. "I didn't think I'd like anything as much as the black. But you in that dress? Ah, baby, you're glowing!"

I looked in the mirror and could immediately see what she meant. My skin was aglow, and I didn't know if it was the way the deep pink enriched my skin tone—or maybe how the dress made me feel inside was shining through on the outside.

The sales lady smiled as she walked by. "Told you it was your size."

"You did," I agreed.

"Your killer curves are exactly what that dress needs."

I blushed at the compliment.

"Thank you, I really do love it." My eyes went wide as I spotted the price tag for the first time. "But er…I didn't realize how much it was. I'm sure another one will—"

Mom slapped her thighs. "We'll take it."

I blinked at her. "But Mom, it's a lot—"

"I don't care how much it is," she said and handed the lady her card. "You love it. You look like a goddess in it. I'm getting you the dress."

Toni threw me a smile. "Your mom rocks."

"I know," I said.

"Okay, now that you're good, I'm going to have a little look around," Toni said. "I spotted a skirt that I know will drive Ben wild. See you in a few!"

As she skipped away, I turned back to my mother. Her eyes were glassy as she looked at me.

"Mom, thank you so much, but you really shouldn't have."

"Yes, I should," she said, wiping away a tear. "You have no idea how good it makes me feel to see you so happy. I'd give anything for that."

I smiled, pointing to her face. "Is that what the tears are for—or did you see the price?"

She laughed. "That bad, huh?"

"I'll pay you back someday," I said.

"You pay me back every day by being a wonderful daughter," Mom retorted. "Now, stop it with that. Get changed—we still have to find you shoes—and let's go grab Toni before that saleswoman convinces her to buy everything in the store."

Toni only ended up buying the skirt. I got Mom a pair of earrings I saw her eyeing, and we all went home with something. The search for a Homecoming dress was an undeniable success.

I should've been ecstatic. We'd had an awesome day. I loved my dress. It made my body look wonderful and accentuated every one of my favorite attributes about myself.

But hours later, as Mom and I were sitting on the couch, I couldn't shake this feeling that something was off.

My phone pinged, and I looked down to find a text from Rhys.

Rhys: Looked for you at the grocery store today.

I smiled as I sent my response.

Me: Did you? Sorry I wasn't there.

Rhys: The peas and I were disappointed.

He sent me a picture of him, looking into the camera as he leaned back against the freezer. Man, I thought. Even when he frowns, he's lovely.

Realizing I hadn't answered, I typed a quick reply.

Me: Apologies to you and the peas. I had to shop for a dress today.

Rhys: Really? You got something special coming up? ;)

Me: As a matter of fact, I do.

Rhys: Well? Don't hold out on me, Princess. Did you find a dress or not?

I smiled at that.

Me: Yes, I did :).

Rhys: And??

Me: Not to sound too girly, but I love it!!! It's actually pink, and it makes me feel pretty.

Rhys: Well, that makes sense. You are pretty.

I read the words again and again until a new text came through.

Rhys: So…are we talking pink like Pepto-Bismol?

Me: No!!! What the heck, Rhys?

Rhys: Sorry, sorry. That's just all I can see.

I rolled my eyes.

Me: Well, it's not that, lol. My dress is a darker shade of pink.

Rhys: Still having trouble. Any chance you'll send me a pic?

My heart got stuck in my throat, and I didn't know what to say. It was a simple request. There was no reason for the wave of dread that overtook me. But for some reason, my fingers were frozen.

Rhys: Princess?

With a swallow, I forced myself to type one last reply.

Me: Sorry, Rhys. My mom's calling. Talk later.

I locked my screen then turned it facedown—but a new text came through a second later.

Rhys: No worries. Sweet dreams, Princess.

My groan drew Mom's attention.

"Everything okay?" she asked.

It obviously wasn't. She knew that, which was why she asked the question.

"Not really," I said. "Mom, can I get your opinion on something?"

"Sure."

"It's about Rhys."

Mom nodded. "I thought it might be. What's up?"

"He asked me out," I said while flipping the phone between my hands. "He's asked me a couple times actually."

"Oh," she said as I paused. "Well, what did you say?"

"I told him I need more time."

"Nothing wrong with that. If you're unsure how you feel about him, it's a totally reasonable request."

"That's just it." I sighed and rested my head against the couch cushion. "I know how I feel. I like him, Mom. I *really* like him."

Mom turned to face me better. "Then why didn't you say yes?"

"I'm not sure," I said. "I wanted to. I wanted to so badly. Toni asked me that, too, and I couldn't explain it. I told Rhys it was because I had to prepare for the charity bake-off."

Her brows lifted. "You've been ready for that for months."

"I know." I groaned again. "What the heck is wrong with me, Mom? Rhys is amazing. I have no idea why he'd want to date me, but he does. Isn't that unbelievable?"

"I don't think it's unbelievable at all," she said.

"You don't?"

Mom shook her head. "Baby, you're beautiful inside and out. You're smart, kind, have the best taste in movies of anyone I know—besides myself. Of course Rhys likes you. What's not to like?"

I shrugged. "It's just hard to believe. We're so different."

"Are you really, though? I don't think you give yourself or him enough credit."

"You may be right," I said. "Just now, we were texting about my dress. Rhys wanted a picture, and I froze, made some terrible excuse. I felt so beautiful today. But when Rhys asked, it was like the only things going through my mind were: What will he think? Will he like it on me as much as I do? What if he hates it?"

Mom shook her head. "If Rhys hates that dress, he's crazy."

"I agree," I said. "But Mom, I'm so not that girl. My body isn't perfect, but I love it. I pretty much always have. So why do I feel like this?"

"Ah baby, listen," she said. "This is a lesson that took me a while to learn. It's only natural to care what people think. You just can't let that dictate or change how you feel about yourself."

I nodded and lay my head on her shoulder.

"Did I help you at all?" she said.

"Yes," I said, sighing. "Isn't it funny how you can be okay and love yourself, but still not think anyone will ever love you back?"

"If by funny you mean sad, then yeah. It's hilarious."

We were silent a beat.

"Ariel, you have to know that's total bull, right? Someone will love you. So many people already do, in fact."

"Yeah, I know," I said. "And for the record, even after all that, you still don't think Rhys is crazy for wanting to date me?"

"No." Mom rested her head on top of mine. "I think he'd be crazy not to."

Chapter 27

*I*t was finally here.

Homecoming week.

Reminders for the dance were everywhere. A massive banner hung from the ceiling of the main entrance. Green and white streamers—HHS's school colors—made the halls seem brighter. The cheer squad was full of extra pep. At random times, members of the band marched through the school, playing fight songs to keep everyone's spirits high.

"I feel like I'm in a teen movie," Toni said as we walked down the hall.

"Is that a good or bad thing?" I asked.

"I'll let you know." She glanced around. "I'm waiting for the moment where everyone busts out into an unexpected dance scene."

"Like in *La La Land*?"

"I was thinking more *Breakfast Club*, but yeah. I guess."

I smiled at the note of skepticism in her voice. "Hey,

remind me again. Wasn't it you who roped me into this Homecoming stuff in the first place?"

Toni feigned a sigh. "Alas, you were destined to be a princess."

"Whatever," I said.

"And I, your lowly but loyal subject."

"Toni, stop." I laughed. "We both would've been happy being sarcastic bystanders like every other year, and you know it."

At that moment, a cheerleader zoomed by doing a series of flips down the center of the hall, forcing everyone to stand aside or be run down.

"Okay, that was awesome." I shook my head. "But man, back pain, anyone?"

"Um, one, I think you just proved we still are," Toni said. "Sarcastic that is. And two, if I hadn't nominated you, something like this"—she held up her phone—"might've never happened."

The screen showed a picture of Rhys and me. It was taken at the parade, post-ankle roll, so I was in Rhys's arms. I didn't know who'd taken it, but they'd captured the moment when I placed my head on his shoulder, and Rhys was gazing down at me. The overall effect was undeniably romantic. It took my breath away.

"Ms. Weaver posted pics of the Court this morning," I mumbled. "I didn't even know the picture existed before that."

"Again," Toni said, "you're welcome."

I wasn't sure if that meant she'd taken the photo or if she was just taking credit for setting everything in motion.

Still, I smiled.

"Thanks, Toni," I said. "I can't lie. I've had a good time."

She shot me a look. "I'm glad. Any news on you and Prince Rhys?"

"Well, I think I finally realized why I was hesitant to go on that date."

"You did?"

"Yeah, Mom helped." I gave a shrug. "Pretty sure I'm ready now, though."

Toni smiled. "Tell me something I don't know."

"Okay." I lifted my chin. "Rhys is standing at his locker a little way down the hall. We're about to pass him. But instead, I'm going to stop and talk to him."

"That's big," she commented. "You making the first move."

"I know." I released a heavy exhale. "Wish me luck?"

Toni laughed, bumping her shoulder with mine. "You don't need it, A. Just do your thing."

She gave me a thumbs-up, then called Ben's name and kept walking. I stood there a minute gathering my courage before taking the last few steps to Rhys's locker. His back was to me as he switched out his books.

"Hey Rhys," I said, trying not to sound as nervous as I felt.

"Princess," he said, his back still to me. "I have to be honest. For a second, I wasn't sure if you were going to talk to me or bolt."

I blinked. "How did you…"

"Good peripheral vision." Rhys nodded, then shut his locker, turning to face me with a small smile. "It's one of the things that make a quarterback successful."

"Oh," I said, then shook my head. "That makes sense."

"So how's it going?" he said.

"Good. And you?"

"Fine."

 I nodded.

"Was there a reason for this unexpected visit?" he asked.

 Okay, so this was painful. Whenever Rhys came to talk to me, he was confident in himself, but I was all tongue-tied. What I really wanted to say was: *I'm ready now. Let's go out.* It was simple, sounded good in my head, but in real life? Ugh. I didn't want to come off as strange and/or desperate. How did other people do this all the time? I wondered.

 Squaring my shoulders, I decided to just say it.

"Okay, I'm ready. Let's go—"

"Hey," he cut in, "did you see the picture of us this morning?"

 I hadn't expected that, but I nodded. "Yeah, I did."

"I'm not usually big on photos," he said. "But that's one of my favorites."

"Same here," I said, fighting down a blush. "Though I think if I had your looks, I'd take selfies every day."

"I'm flattered, Princess," he said. "But no, that was Lana's thing. When we were together, that's all she did. Take pics and selfies."

 My heart dropped a little. "Really?"

"Yeah, I think she spent more time posting on social media than talking to me." He shrugged, pushed his hands into his pockets. "Guess I'm not that interesting."

"Yes you are," I said. "I love talking to you."

"Thanks," he said in a soft voice.

Rhys stared at me, and there was no chance of my blush fading now. I was just about to bring up the date, try a second time, when he spoke again.

"I'm glad you're here, actually," he said. "Mom's birthday is tomorrow night. It's at my house, just a small thing, family mostly. I was wondering if you'd like to come."

"To your mom's birthday?" I asked.

He nodded. "I may need your help on the cake, but that's not why I'm asking."

"Yeah, I would love to. I love birthdays."

"Cool." Rhys gave me a wink. "Don't worry, Princess. We'll just think of it as another pre-date."

"I wasn't worried," I mumbled. "Rhys, I want—"

He stepped closer, and my breath caught in my throat. "You know that picture made me realize something."

"Oh yeah?" I said. "What?"

"It's the only one of us together." He lifted his phone and nodded for me to turn. "Until now."

I didn't look away from him. "I thought you didn't like pictures."

He shrugged. "I don't. But I'll like this one because you're in it. Smile, Princess."

I kissed his cheek instead, and as the click sounded, I wasn't even mad about it.

The day went by fast after that. My brain didn't want to focus on schoolwork, but I did my best to pay attention.

Before I knew it, the final bell rang, and I was on my way to the cafeteria. Ms. Weaver had arranged one last get-together with the members of Homecoming Court. And yes, my feet might have carried me there faster in anticipation of seeing Rhys.

Unfortunately, he wasn't there.

"Okay, princesses and princes, Homecoming week is officially upon us!"

She nodded once we'd all been seated.

"You'll notice this is the final event on the itinerary before Friday," she said. "We try to keep it open because a lot of you are involved in other activities. But I wanted a quick word to send us off."

Lana raised her hand. "Ms. Weaver, if it's our last meeting, why aren't all the Court members present?"

I'd been wondering that as well.

"Zander and Rhys were excused because of football," she said.

"Of course they were," Lana mumbled.

More mutterings went through the group, but Ms. Weaver wasn't deterred.

"Everyone will be here Friday, however, which is when we'll take a group picture followed by the pep rally," she said. "The Homecoming game is that night, and by halftime, we'll know who this year's king and queen will be!"

Ms. Weaver cleared her throat.

"I simply wanted to say thank you for being such a wonderful group to work with!" Her eyes had gone misty, and I couldn't help but like her for all the effort she'd put into this. "I hope you've been practicing your dances. Don't forget your tiaras and scepters on Friday. And finally, good luck!"

Everyone cheered while Ms. Weaver performed a little curtsy.

"Thank you for everything you did to make this special for us," I said to her as I was leaving.

"Ah, Ariel." Ms. Weaver put a hand on my arm. "I'm so glad you could be a part of it!"

"Me too," I said and meant it.

Shopping for a Homecoming dress (the second time around with Mom and Toni) had been awesome. Learning how to dance, even the stressful bits with Lana, were fun. And of course, getting to know Rhys was amazing—but I'd learned a lot about myself, too.

I could walk down the halls in a tiara and not feel like an imposter.

I could do something completely outside my comfort zone (like be on Homecoming Court) and overcome my doubts.

I'd already touched a lot of lives with my baking. They enjoyed the sweets, yes—but the other students at HHS must've seen my heart…which was why they'd voted for me.

Though I'd been reticent at first, being a member of Homecoming Court had been a humbling, overall positive experience. I'd have to thank Toni later.

I was walking toward the parking lot when Lana caught up to me and thrust a square piece of paper into my hands.

"What's this?" I asked.

"An invitation," she said. "I'm having a princess party at my house on Thursday."

I blinked. "And you're inviting me?"

Lana sighed. "Don't make it a big deal, Cupcake. I invited every girl on the court."

"Oh, well, thanks, Lana," I said. "I can't believe I was invited to two parties today. That never happens."

"Color me unsurprised," she said and crossed her arms. "Out of curiosity, what is this other invite?"

"Um, Rhys kind of asked me to come to his mom's birthday."

"He did?" Lana looked surprised a second, but she managed to hide it with a flip of her hair. "I'm glad you two are hitting it off. I know it must be hard with the dancing."

"He's actually much better," I said. She looked dubious, so I added, "Seriously. He practiced, and then we practiced together. Rhys is wonderful now."

"Wonderful?" she repeated. "At dancing?"

I nodded.

"I'll have to see it to believe it."

"You and Zander seem to be getting along," I said.

She rolled her eyes. "That guy? He's so annoying."

"But he seems to like you."

"Well." Lana sniffed. "He's annoying with good taste."

I laughed, and she seemed to shake herself out of it.

"Anyway, you're a princess, so you're invited to the party," she said. "Come or don't, Cupcake. It's up to you."

With that, she walked away and didn't look back.

It was the first semi-normal conversation I'd had with

Lana. If I hadn't been holding the invitation as proof, I would've thought I'd imagined the whole thing. But nope. The little silver envelope was still there in my palm.

One birthday and one princess party.

My mind was already running rampant with all the baked goods and treats I could make.

Chapter 28

I didn't know much about Rhys's mom. In fact, I could list everything I knew on one hand.

1) She loved English things.

2) She loved chocolate.

3) She was a romantic (I vaguely remembered Rhys saying something about her liking Hallmark).

4) She'd raised Rhys (which meant she had to be an awesome mom).

5) She'd called me pretty…

…and I desperately wanted to impress her.

Okay, so I guess technically that was six things.

Since Rhys was already baking the cake, I had to go another route. I'd met his mom only the one time, but she'd been so kind. I liked her and wanted to give her a great gift. After much thought, I finally decided what to bring.

I just hoped she would like it.

When her birthday finally rolled around, I had wavered,

rethinking the gift about a million times on the drive over. But the truth was I couldn't think of anything better.

"Glad to see you, Princess," Rhys said as he opened the door to let me in. Hercules came barreling over to see me, and I bent down to pet his tummy and say hi. "Come on in—I'm in the middle of baking."

"How is it?" I asked as I straightened. "Did you remember to add the coffee?"

He rolled his eyes but grinned. "Yes."

"Did you put in enough cocoa?"

"Yep."

"Did you grease the pans and put flour in them, so the cake won't stick?"

His eyes went wide. "Oh my God."

"Rhys!"

"Just kidding," he said with a laugh. "I did all that, Princess. You taught me well."

I shot him a frown. "Not funny. You had me worried for a second."

"Ah, don't be mad. I need all the good vibes I can get."

Grandma D's words came back to me then: *you eat with your eyes first.*

She'd been so right about that one. My favorite chef had drilled it into me over and over as I sat in her kitchen, watching her put together some of the best food I'd ever eaten (or seen), the Food Network playing in the background. The weird thing was the saying could be applied to a ton of things. Looks counted for a lot—in food and in life.

If she could've seen the cake Rhys baked for his mom, I

knew Grandma would've said it was love at first sight.

"There's no way you made that by yourself," Zach said to his brother. "You can't even boil decent pasta."

Rhys shot me a smile. "I had a good teacher."

"Ah, I get it now. Ariel, tell the truth." Zach turned to me. "You made the cake, didn't you?"

I shook my head. "Nope, it was all Rhys. I gave him the recipe, but he did the baking."

"Seriously?"

At my nod, the kid groaned.

"Well, if you'll excuse me, I need to go upstairs and redraw the artwork for my card." Zach frowned, shooting Rhys a glare over his shoulder. "You're lucky you have a girl who can cook, bro. My handmade card is going to make Mom's heart melt. It would've been the clear winner if it wasn't for her."

"It's not a competition," Rhys called to his brother's retreating back.

Once he was far enough away, though, Rhys turned to me.

"But if it was, our cake would definitely win."

My heart warmed at his use of the word "our." Rhys really had done all the work. The pans were already in the oven when I arrived, but I could tell he'd followed Grandma D's recipe to the letter, and the result was a delicious-looking chocolate cake now covered in vanilla frosting. Rhys's parents were currently out while the boys got everything ready for her birthday.

"Rhys, your Mom is going to love it," I said. "Awesome job."

He shrugged. "I couldn't figure out how to do those fancy letters, so I bought a cake topper from the store. Pretty sure it'll taste good, though."

"Oh, I know it will. Maybe you should stop playing football and become a chef."

"Yeah, right," he said. "You're the baker, Princess, not me."

I pointed to the counter. "That cake says otherwise."

If I didn't know better, I would've sworn he was blushing.

"Okay, I have a confession. I bought a backup cake from Publix," he admitted. "It's in the fridge."

"Why?"

"To be prepared in case I failed."

I laughed as Rhys grinned. "Well, luckily you won't need it."

"Like I said, I had a good teacher."

"I really shouldn't like you so much," I said. "It's not fair. You're good at everything."

"Not everything," he said.

I raised a brow as he held out a hand.

"Dance with me, Princess?"

Heart pounding, I placed my palm on top of his and let him pull me in.

"I could say this is practice for Homecoming," he murmured, "but that would be a lie."

The kitchen was silent as we swayed together.

"I just wanted to hold you."

Rhys's words caressed the top of my ear as I shivered.

"You're really good at that, too," I said.

"What?" he asked.

"Making me want you."

"Ah, but if I was good at that, you would've said yes to the date."

I bit my lip. "I am," I said.

Rhys pulled back a bit. "You are what?"

"Saying yes. I want to go out with you, Rhys."

His eyes looked brighter than they had a second ago. "Is that right?"

I nodded and pressed my cheek against his shoulder.

"Don't make me say it again," I mumbled. "It was hard enough the first time."

Rhys laughed. "But I loved hearing it."

I nudged him instead of answering.

"I know this may sound odd, considering we were already paired up," he said. "But I've wanted to ask you this for a while."

My heart was beating triple-time as Rhys placed his hand gently under my chin and lifted until I met his eyes.

"Will you go to Homecoming with me?"

And there it was.

The question, that one question I hadn't realized I'd been waiting for, wanting him to say for so long until he actually said it.

"Yes," I said.

"One more time, Princess."

"Yes, Rhys! I'll go to Homecoming with you!"

I laughed as he twirled me around, feeling dizzy and wonderful at the same time.

Chapter 29

A day later, I still couldn't believe it.

A guy—not just any guy but the one I was pretty sure I was falling for—had asked me to Homecoming. And he hadn't done it in a big, flashy way. There were no bells and whistles. Rhys waited for the perfect moment when we were alone in his kitchen, the yummy smell of baking and chocolate in the air, to sweep me off my feet.

It was like I was living someone else's life.

"Why can't you believe it?" Toni said after I told her everything. "I knew Rhys liked you. I told you that."

I sighed. "Yeah, but stuff like this doesn't happen to me."

She rolled her eyes. "Except that it does. It happened."

She was right. It had.

And I was left reeling as we sat discussing it in home-room.

"Did his mom like the gift?" she asked.

I thought back, remembering Mrs. Castle's face as she

opened the bag.

"Yeah, she did." I'd included three scones, clotted cream, strawberry jam, and a box of Earl Grey tea along with the *North & South* mini-series. Mom and I kept a brand-new, unopened set of the DVDs on hand in case the series ever dropped off a streaming service. "Her eyes lit up when she read the description, and she said she couldn't wait to watch. But she cried when she found out Rhys made the cake."

"Must've been pretty tasty."

"It was so good, Toni," I said. "All chocolaty and rich. Her younger son, Zach, made her a card, and that definitely brought on the waterworks, too."

Toni gave a sniff. "Yeah well, that's because they're her kids. *North & South* is like *Pride & Prejudice* but better. She just doesn't know it yet."

"True," I said. "She may need moral support when she falls head over heels for Mr. Thornton."

"Oh, she definitely will."

"I know I did."

We sighed in unison.

"Who would you choose?" I asked. "Darcy or Mr. Thornton?"

Toni shot me a look. "Thornton, duh."

"Same. He's so lovely."

"Ooh, I have a better one," Toni said. "Who would you pick: Darcy, Thornton…or Rhys?"

If she'd asked me that question three weeks ago, I would've had a very different answer. But now…

"That's a hard one." Toni waited as a blush stole up my cheeks. "Okay, so no one beats Mr. Thornton in the movie world. His accent alone would kill me. But—"

"But?"

"I'd have to say Rhys," I said, and Toni squealed.

"You're totally in love with him," she declared.

I was shaking my head before she even finished.

"Yes, you are. Ariel, you chose him over Mr. Thornton. That's serious stuff." Toni's smile was bright as she shrugged. "It has to be love."

The strange thing was that I didn't fight her on it. Even though my brain was saying *there's no way you can be in love with this guy—you don't even really know him*, my heart was singing a different tune.

You do know him, it said.

You've gone to his games. He's been over to your house and met your mother. He felt comfortable enough to tell you about therapy. You watched the first two episodes of your favorite mini-series. You even showed him your baking challenge and baked Grandma's cake together.

My heart was right.

I knew him, and I liked him—and right then, all I wanted to do was see Rhys.

Hoping to catch him at his locker again, I walked that way when the bell rang to change classes. The idea was to surprise him, so I was careful to keep my distance. Rhys was talking to Zander, both of them leaning against the wall. I was just about to walk over when their conversation filtered to me.

"I don't think it's going to work," Rhys said.

"But I thought you liked her," was Zander's reply.

"I do like her. She's great. She's done a lot for me."

I frowned, deciding to remain where I was. What were they talking about?

"I don't get it," Zander said. "If she's great, then what's the problem?"

Rhys ran a hand along the back of his neck. "She's so...big. I don't know about bringing her out in public—especially to Homecoming. People might stare."

His words felt like a dagger to the chest.

But like the coward I was, I stayed to listen, hoping I was wrong, that I'd misunderstood.

"Why did you say you'd bring her to Homecoming then?"

Rhys shrugged. "It felt like I owed her."

Zander put a hand on Rhys's shoulder. "I got you, man. I feel your pain," he said. "But a bet's a bet. If you don't bring her, you lose, and I win."

Rhys grimaced.

"And I know how much you hate to lose."

"You're right. I'll take her," Rhys said. "What's a few more days?"

As they moved to walk away, I stayed out of sight.

"I just hope she doesn't humiliate me too much."

A wet drop hit my cheek, and it was then I realized I was crying.

Hurrying to the bathroom, I quickly cleaned my face. Or at least, I tried to. The tears were running fast now like a river. Maybe a braver person would've stepped up to him right then and demanded an explanation, but I knew what I'd heard. It felt like history repeating itself. Maybe I had a thing for guys who seemed sweet but were actually vile. Ugh. I didn't need him making excuses to soften the blow or to make himself feel better. It would only mortify me more.

There's no bet.

I remembered Rhys saying those exact words when he first asked me out.

He'd joked about it, made me feel silly for bringing it up, said I'd watched too many movies.

But the joke was on him.

I found out about his little bet with Zander. Yes, it was completely by accident, and the truth stung like a mother. It hurt even worse because I hadn't seen this coming.

My heart felt battered, bruised beyond recognition. But that meant it was still beating. I looked at my reflection in the mirror and made my decision.

I wouldn't let this break me.

Wouldn't let Rhys have that much power over me.

My prince wasn't a prince at all. He was a jerk.

He didn't deserve my tears or a chance to explain.

So, he felt like he owed me?

Too bad, I thought. I didn't want anything to do with him. Rhys Castle and I were over—and we'd never even really gotten started.

Chapter 30

*A*voiding Rhys was far easier than I thought it would be. Two days later, I hadn't even run into him. That was mostly by applying the following tactics: I stayed away from his and my lockers as much as possible, ignored his texts, and made sure to check around corners whenever I was traversing the halls. Piece of seven-layer cake.

"I still say you should talk to him," Toni sighed.

"Why?" I asked, checking ahead before turning the corner. "My strategy's worked great so far."

"What strategy is that?" she said. "The one where you run in the other direction whenever you see him?"

I shot her a glare. "That was one time—and I hardly ran. It was more like a brisk walk if anything."

"Ariel."

"Toni," I said back. "I don't want to see him. Ever. Why can't you understand that?"

My bestie shook her head. "Maybe it wasn't as bad as

you think."

I scoffed. "Trust me, it was bad."

"But you're a good judge of character," she persisted. "And you really liked Rhys. Don't you think you would've suspected something before this?"

"I guess that means I'm losing my touch," I said. "Or he's a really good liar."

"But—"

"Toni, whose side are you on?" I asked.

"Yours," she said in surprise. "I always have your back, A. You know that."

I nodded. "It was getting kind of hard to tell."

"I just want my happy, innocent, totally lovable best friend back," she said. "You've been stressed the past few days, and I'm worried."

"I'm fine," I said in a cool voice.

Toni held up the container of cupcakes I'd baked last night. It was one of five.

"Okay, I'm not fine," I corrected. There was no hiding the results of my stress baking. "But I will be, no need to worry. Homecoming will be over in a couple of days, and I'll be back to normal."

"You think it's that easy?" she said.

"Yeah. I mean, Rhys will forget about me—"

"He's been hanging out at your locker a lot," Toni put in.

"—and I'll forget, too."

I took a deep breath.

"Though I'll probably have a harder time getting over him. Even if he is a jerk."

"I wouldn't be so sure," she said. "Rhys was exposed

to all your awesomeness. Mark my words, Cupcake—he's going to find it very difficult to recover."

Toni gave me a smile before heading to her next class.

Even if it wasn't true, I appreciated the pep talk. I was still thinking about what she said, not paying attention, when I bumped into something—or to be accurate, *someone*.

"Princess," Rhys said with a frown. "Long time no see."

Exactly, I thought as I went to move around him, but he blocked my path.

"Is something going on?" he asked. "I've been trying to talk to you, but you never return my calls."

"Everything's fine," I said.

"Did you break your phone or something?"

My brow furrowed. "No."

Rhys leaned back. "Well, my mom loved the *North & South* movie you got her. She's basically in love with that Mr. Thornton guy. Won't shut up about it."

"Mini-series," I mumbled. "And I'm glad she liked it."

"I wanted to see if I could come by your house tonight," he said.

"What?" I squeaked. "I mean, why would you?"

He gave me a half smile, and I cursed my heart when it fluttered in response.

"To see how it ends," Rhys said. "We only watched the first two hours, remember?"

"Now that your mom has her own copy," I said, "I'm sure she'll let you watch hers."

Rhys shook his head slowly. "I don't know about that. She seems pretty attached."

Mr. Thornton would do that to you, I thought.

Remembering how I'd picked the liar in front of me over him, I wanted to knock myself over the head.

"And besides," he added, "I'd rather watch it with you."

As he took a step closer, I backed away.

"Well, sorry, but I can't tonight," I said. *Or any other night*, I silently added.

"Why not?" he asked.

Because you lied to me. You made a bet with your friend and told him you're embarrassed to be seen with me. Because it's breaking my heart right now just looking at you.

Lana saved me from the painful truth. I caught sight of her coming toward us down the hall and remembered something I hadn't before. I actually *did* have plans.

"I have a princess party to go to," I said suddenly.

"Are you for real right now?"

"Yeah, it's at Lana's house." I smiled at the other girl. "Can't wait for tonight. Thanks again for inviting me."

Lana seemed surprised I was addressing her, but she nodded.

"Don't forget your pajamas," she said. "And for the love of all that's holy, please don't bring your prince with you. This party is girls only."

She kept walking. Her tone wasn't overly friendly, but I swear I could've kissed her right then. Turning back to Rhys, I shrugged.

"What are you guys doing?" he asked.

"Having a movie night," I said. It was the thing that convinced me to go in the first place. "We're supposed to watch the *Princess Diaries*. It's awesome, and appropriate for this week, too."

Rhys nodded. "Maybe we can get together some other time, then."

Or maybe not.

"Princess, I—"

He reached for my hand but let it fall when I pulled away.

"Rhys, we're in public," I said quietly.

"So?" he said.

"People can see. I just don't want to embarrass anyone."

The line between his brows grew as his frown deepened. "What does that mean?"

"I don't think we should hang out anymore," I said. "That goes for Homecoming, too—other than the required bits, I mean."

"Hold up. Where is this coming from?"

I forced myself to meet his eyes. "I think you know."

"I really don't." He looked so confused, I almost believed him. "Did I do something wrong?"

No, I thought. I did. I was wrong to fall for someone who couldn't fall back.

"It's not your fault, Rhys," I said, realizing in some ways that it was true. "You can't help how you feel."

Before he could say anything, I left.

It was better this way, good that we had talked and put a definite end to things. Rhys had to be relieved that he didn't need to pretend anymore, and I could begin the long process of healing my heart. This was for the best.

But then why didn't I feel any better?

Chapter 31

*M*om could tell something was wrong the minute she got home. Granted, it wasn't hard to guess. I had the freezer open and was resting my head on the bag of frozen peas when she walked in.

Probably not the best move, I thought. It reminded me so much of Rhys. With a sigh, I went straight from that to baking—which was one of my worst tells.

"Do you want to talk about it?" she said.

"Nope," I replied, reaching into different cabinets and pulling things down.

"Since you asked, I had an interesting day, too."

I stopped everything and gave her a sheepish look.

"Sorry, Mom," I said. "I wasn't thinking. How was your day?"

"It's fine, baby." She rubbed my back as she passed by. "I remember what it was like to be in high school. There were days—a lot of them—when I didn't want to talk, either."

I sent her a grateful nod.

"I'll be honest, my day was a doozie. One of my kids started eating the macaroni art then promptly threw it up everywhere. Guess who had to clean that up?"

"Ugh, I'm sorry, Mom."

"And then to make things more fun, throughout the day, different kids started crying for no reason."

"Must be something in the air," I mumbled.

"What did you say?"

"Oh." I gave a shrug. "Well, maybe they had a reason, and you weren't aware of it."

"Could be," she agreed. "I love them, though. Shamika, the little girl you met, drew me a picture and said I made her whole day brighter. That felt good."

I smiled. "She's right, you know. This has been the best part of my day by far."

"Oh hush." Her eyes moved over the items on the counter. "What are you making?"

"Princess pretzel rods covered in white chocolate. I thought I'd use different colored sprinkles and things to represent the different princesses."

Her eyes lit up. "That sounds fun. Is this something for your vlog?"

"No, actually." I wiped my hands on my jeans. "I have a party tonight that I forgot about. One of the girls on Homecoming Court is hosting it."

"Well, aren't you popular," she said. "First, Rhys's mom's birthday"—I couldn't help my wince—"and now, this. When is he coming over again anyway?"

My sigh was way too dramatic, but I couldn't help it.

"I don't think he'll be back, Mom."

"Ah," she said, "that's too bad. He seemed nice."

She would've been so disappointed to know he wasn't.

Almost as disappointed as I was.

I decided not to burden her with that knowledge and nodded instead.

"I guess he has other things to do," I said.

She studied me a beat then said, "You know, boys can be confusing. They mess up just like girls do, make bad mistakes. But the good ones realize it and try to fix things."

I lifted a brow. "I get what you're saying, Mom. But I don't see how it applies here."

"Hey, what do you expect? I'm working on very little info." She held out her hands. "If I knew the details, my advice would be spot-on."

Despite my rotten mood, I laughed.

"You do give the best advice," I said.

"You're darn right."

My hands went to the counter as I thought about what I'd heard. "I'm sure I'll tell you everything. It's just a little raw right now, you know?"

"I do," she said. "I'm here if you need to talk."

"I love you, too, Mom."

"And baby," she said.

"Hmm?"

"I hope Rhys is one of the good ones."

It was a vain hope, but I didn't say so. Secretly, a part of me wanted that, too. Rhys had seemed like such a decent guy; it was hard to believe he was a superficial jerk like

so many other people. But the words he'd said still tore
at my heart.

Putting everything else out of my mind, I focused on
the pretzel rods.

They were one of the easiest desserts to make. Sprinkles,
edible pearls, and colored sugar took it up a notch. I went
ahead and frosted some of the cupcakes I made yesterday
with a princess theme in mind. Even with my inner turmoil,
the sweets ended up looking good. My cooking skills didn't
fail me, and for that I was thankful.

At seven o'clock, I rang the doorbell to Lana's house.
Her mother answered and smiled as she led me inside.

"Welcome, Ariel, we're so glad you could make it," she
said. "If you'll just leave your shoes by the door, Lana and
the other girls are in the living room."

"Thanks, Mrs. Leavengood." I did as she asked, slipping
off my tennis shoes, staring at my surroundings. "Your
house is really nice."

Her mouth pursed. "I've been asking my husband
forever to make improvements. But thank you, dear, that's
kind of you to say."

Lana and the other princesses came over to greet me
as I walked in.

"Hey Cupcake," Bryleigh said with a smile. "I like your
pajamas."

Looking down at myself, I grinned. My nightshirt had
little Princess Leia buns and the words *Rebel Princess* on
it. "Thanks, I was feeling the Force." I gestured to her outfit.
"Nice onesie."

"What do you have there?" Lana asked.

"Just some stuff I made." I lifted the cover and showed her the treats.

"You didn't have to bring anything."

I shrugged. "I always do. It's no big deal."

Tessandra reached forward to take a pretzel rod and smiled. "Thank goodness, real food!" She dropped her voice to a whisper. "Lana's mom insisted on veggie platters, fruit salad, and lettuce wraps."

Bryleigh nodded as she took a cupcake. "We're all starving."

"Exaggerate much?" Lana said.

"Well, I'm almost there."

"Me too," Tessandra said. She was halfway through her first pretzel rod and was reaching for a second.

"Face it, Lana," Bryleigh said. "Your mom's a health nut."

Lana sniffed. "She wants us to eat right. There's nothing wrong with that."

Tess just shook her head. "I'm all for healthy eating, but this is ridiculous. It's movie night for crying out loud! Where's the popcorn, the candy, the snacks?"

Bryleigh was nearly done with her cupcake, and I looked down at my tray.

"I hope I brought enough for everyone," I said.

That was actually one of my worst fears as a baker, that I wouldn't have enough food to go around. But as I looked past the girls in front of me, I saw there wasn't anyone else behind them. The living room was empty.

"Oh, it's just us," Bryleigh said as she polished off her cupcake. "I'm sure this will be more than enough."

My brow scrunched as I looked at Lana. "But I thought

you invited all the girls on the court."

"She did," Tess put in. "They just didn't come."

"Why not?" I asked.

Lana huffed and rolled her eyes. "Because underclassmen are annoying little brats."

Bryleigh leaned toward me then added, "Also, I'm not sure if you've noticed, but Lana can be a little scary."

Just a little, I thought.

"We figured they were probably too afraid to come, convinced this was some sort of hazing ritual. Hilarious, right?"

"Yeah." I forced a laugh like I hadn't had that same thought go through my head about a dozen times. "Hilarious."

Lana was apparently done with the chitchat. "Come on, girls," she said. "It's a freaking princess party. Are we watching this movie or not?"

Feeling like I was in a dream, I stepped farther inside, hoping for the best. My plan was to check things out and leave if I felt uncomfortable. It wasn't a crime to leave a party early. Since Bryleigh and Tess were on the brink of starvation, and Lana was Lana, I didn't think anyone would try to make me stay.

Besides, I loved movies.

Everything would be fine…hopefully.

Chapter 32

"Do you think that's Anne Hathaway's real hair?" Bryleigh's face was thoughtful as she asked the question. It was during the first twenty minutes of *The Princess Diaries*, so pre-makeover. Anne (aka Mia in the movie) still had a head of long, frizzy curls.

"No way," Lana said.

"I'm not sure," Tess said back. "It could be."

Lana took a bite of her celery stick. "It's too poufy and thick. They probably used a wig—or at least some extensions. The real question is: Are those eyebrows legit?"

We all studied the actress a bit closer.

"Eyebrow wax and tweezers work wonders," I said.

"Now *that* we can agree on, Cupcake."

She offered me the veggie tray and I took a piece of broccoli. It was raw with no dip, but I didn't want to ruin our precarious truce. After we settled on the couch and started the movie, she'd been less icy than usual. So yeah, I ate the broccoli with a smile.

I leaned forward and held out the tray of pretzels and cupcakes to her.

"You want one?" I asked.

Lana looked at me then to the desserts and shrugged. She was about to take something when Mrs. Leavengood suddenly joined us.

"Lana," she said in a sharp tone. "What do you think you're doing?"

"Nothing."

"Are my wholesome choices not good enough for you?"

Lana's face went red, but before she could answer, another little girl ran into the room and grabbed Mrs. Leavengood's hand. She looked familiar, but I couldn't place her for a second.

"Lana, I asked you a question," Mrs. Leavengood said. "Is there something wrong with my snacks?"

"No, Mom," Lana replied. "I was just thinking about having a cupcake."

"Oh honey. What have I told you about making good choices with food?" she said.

The little girl was the one who answered. "Eating bad things is the first step to a lifetime of sadness."

"Well said, Ashley." Mrs. Leavengood gave her a nod. "At least one of my daughters listens to me."

Ashley? Now why…

Ah, right! This was the little girl from my mom's class, the one who said the thing about how there were no fat princesses. When I looked closer at her and Lana, I could see the family resemblance. Ashley was currently staring at me with a tiny frown on her face.

"Hi," I said. "I think we've met before. Do you remember me?"

"Yes," she said. "You brought the cake for Shamika's birthday."

I nodded. "That's right. It's nice to see you again, Ashley."

She tilted her head. "Why are you at my sister's princess party?"

"Lana invited me," I said. "We're on Homecoming Court together."

"How exactly do you know my baby sister?" Lana asked.

I gave a shrug. "My mom's her teacher at school. I bring the kids cake sometimes for their birthdays."

Ashley was still frowning as her mother spoke again.

"Unhealthy eating leads to poor living in general, Lana." Mrs. Leavengood shook her head. "It's a fact. How many times must I tell you this?"

"Actually," I said, "the cupcakes are gluten free."

"They are?" Lana asked.

I nodded. "Also, free of refined sugars or oil. I make a lot of different ones, but I know you're always mentioning eating well. So I brought my healthiest choice."

Lana blinked. "That was nice of you."

"Well," her mom laughed, "Ashley and I have some errands to run. Do you girls need anything?"

"No, we're fine," Lana said.

Mrs. Leavengood nodded. "No offense, Ariel, but I remain unconvinced. Desserts will never be the best choice."

At the door she turned back to deliver her last word.

"Lana, I hope you'll set a good example for your sister.

And don't forget you have Homecoming," she said. "You want to make sure that dress still fits."

With a wave, she and Ashley left. I was too nervous to look at Lana, suffering from a kind of secondhand embarrassment. I didn't know how the others felt, but Bryleigh and Tess didn't say anything, either.

"You say these are gluten-free?" she asked.

My eyes shot to hers in surprise. "Yeah, but you don't have to eat any if you don't want to."

Honestly, after that uncomfortable exchange, I was sorry I'd even brought them.

Lana stared at the front door a second longer before rolling her eyes. She turned back to me and grabbed a cupcake out of the tray.

"My mom's sensitive about food," she said. "She used to be very overweight and got a lot of crap about it. I don't think one cupcake will hurt."

After she took the first bite, her eyes closed.

"Especially when it's this good."

I hid a smile behind my hand. "So glad you like it."

"Yeah well," Lana said, "don't get a big head, Cupcake. This is the first sweet I've had in like a hundred years. So…"

"I've had three in the last hour," Bryleigh said. "And I'm not even sorry."

The tension broke as everyone laughed. Lana brought out some cute princess-themed face masks, and we rewound the movie a little to see what we'd missed. The mask was supposed to clean out pores while calming the skin, but maybe it was magical. I found myself more at ease, enjoying this time with these girls I barely knew.

This isn't so bad, I thought as the green tea mixture seeped into my skin.

"This is so unrealistic," Tess pointed out once we got past the movie's makeover scene. "Anne's gorgeous. Are we supposed to believe no one saw how pretty she was before?"

"It's the Clark Kent effect," I said.

"Like Superman?"

"Yeah, in movies, no one acknowledges the girl's pretty until she ditches the glasses and gets a makeover." I shrugged. "But a lot of people look good in glasses."

"Total cliché," Bryleigh agreed. "Though I do like makeovers."

"Who doesn't?" Lana said. She was just finishing up her cupcake and looked a lot happier. "And anyway, that one guy saw how pretty she was. He liked her the whole time."

"That's a bit unrealistic, too, if you ask me." Tess chewed her pretzel thoughtfully. "Why couldn't it have been her crush, the popular athletic one?"

"Because," I said, "the popular jocks can only see skin-deep. They're pretty but shallow."

Lana scoffed. "Another freaking cliché."

I gave her a sad smile. "I don't know. Some guys are like that."

"Yeah, but it doesn't matter if they're popular or not," she said.

"She's right," Bryleigh put in. "Boys are much more superficial than girls. Especially when it comes to height or weight."

Tess wasn't having it. "Not all guys feel that way."

"More than you might think," I muttered.

"It probably has something to do with my mom," Lana said. "But my worst fear is getting fat."

The movie was forgotten once more as I pulled off my face mask and turned to her.

"That's ridiculous," I said. "There are way worse things than being overweight."

Lana crossed her arms as she stared me down. "Oh yeah? Name one."

She reminded me so much of her little sister that I wanted to laugh. But I didn't, because this was an important issue, and I actually had an answer.

"Um, I can think of a ton of things that are worse," I said.

Lana rolled her eyes, gesturing for me to go on.

"Being hateful for one," I said.

"Or a bully," Tess added.

"Or prejudiced," Bryleigh put in.

"Or homeless, or incarcerated, or sick, or living in a war-torn country—"

"Okay, okay," Lana cut in, stopping my words. Too bad, I had a lot more. "I get it. I guess there are worse things."

I gave her a nod. "There really are."

The movie was still rolling, so we sat back again to watch. Only a few minutes had gone by when Lana leaned over and beckoned me closer. Bryleigh and Tessandra were having a deep conversation about whether or not they'd want to be an actual princess if that meant they had to move all the way to an unknown country.

"What's up?" I asked Lana.

She kept her voice low. "How do you do it?"

"Do what?"

"How are you so confident about your weight?" Seeing the look on my face, Lana sighed. "I'm not trying to be mean, Cupcake—I'm honestly curious. Mom has told me so many horror stories, and she blames them all on her weight. It's totally overboard. I honestly want to know why she's like that and you're not."

"Okay," I said frowning, "but if you're doing this to tease me..."

"I'm not," she said. "I swear."

"Swear on the Homecoming crown."

She rolled her eyes. "I swear on the crown. Now, will you just answer?"

I knew she cared a lot about being queen. Whether she was doing this to be mean or not, the fact that she'd sworn made me feel better about our conversation. Maybe Lana really did want to know. I settled farther into the couch.

"I guess one reason is because my mom's never made a big deal about it," I said. "She loves herself—and me—no matter how we look."

"Must be nice," Lana murmured. "What's the other reason?"

I took a deep breath.

"Well, I had a friend who went through a bad time," I said, intentionally leaving Toni's name out. I wasn't sure if she'd want to be a part of this conversation, but I couldn't fully answer Lana without bringing up the past. "This was years ago. You never met her."

"Okaaay," she said, sounding impatient. "Like I care about your long-lost friend. Jeez, Cupcake. Can we move on?"

That made me smile because I knew she didn't care.

"I've always been chubby," I said. "She was smaller than me, but we were both teased. A lot." My thoughts drifted back to those days, and a tremor worked its way down my spine. "At some point, we started believing the insults. They sort of get in your head, you know?"

Lana nodded, and I went on.

"We started complaining all the time, downing ourselves, finding flaws—about weight mostly." I cleared my throat. "I hadn't realized she'd stopped eating, that it was that serious. But at one point, she got sick and ended up in the hospital. It was…bad."

I still had nightmares about seeing Toni in that hospital bed, how small and frail she'd looked.

Shaking myself, I said, "Luckily, she got better. We both went to therapy—which helped. And I decided to never put myself down again."

"You just decided?" Lana said doubtfully. "How's that working out?"

"I still have insecurities, if that's what you're asking." I gave her a smile. "I just try to be kinder to myself."

"That's not the easiest thing to do."

I nodded. "It's not. Especially in high school."

"I'm glad your friend's okay," she said.

"I am, too."

Lana and I stared at each other for a moment. I'd always thought we were so different, but maybe we had a few things in common.

"It's good that you came," she said. My heart started to warm—but then she reached past me, coming back with another cupcake, and added, "These desserts are awesome."

If Lana wanted to make it about the sweets, that was fine by me. Our little moment didn't need to go any further than this couch. Bryleigh and Tess were still talking about the movie when I took a pretzel from the tray.

"He's so much cuter than that other guy," Bryleigh was saying.

"But he's not her crush," Tess said, "who, granted, turned out to be an ass."

"I don't care what you think—Princess Mia should've been with the nice guy from the beginning. Lana, Cupcake, what do you say? Should she have chosen the cocky jock or the sweet musician?"

"Maybe," Lana said, "she should've gone with her cat and ended up single."

Bryleigh groaned. "That's not romantic."

"Possibly more realistic, though," Tess said.

"Cupcake?"

"I like the cat idea," I replied. "Boys can be...more trouble than they're worth."

"I hear that," Tess said. "Speaking of which, who do you guys think is the hottest prince on the court?"

The girls were silent a beat, then...

"Rhys," they said in unison, followed by a bout of giggles.

"He's gorgeous," Tess said.

Bryleigh nodded. "Oh, you are so lucky you got to partner with him, Cupcake."

"I agree," Lana said. "I've been working toward being Homecoming queen since I was a freshman. But with Rhys on your arm? There might be some competition."

"Yeah right," I said. "We're not even really going together."

"What do you mean?"

"We're required to go as a couple because of Court, but I'm sure he'll find someone else to take as his real date."

Lana rolled her eyes. "Oh please, if he hasn't asked you yet, he will."

He did ask, I thought. He just didn't mean it.

"We've all noticed how the two of you look at each other," Bryleigh said. "It's sweet."

"It's nauseating," Lana retorted.

"Like you have room to talk," Bryleigh said. "Do I really need to comment on your and Zander's little romance? The way you pretend not to like him, and he keeps gazing at you as if you're a queen already?" Lana's mouth fell open as Bryleigh grinned. "That's what I thought."

"Zander's intentions are suspect," she said breezily. "But Rhys is so easy to read. He's too honest for games, and he's been flirting with Cupcake for a while."

I shrugged her off. "I think Rhys likes games."

"No, he doesn't."

"I hear you, but I just disagree," I said. "He's good at pretending."

"Please, he's, like, the most sincere guy I know. He can't lie for anything."

"Hmm, I wouldn't be so sure of that."

Lana looked at me like I'd grown a second head. "Are you serious right now? Cupcake, Rhys hates games. It's one of the many reasons he broke up with me. I played around too much trying to make him jealous."

Throat suddenly tight, I took that in.

"Sorry," I said, "I didn't know."

"It's fine." She waved me off. "I was planning on breaking up with him anyway. He doesn't talk much. Honestly, I don't think he has a lot going on upstairs. He's hot, but he's just so boring, and—"

"Rhys isn't boring," I retorted, my cheeks hot with indignation.

"Really?"

"He's smart, thoughtful, and kind, too."

"Okay, whatever."

"And you're wrong about him not talking," I said, remembering all the fun we'd had. "Rhys has a ton of opinions, and he's so funny. I loved our conversations. I loved hanging out with him. I loved…basically every second we had together."

Lana yawned. "Like I said, he's too nice."

She gave me a once-over.

"Actually, now that I think about it, you two are probably perfect for each other."

Of all the things she could've said, that one cut the deepest.

If only it were true, I thought.

If only Rhys hadn't lied to me, maybe we could've been something more.

If only my confidence was as unshakable as Lana believed it was, maybe his words wouldn't have hit me so hard.

If only.

Chapter 33

The rest of the night was a bust because I couldn't stop thinking about Rhys. I was irked that Lana thought she knew him better than I did, but it also made me mad at myself for caring. Even after the lies, I still stuck up for Rhys. And that made me hate myself a little.

Other than that, though, the princess party was a good one. The movie still made me laugh (though I'd seen it a million times). The girls and I had had some fun conversations. Plus, they ate all the desserts, which made me feel good. But tomorrow we had the pep rally and then the Homecoming game. On Saturday, we'd have the dance.

It felt like everything was about to end.

On the drive to school Friday, I kept hoping I could get through it all, interacting with Rhys as little as possible, and come out with my heart intact.

"Please line up next to your partner for the group picture," Ms. Weaver said.

So much for not interacting with Rhys.

"Princesses in the front and princes in the back."

We were all standing outside the gym as other students filtered in for the pep rally. I could feel the humidity coming from inside the building. Out here it was windy, which made it quite cool.

Or that could've been my prince's frosty attitude.

I was sure I felt the temperature drop as he came to stand behind me.

"Okay, everyone look at the camera! On the count of three, we'll take the picture," Ms. Weaver said. "And one… two…three!"

A click sounded. The photographer looked down to check the viewer but shook his head, whispering something to Ms. Weaver, who nodded.

"Mr. Castle," she said, "can you try to be ready this time?"

"I was," Rhys said.

"You were frowning. Let's just try again!"

A deep sigh came from behind me, and I shivered.

"Can you stop that?" I said.

"Ah, she can speak," was Rhys's response.

"Just stop."

"I'm not doing anything," he said.

"You're breathing on my neck," I retorted.

"Trust me, Princess," he said. "If I was breathing down your neck, you wouldn't be asking me to stop."

Gah. I was sure my face was beet red, but I couldn't help it. The next time the camera clicked, I knew my smile was off. Ms. Weaver and the photographer shook their heads again.

"Third time's the charm!" she said. "Mr. Castle, could you please try to look less broody? It's throwing off the entire happy mood of the Homecoming photo."

I sighed.

"Just do it so we can go, man," Zander said.

"Yeah," Lana hissed. "We still have to walk into the pep rally. Everyone's waiting. We're the honored guests."

I couldn't see it, but I knew Rhys was rolling his eyes.

"Whatever, Lana. No one's waiting for us," he said. "Stop being a brat."

"Don't call her that," I said.

"What?"

"Don't call Lana a brat," I repeated. "You're the one who's acting like a jerk. Just smile for the dang picture so we can get this over with."

"Whatever you say, Princess."

It turned out the third time was the charm—or maybe Ms. Weaver had accepted that Rhys's expression wasn't going to improve anytime soon. She lined us up by class outside the gym doors. Rhys and I were next to last again, and we had to wait until we were announced to walk inside.

Rhys settled in next to me, but I took a couple steps to the side and widened the gap between us.

He shook his head. "You're such a hypocrite."

"Excuse me?" I said as my eyes shot to his. "What's that supposed to mean?"

"You calling me a jerk," he said. "You were the one who agreed to go to Homecoming with me and then canceled for no reason."

I scoffed.

"The line's moving," Lana said from behind us.

Rhys and I stepped forward, but I couldn't let what he'd said go.

"Oh, I had a very good reason," I said.

"Really?" he asked. "Is it the same reason you stopped talking to me without a word? The same reason you keep trying to put more distance between us?"

"Yes, it is."

Zander cleared his throat, and Rhys and I moved again to keep up with the line.

"You're really good at pretending," I said.

"What are you talking about?"

I was about to respond when something buzzed near my ear. Eyes wide, I squeaked and jumped away. But the fly wasn't done with me. I bobbed to the left as it zoomed by again—and suddenly Rhys was there. He swatted the fly away and then frowned at me.

"All clear, Princess," he said. "Go on. You were telling me what a jerk I am."

But I shook my head. Gah, this was what confused me in the first place.

"Why did you do that?" I asked.

"Because you hate bugs."

"Ugh, I don't understand you, Rhys," I said. "You have two faces, and I can't figure out which one is real. Are you this guy who protects girls from evil bugs? Or are you the guy who talks behind a girl's back about how embarrassing she is?"

Rhys's look grew concerned as he took a step toward me. "Princess, I really don't know what you're talking about."

I looked away, widening the gap again.

"Stop doing that," he said.

"Doing what?" I asked.

"Pulling away."

Lana muttered something about the line again, but she didn't need to because I was already in motion, trying to outpace Rhys. It turned out to be futile. His legs ate up the distance, and soon he had grabbed ahold of my hand.

"Let go," I said quietly. "Or people will see."

Rhys scoffed. "Like I care."

"I think you do." My eyes moved up to meet his, even though I could feel mine growing wet with unshed tears. "You're really going to make me say it?"

"Say what?" he asked.

"I heard you and Zander," I said, "talking by your locker, saying how you didn't want to bring me to Homecoming."

"What?" Rhys's face contorted as he shook his head. "I never said that. I would never say anything even close to that, because it's not true."

I shook my head. "I heard everything, Rhys. You said I was so big that you didn't want to be seen with me in public. That—" I paused to take a breath because this was more painful than I could've imagined. "That it would be humiliating."

"I didn't—"

Rhys's face cleared a moment later.

"Oh."

"You remember now?" I said.

"Yes, I remember," he said. "But I wasn't talking about you."

I frowned at him because how dare he deny it? "But you made a bet with Zander that you'd take me to Homecoming."

Rhys bit back a smile. "Like I said, that wasn't about you. Ask Zander if you don't believe me."

Turning, I looked at the other boy, and he grinned at me in return.

"He's not lying, Cupcake," Zander said. "The bet wasn't about you. It was about Selene."

The name didn't ring any bells.

"But that doesn't make sense," I said. "Rhys asked me to Homecoming, not someone named Selene."

The guys laughed as I looked back and forth between the two of them.

"Selene's not a someone," Rhys said. "She's my 1957 Chevy Bel Air."

"But you drive a truck," I said.

"Yeah, because Selene's still in the garage. I've been fixing her up for a while. The parts are hard to find. I had a bet with Zander that she'd be ready to go by Homecoming."

"She's a real beauty," Zander said. "Total classic. I'd give my left nut to drive that car."

"Ew," Lana said, but he just shrugged.

"The right one, too, if I'm being honest."

"She is really big," Rhys said with a shrug. "Not exactly a car you'd typically see at a dance. I didn't want to embarrass my date—not that I have one anymore."

Reeling, I shook my head in disbelief. "But you said she'd done a lot for you, that you felt like you owed her."

Rhys nodded. "My grandfather left her to me when he passed away a couple years ago. Of course I feel like I owe her—or really him."

How could I have gotten this so wrong? I wondered. A car? Seriously?

"Are you lying right now?" I asked.

He tilted his head. "I've never lied to you, Princess. Why would I start now?"

Lana spoke up from behind us then. "You really should believe him, Cupcake. Rhys isn't a liar—I told you that already."

Her words shocked and exhilarated me, but I still had one last question.

"So…you're not embarrassed to be seen with me?"

"No, and I never have been," Rhys said as I swallowed. "How could you even think that?"

"I don't know," I murmured.

Lana sighed. "I hate to interrupt this little soap opera again, but you're next," she said.

There was no one left in front of us. As we'd been speaking, the other nominees must've been announced and moved along. Ms. Weaver was gesturing to us, frantically trying to get our attention. Rhys and I walked more sedately this time.

"Why would I be embarrassed?" he said. "I wanted people to know we were together."

"You did?" I asked, hearing the hopeful note in my voice.

"Of course. You're beautiful, kind, fun to be around. Not to mention, I love the things you bake." Rhys shrugged. "I like everything about you."

I sighed. "I like everything about you, too."

He held up a hand.

"But…then how could you think I'd say something like that?" he asked. "Or even feel that way? Do you really think I'm that shallow?"

I honestly didn't know what to say.

Principal Maxine announced our names over the loudspeaker, and Rhys and I walked out. The cheers were loud, the crowd going wild over their star quarterback. But I barely heard any of it. I couldn't recall much of what happened after that. Rhys's words kept replaying in my mind, and I had no idea how to make this right. "I'm sorry" sounded so inadequate.

After the pep rally ended, amid the chaos of everyone trying to exit the stands at once, I turned to Rhys.

"I'm sorry," I said to him. "It's not enough, but I'm so sorry."

He stayed silent.

"I misinterpreted what I heard. I totally misjudged the situation. How was I supposed to know you were talking about a car?"

"You could've asked," he said.

"But I didn't even know you had another—"

Rhys's intense gaze bore into mine. "Right after you heard the conversation between me and Zander, you should've come to me. But instead, you assumed the worst."

I winced. "You have to admit it wasn't that farfetched. I—"

"Wow, Princess." The word lacked any of its former warmth. It made my chest ache to hear him say it with such coldness. "I must've made a pretty bad impression if you thought I was capable of being that cruel."

I had so much to say, but not one word escaped.

He was wrong. He didn't understand. Yes, I had doubted him, but mostly…I had doubted *myself*.

Rhys leaned down and spoke directly in my ear.

"Just so you know," he said, "it wasn't embarrassment or humiliation I felt when you said yes. My first thought was: I can't believe I get to take the most amazing girl to Homecoming. I felt so lucky, I wanted to shout it from the rooftops."

My eyes filled as he drew away.

"Maybe you're the one who's embarrassed," he said. "Since I'm such a bad person."

He walked away…and it was like he took my heart with him. My hand traveled to where the muscle should've been, but instead, there was just a Rhys-sized hole. It hurt. I didn't know how to fill it or if that was even possible. The worst part was I couldn't stop seeing Rhys's eyes, and the wounded look I'd put there.

It wasn't until Toni came to get me that I realized everyone else had already gone. Who knew what would've happened if she hadn't? I might've stood there all day, picturing Rhys's back as he left me in the dust.

"Bad talk with the prince?" Toni asked.

"The worst," I said then looked up at her. "Oh Toni, I was so wrong. Now Rhys hates me, and I have no idea what to do."

She linked her arm with mine and tugged me along.

"No problem," she said. "Just tell me all about it, and we'll come up with a plan."

"A plan for what?"

Toni rolled her eyes. "To get him back, silly."

"I don't think that's possible," I said.

"Nothing's impossible when it comes to true love," she retorted. "Start from the beginning."

I was desperate to believe her, so I nodded, filling her in on everything that had been revealed, every piece of new info, and of course, how disheartened Rhys had looked. We talked the whole time on the ride to my house. Toni had left her car behind. She'd planned to help me get ready anyway, and we'd drive to the game together. When I parked the car in the driveway and turned to her, her jaw was hanging open.

"A car?" she asked. "All this trouble was caused by a car?"

I nodded.

"Ugh. Well, the good news is it's obvious he still cares about you."

"How?" I asked. "Rhys could barely stand to look at me, and then he left."

"That's because you hurt his feelings." Toni held up a finger for each point. "Rhys was upset about you ghosting him."

"That's true."

"And he said a bunch of nice things about you—even when he was mad. Most guys don't do that very often."

I nodded for her to go on.

"He wanted everyone to know you were going to Homecoming together," she said. "The fact that you could think he's a jerk obviously upset him. And he even admitted that he thinks you might be the one who's embarrassed."

Toni seemed to think this meant something, but I didn't know what.

"Don't you see?" she said. "He wants to know you like him."

"I do," I said immediately. "Rhys is the best guy I've ever met. He puts up this strong front, but beneath that, he's so much more. Sweet, smart, and thoughtful—the kind of guy who tells you when he's going to be late. He's brave, too, even around bugs. I love how we can talk, like really talk, about important things. And we have! He has this delicious soft side. And gah...Rhys is everything."

"Don't tell me that. Tell Rhys!"

I shook my head. "You didn't see his face, Toni. I don't think he'll believe me."

"Well, show him, then," she said, grabbing my hands. "He needs to know you're not embarrassed. Make him understand how you feel. Show everyone he's yours."

"Okay," I said, beginning to understand. "But how?"

"I'm sure you'll come up with something." She gave me a wink. "A little romance goes a long way."

Could I do that? I wondered as my mind ran wild. Was I brave enough to put everything on the line, risk rejection, just to let Rhys know my true feelings?

There was only one way to find out.

Chapter 34

*T*he football field lights never shined brighter.

The stadium was packed; current students, teachers, alumni, fans, parents and other family members filled up the seats. It looked like the Honeycomb Trojans were playing for a sold-out crowd. At halftime, our boys were up 37-7, and I didn't see the other team closing that gap anytime soon. HHS was playing great today, and Rhys looked fantastic.

Like always, I thought.

Ms. Weaver stood with the Homecoming nominees along the sidelines of the field as we waited for everyone to be assembled. I was wearing my dress, though Rhys hadn't seen me in it yet. He and Zander were still in the locker rooms with the rest of the team. They'd be out any minute.

Looking up into the stands, I saw Rhys's mom and dad; even Zach was there to support his brother. Mom and Toni were a few stands up from them, and when we made eye contact, they both started waving like mad. I smiled and waved back, glad they were here.

Even if I was planning something kind of reckless.

Okay, for anyone else, it probably wouldn't have been a big deal.

But for me? It was colossal, a gesture of *Titanic*-size proportions.

I just hoped it didn't end in disaster.

My palms were sweaty, my heart beating too fast. I had to grip my hands to stop them from shaking—which they'd been doing since I got to the field. But I forced myself to be calm. Mentally going over the plan for the millionth time helped.

A little.

But I was still nervous.

"Nice dress, Cupcake," Lana said as she stood next to me. "Where did you get it?"

"A place called Glitter & Glam," I said, thankful for the distraction. "The staff was really nice, and the dresses were gorgeous."

"I'll have to check it out."

"You look beautiful, Lana," I said. "Like a queen."

She sniffed. "Naturally."

Tessandra readjusted her strapless dress. "I wish we could get started already. My arms are starting to chafe from pulling this thing up so much."

"Ah, come on, Tess." Bryleigh smiled at her. "This is it! Aren't you excited to know who won?"

"Uh, no."

"Finally," Lana said in exasperation, "what took you so long? All you did was go into the locker room and come back out."

Zander came up beside her, running a hand through his hair. "Beauty takes time, my lady. I have to look good if I'm going to have you on my arm."

She tried not to, but I saw Lana's smile break through.

"Good answer," she said.

"True answer," he said back.

If Zander was out here, I realized with a jolt, then Rhys must be…

I turned around slowly and caught sight of him. Like Zander, he was dressed in the standard Honeycomb football uniform, which had a few grass stains on it. But my goodness. Rhys looked amazing.

He was standing a few feet away, staring at me with this expression of awe on his face, his mouth slightly open. His eyes traveled my frame, and I swear I felt that look all over. When his gaze finally met mine, my heart was pounding. He swallowed, then made his way to me.

"Princess," he said.

"Rhys."

When he didn't say anything else, I started to get nervous. "Do you like the dress?" I asked.

"I do," he said, "but I like the girl in it more—even if she thinks I'm some cliché from one of her movies."

A smile worked its way up my lips as I sighed in relief.

"You happy about that?"

I turned to him, bolstered by his response. "Yes, absolutely. Rhys, I don't think you're shallow or a cliché at all. You're more than that. So much more."

Rhys looked at me a second but shook his head.

"Pretty words," he said, "but your actions speak louder, Princess."

"I know. But Rhys—"

A new voice intruded before I could say more.

"Hey Cupcake," Kendall called from a few paces away. She was standing in a group with the other cheerleaders. "Try not to fall this time, okay? You don't want to make Rhys look bad in front of all these people."

I put a hand on Rhys's chest when he went to argue.

"Yeah, thanks," I said, brushing her off.

"That dress is really pretty," she went on. "It would look better on someone else, but whatever. You obviously tried. But I hope you don't actually think you have a chance at winning."

Kendall smirked and shook her head.

"Pathetic."

The word that put me off-balance before only served to fortify me now.

"I see what you're doing," I said. "But it won't work."

Kendall frowned. "What?"

"You want me to feel bad or unworthy." My smile was bright. "But I don't even want that crown. At least I have a shot, though, unlike you."

Kendall's eyes flared. "Wow, I didn't know pigs could talk."

"Ken," Lana said sharply. "Enough."

The other girl's eyes shot to her. "Stay out of it, Lana. This isn't about you."

Lana gave her a bored look. "Cupcake's right. You're just jealous because she's a princess and you're not. Stop embarrassing yourself."

Shaking her head, Kendall said, "I can't believe you're standing up for her."

Lana stayed silent, staring down her friend.

"Well, screw you. Both of you." Kendall gave us a sickly sweet smile. "Oh, and Lana? That dress makes you look fat."

With that parting shot, she turned away to gossip with her friends, and I leaned toward Lana.

"You didn't have to do that," I said, "but thanks. Also, what Kendall said is crap. You look amazing."

Lana looked down at herself. "I know, right? I'm so winning this year."

I laughed as she threw me a grin. "I really hope you do. Good luck, Lana."

"Like I'll need it," she said. "Good luck with Rhys."

"Thanks," I repeated.

Turning back around, I looked up at the guy in question. He was staring down at me with a scowl on his face. His displeasure wasn't directed at me, though, but at what just went down. Rhys made that clear with his next words.

"You okay?" he said.

I waved a hand, touched by his concern. "Oh yeah, I'm used to it."

"What Kendall said was messed up. You shouldn't be used to that."

"But I am," I said softly.

Rhys clenched his jaw, nodded once, and then looked straight ahead.

"That's part of what I wanted to tell you earlier," I said. "But I couldn't find the words."

The announcer's voice came over the stadium speakers, and Ms. Weaver jumped into action, making sure we were all in place.

"Sashes, tiaras, and scepters at the ready, everyone!" she said.

"Rhys," I said, waiting until he looked at me, "I'm sorry. For getting it so wrong. For getting *you* wrong. Most of my doubt was about me, not you. I'm confident, but apparently I still have some doubts. I just couldn't believe someone as wonderful as you would be into me. Sounds unbelievable, but it's the truth."

"You're right," he said. "That does sound unbelievable."

Before he could turn away, I stopped him with a hand on his arm.

"Wait. Could you check my tiara?"

I held his gaze as he reached up. He moved the little crown on my head, fingertips brushing lightly through the ends of my hair as he finished.

"Looks good," Rhys said.

"Thank you," I replied.

I moved my hand down to grip his, and his eyes followed.

"Careful, Princess," he murmured. "People can see us. I know you're weird about that."

"I don't care."

"Don't you?"

"No," I said, then shook my head. "Or actually yes."

Rhys's face filled with confusion.

The announcer's voice intruded once more as he called my name followed by Rhys's. We walked down the fifty-yard line, my arm resting on top of his, doing the slow glide like Ms. Weaver taught us. I was still so focused on the guy next to me, I hardly noticed the grass beneath my feet.

"Which is it?" Rhys said finally. "Do you care or don't you?"

I smiled, glad that he'd asked, because that meant he was invested. He still cared, even if he was trying not to.

"It's both," I said. "I don't care what they think, but I do want them to see us together."

"Why?"

"Because"—I took a deep breath—"I want everyone to know you're mine. And that I'm yours."

I stopped in the middle of the field. Rhys took a few more steps before he noticed I wasn't moving. He looked at me in question, but I held up a hand.

"What are you doing?" he asked.

"Showing you how I feel," I said.

As I lowered my arm and gave the signal to Jon Wu, the drum major nodded. The marching band burst to life, music filling the stadium from every corner. "Can't Take My Eyes Off of You" had never sounded better. While Rhys and everyone were looking around, Lana walked out onto the field, stopped at my side, and handed me a microphone.

Her smile was bright even as she said, "If I lose my crown over this, Cupcake, you are so dead. Now, go get him." I nodded as she walked away. Sending up a little prayer, I turned on the microphone. I'd enlisted Mrs. Reeve's help with making sure it was wired into the stadium's sound system.

"Hello," I said, shocked by the loudness of my voice. "My name is Ariel Duncan, and I just wanted to say a few things to someone I care about very much."

My prince's eyes met mine.

"Rhys, I'm so sorry for misjudging you," I said. "You're the kindest, sweetest, best guy I've ever known. There's not ten things I hate about you. There's not even one. I like everything about you."

Cheers went up at that, but I wasn't done. As the song changed to "In Your Eyes" by Peter Gabriel, I took a deep breath.

"And I don't just mean in a you're-totally-hot kind of way. I mean in the I'd-stand-outside-your-window-holding-a-boom-box-over-my-head-for-hours kind of way. I'd be doing that now if I could've found a boom box on such short notice—do they even make those anymore?—and if I wasn't wearing this dress," I added.

I heard a bit of laughter at that.

"My point is I'd want to listen to you say anything."

I nodded.

"I'd say you had me at hello. But I actually think you had me at Sarah J. Maas. When I found out you'd read my favorite book series, some part of me knew you were the one."

Rhys's eyes seemed to sparkle, and I hoped that was a good sign.

"The point is"—I said as the song changed once again to the final selection: "Don't Worry Baby" by the Beatles—"before you, I'd never been kissed."

I swallowed.

"But if you accept my apology, I invite you to come kiss me—again. And even if you don't, I want you to know: I'm pretty sure I'm in love with you. I know now that you could love me back. And I hope you do."

The band was still playing, the crowd had gone quiet, and I had no idea what was going through Rhys's head. I didn't know if he'd gotten any of my movie references, let alone if he'd take me up on my offer. But at least I'd tried. I'd put my heart out there…

And now, I was just waiting to see if he'd accept it.

Rhys was silent a whole five seconds. I counted every one of them and the beats of my heart. It was a hard thing, but I stayed silent. How would he react? What would he say? Would he give us another chance?

"Rhys?" I said nervously, when it became unbearable to wait any longer. "Do you have any thoughts about that?"

"So many, Princess," he said in a deep voice. "I have so much to say, but I can't say any of it because we're on this damn field. I wish we were alone."

My eyes met his as he walked toward me, and they were filled with fire.

"I don't want to wait," I said, heart pounding like a drum in my chest.

Putting my hands on his shoulders, I rose to my tiptoes, gently guiding him down to meet me. My heart flooded with joy as his hands circled my waist.

"Hey," he said, "I thought I was supposed to be the one kissing you."

"You are," I said, unable to hold back a smile. "My whole heart is yours, Rhys Castle. I want you and everyone else to know it."

"That's good," Rhys said as he gazed into my eyes.

"Because I'm yours, Princess. All yours."

"I'm going to kiss you now, okay?"

He grinned. "Well, it's hard to say no to you in that dress."

"Rhys."

"Just kidding. I might kiss you back. Are you ready for that?"

"Oh yes, please," I said.

My lips met his in a kiss that was like fire touching tinder. I went up in flames right there in front of everyone. And I knew Rhys burned for me, too.

One of his arms went around my waist as his other hand cupped my cheek. My own hands were wrapped around his neck. His mouth danced with mine, moving together with a tenderness that I felt down to my soul. Our lips parted and came back together again and again. I was distantly aware of the crowd cheering.

But I just kept kissing him.

Rhys.

My prince.

Homecoming had thrown us together, but it grew into more than that. It helped me realize my feelings about Rhys—and myself. This experience had made me brave enough to say them.

For the first time in my life, I actually felt like a princess.

And it had nothing to do with the tiara. Or even the boy.

It was all me.

Chapter 35

"*I* can't believe Lana won," Toni said.

"I can," I said, smiling as Lana danced with Zander. It wasn't one of our choreographed ones—we'd done those earlier when the Homecoming dance first started. Rhys hadn't missed a step—and it looked like both of them were having a good time. Lana's crown glinted under the lights. "I'm glad she won."

"You are?" My best friend sniffed as I nodded. "Well, I guess it's fine. Nothing surprising or original, but if you're good, then I'm good."

I shot her a grin. "I am *so* good."

Toni laughed. "I can see that. So, I gotta say, that kiss was unexpected. I know we talked about showing Rhys your feelings, but I thought you'd bake him a cake or something."

"I thought about it," I said, "but that wouldn't have been enough."

"Hey, no complaints here," she said. "Hooray for PDA!"

Rolling my eyes, I shook my head.

"Your mom took it pretty well."

"I know," I said. We'd had a big talk about it before the dance, and she'd been of two minds. "Part of her was shocked that I did it at all. The other part was glad because it reminded her of some of our favorite rom-coms. Before I left, she told me, in no uncertain terms, to be home by midnight. Pretty sure the kiss inspired that as well."

Toni laughed at that. "You should've heard her when it happened. She was cheering louder than anybody else. I thought I saw a few tears, too."

"Probably." I lifted my chin, gesturing to something behind her shoulder. "It looks like Ben's coming back. How do you keep convincing him to get you punch all the time instead of walking over there yourself?"

"It's a gift," she said.

Rhys was walking next to him. He'd gone over with Ben, and I had to admit, I may have been ogling him every chance I got. Rhys in a football uniform was one thing, but Rhys in a suit? Lord help me.

"Your man is looking mighty fine," Toni remarked.

"Hey, eyes to yourself," I said then sighed. "But yeah, he totally is."

Rhys gave me a half smile as he got closer. I was surprised I didn't melt on the spot.

"Ben's looking good, too."

"I know this," she said. "Can you believe he got a tailor to match his tie to the exact color and material of my dress? So above and beyond."

I could believe it, I thought. Ben was all about Toni, and

my best friend was head over heels for him.

The guys joined us, and Rhys sidled up beside me.

"Have I told you how beautiful you look, Princess?" he asked.

I gave him a look but couldn't help my smile. "Only about a dozen times."

"Ah well, that's not nearly enough." Rhys looked at me, his eyes bright. "You look gorgeous."

Strangely enough, I had no trouble believing he meant it.

"So do you," I said. "You're almost too pretty to look at."

Toni groaned. "Ugh, please. No more. Ben, let's go before their mushy ways rub off on us."

"Whatever you say, love," Ben said, and Toni blushed to high heaven.

"Catch you later, A," my BFF said.

"Sounds good, *love*," I said back.

The two scurried away without another word. They were cute together, and I was glad we had come as a group. I couldn't imagine this night without my best friend.

Then Rhys stepped in front of me, and a new thought formed. The truth was: I couldn't imagine it without him, either.

"I'm glad you were able to get Selene up and running for tonight," I said. "Zander was right. That is a beautiful car."

"A gas-guzzling tank of a car, but yeah," Rhys said. "Me too."

"You think she'll be able to get us home?"

"You know it. I wouldn't have taken her out if I thought she'd break down. Not with you in the car."

The flutters in my stomach couldn't be controlled.

Rhys sent me that little smile again. "Do you think your mom got enough pictures?"

My smile grew as I remembered her asking us for "just one more" about a million times.

"She wanted to get us from every angle," I said. "I know neither one of us liked it, but this is one time I'm glad she got a ton of pics. They'll be put in a photo album, so we can look back on tonight. When it's over"—I shrugged—"I want to remember everything."

"So do I," he said and took a step closer. The song had changed to a slow one. "Care for a dance, Princess?"

"Of course," I said.

As we walked to the dance floor and began to sway, I closed my eyes, wanting to drink in every part of this moment.

"You know," Rhys said, "it's not going to be that easy."

"What's not?"

"Getting rid of me. I'll still be around after Homecoming. You know that, right?"

"I do." I smiled as I peeked up at him. "And I hope you know I'm not letting you go that easily, either."

Rhys chuckled, but my face sunk into a frown.

"Not in a creepy way or anything," I added. "Gah, that sounded weird. I didn't mean I'd hold you against your will."

"I know." He pulled me closer, and my mouth snapped shut. "I got what you meant, Princess. My will is urging me to keep you as close as possible, too."

We moved together, letting the song sink into our bones as we sank farther into each other.

"You really are a prince, Rhys," I murmured. "In every sense of the word."

"I'm actually a king now, but who cares about semantics."

I laughed at that, settling my cheek against his chest.

"Princess," he said quietly, "you know I kind of love you, right?"

A jolt of electricity ran through me, and I was sure Rhys could feel it. The pulse was so strong, I felt it from my forehead to my toes. His words were such a surprise.

"I kind of love you, too," I said back.

Rhys tilted my chin up, and his smile was brilliant. As he kissed me, I knew, pictures or not, I would always remember this night. It was more than a prince kissing his princess. It was better than happily-ever-after.

It was real life. And I could not ask for more.

Acknowledgments

Thank you so much for reading *CUPCAKE*!!! It's my first ever #OwnVoices book, the first I've ever had traditionally published from start to finish, yayyy! There are a lot of people to thank, so here we go!

To Stacy Abrams, thank you for your thoughtful insights, editorial awesomeness, and for helping me make this book the best it can be! You rock, and I'm so grateful I got to work with you!

To Liz Pelletier, thank you so much for taking a chance on *ADORKABLE*—and on me. Thank you for all that you do to get books into the hands of readers who will love them.

To Elizabeth Turner-Stokes, thank you for creating this gorgeous cover for *CUPCAKE*!!!

To Heather, Lydia, Viveca, Curtis, Nancy, Meredith and all of the awesome Entangled team: Thank you for all that you do! For answering this clueless author's questions, lol, for helping with edits, and for making the formatting beautiful: Thank you.

To Aunt Pat, thank you for being my best friend, movie buddy, and my favorite person of all time. I wish you were here to read *CUPCAKE* and see this little romance about a curvy girl get published by an actual publisher! You always said I could do it—even when I didn't believe it myself. I love you and miss you always.

To Aunt Colleen, thank you for believing in me. It means more than you know. I love you.

To Mom, thank you for encouraging my dreams, supporting my writing, and being there. I couldn't ask for a better mom, and I love you so much.

To Mema for being the best ever and for making the best chocolate cake, and to Papa for calling me "princess." I love and miss you both so much.

To romance movies, you rock. Thank you for countless hours of joy, sighs, and happy tears.

To *North & South*, you're still my favorite, and you always will be.

To my dance students, thank you for making my life brighter.

To all the plus-size princesses (like Ariel), you are worthy.

To all the confident best friends who struggled to get there (like Toni), you are worthy.

To all the "mean girls" who actually have good hearts (like Lana), you are worthy.

To all the imperfect princes (like Rhys), you are worthy.

And to YOU, the person reading this book! You are beautiful and worthy of every good thing in life. Thank you so much for giving *CUPCAKE* a chance! I hope you loved Ariel's story as much as I loved writing it! I always knew there was a lack of representation of plus-size girls/women in books and on screen. Particularly in YA! And there are even fewer who just happen to be curvy and are still happy and love themselves. A lot of times the character has to lose the weight before they find their happy ending. And my hope is that this book will be one of many that shows young readers—and all readers—that everyone, regardless of size, is worthy of kindness, love, and happily-ever-after.

Stay safe and happy reading!

Cupcake is a fun, flirty rom-com full of sweet moments and coming-of-age goodness. However, the story includes elements that might not be suitable for some readers. Verbal abuse in a character's back story, bullying, mentions of mental illness, and copious amounts of sugar are included in the novel. Readers who may be sensitive to these elements, please take note.

Cupcake Book Playlist

1. "ily (i love you baby)" by Surf Mesa ft. Emelie
2. "Shape of You" by Ed Sheeran
3. "Roses" by Chainsmokers
4. "I Want You to Want Me" by Cheap Trick
5. "Dance Monkey" by Tones and I
6. "Ice Cream" by BLACKPINK ft. Selena Gomez
7. "Sugar" by Maroon 5
8. "Can't Help Falling In Love" by Kina Grannis
9. "Break My Heart" by Dua Lipa
10. "Shake It Off" by Taylor Swift
11. "Fade Into You" by Mazzy Star
12. "Perfect" by Ed Sheeran
13. "The Way I Am" by Ingrid Michaelson

Black Joe Cake
(aka The Best Chocolate Cake Ever)

Ingredients:

2 cups flour

2 cups sugar

¾ cup cocoa

2 tsp baking soda

1 tsp baking powder

½ tsp salt

2 eggs

1 cup black coffee

½ cup oil

1 tsp vanilla

1 cup milk

Directions:

In large bowl, sift flour, sugar, cocoa, baking soda, baking powder, and salt. Add eggs, black coffee, oil, vanilla, and milk. Set oven to 350°. Mix until blended. Batter will be thin. Pour into a greased and floured 13 x 9 pan (or two circular pans). Bake for 35 minutes or until done.

Frosting
(vanilla)

Ingredients:

1 stick butter (soften)

Confectioner's sugar (start w/half a box)

1 tsp vanilla

1 TBS milk (start with this; add more if necessary)

Mix ingredients then add the rest of the box of powdered sugar. For best results, let chill in fridge for at least 1 hour.

Can be used for cupcakes as well! Makes about 40; stay in for 15 min. Let cool all the way before frosting.

Awesome Vanilla Cupcakes

Ingredients:

1 ⅔ cups all-purpose flour

1 cup granulated sugar

¼ tsp baking soda

1 ½ tsp baking powder

¼ tsp kosher salt

¾ cup unsalted butter (melted)

3 egg whites

1 TBS vanilla extract

½ cup sour cream

½ cup milk

Directions:

Sift flour, sugar, baking soda, baking powder, and salt. In a second bowl, combine butter, egg whites, vanilla extract, sour cream, and milk; once done add to flour mixture. Set oven to 350°. Add batter to your favorite cupcake tins placed in your favorite cupcake pan. Cook for 20 minutes and remove from oven. Recipe makes 16 yummy cupcakes.

Can use same vanilla frosting recipe as the best chocolate cake ever

Yummy Chocolate Chip Cookies

Ingredients

3 cups flour

1 tsp baking soda

¾ tsp salt

1 ⅓ cups butter (softened)

1 ¼ cups sugar

1 cup light brown sugar, packed

2 eggs

4 tsp pure vanilla extract

1 package (12 oz)
  chocolate chips

Directions:

Set oven to 375°. Mix flour, baking soda, and salt. In another bowl, beat butter, sugars, eggs, and vanilla until creamy. Gradually mix in flour mixture. Stir in chocolate chips. Drop dough by rounded tsp on ungreased cookie sheet. Bake 8-10 minutes or until bottom is browned. Makes 3-5 dozen very yummy cookies.

Let's be friends!

 @EntangledTeen

@EntangledTeen

@EntangledTeen

bit.ly/TeenNewsletter